Breaking the Ice

The cold air of calamity had permeated the whole household. Donna Beatrice sat swathed in black georgette, a great silver cross round her neck. Campion remembered with sudden satisfaction that her real name was Harriet Pickering.

"The vibrations in this house are terrible," she said. "The air is full of evil spirits crowding upon one another. We must be very strong. I must be very brave."

Belle dragged her eyes from the fire and let her mild gaze rest upon the other woman.

"Harriet," she said, "*don't* enjoy it."

Donna Beatrice began to sob. The refined sniffing which is perhaps the most irritating sound in the world heightened the tension in the room until it was unbearable.

Max had been temporarily forgotten, so that when he spoke his exaggerated drawl startled them all.

"If you'll permit me to use the phone, Belle, I think everything will be satisfactorily arranged."

He moved over to the instrument and, sitting down before it, dialed a number.

He looked up and spoke half to the room, half to the phone. "I'm going to confess a murder. That's all."

Bantam Crime Line offers the finest in classic and
modern British murder mysteries
Ask your bookseller for the books you have missed

Agatha Christie

Death on the Nile
A Holiday for Murder
The Mousetrap and Other Plays
The Mysterious Affair at Styles
Poirot Investigates
Postern of Fate
The Secret Adversary
The Seven Dials Mystery
Sleeping Murder

Dorothy Simpson

Last Seen Alive
The Night She Died
Puppet for a Corpse
Six Feet Under
Close Her Eyes
Element of Doubt
Dead on Arrival

Elizabeth George

A Great Deliverance
Payment in Blood

Colin Dexter

Last Bus to Woodstock
The Riddle of the Third Mile
The Silent World of Nicholas Quinn
Service of All the Dead
The Dead of Jericho
The Secret of Annexe 3
Last Seen Wearing

Michael Dibdin

Ratking

John Greenwood

The Mind of Mr. Mosley
The Missing Mr. Mosley
Mosley by Moonlight
Murder, Mr. Mosley
Mists Over Mosley
What, Me, Mr. Mosley?

Ruth Rendell

A Dark-Adapted Eye
   (writing as Barbara Vine)
A Fatal Inversion
   (writing as Barbara Vine)

Marian Babson

Death in Fashion
Reel Murder
Murder, Murder Little Star
Murder on a Mystery Tour
Murder Sails at Midnight

Dorothy Cannell

The Widows Club
Down the Garden Path
coming soon: Mum's the Word

Antonia Fraser

Your Royal Hostage
Oxford Blood
A Splash of Red
coming soon:
Cool Repentence
Jemima Shore's First Case
Quiet As A Nun

Margery Allingham

Death of a Ghost
Police at a Funeral

DEATH
OF A
GHOST

MARGERY ALLINGHAM

BANTAM BOOKS
NEW YORK · TORONTO · LONDON · SYDNEY · AUCKLAND

DEATH OF A GHOST
A Bantam Book / published by arrangement with
Doubleday

PRINTING HISTORY
Doubleday edition published April 1934

Bantam edition / June 1985
5 printings through November 1989

*Bantam Books are published by Bantam Books, a division of
Bantam Doubleday Dell Publishing Group, Inc. Its trade-
mark, consisting of the words "Bantam Books" and the
portrayal of a rooster, is Registered in the U.S. Patent and
Trademark Office and in other countries. Marca Registrada.
Bantam Books, 666 Fifth Avenue, New York, New York 10103.*

PRINTED IN THE UNITED STATES OF AMERICA

O   14 13 12 11 10 9 8 7 6 5

LAFCADIO, John Sebastian, R.A., b. 1845, d. 1912. Painter. Entered studio of William Pakenham, R.A., 1861. Lived in Italy, 1865–1878. First exhibited Royal Academy, 1871; A.R.A., 1881; R.A., 1900; m. 1880, Arabella Theodora, d. of Sir J. and Lady Reid of Wendon Parva, Sussex. One son, John Sebastian, b. 1890. Killed in action, 1916. Best known works include: "The Girl at the Pool" (Nat. Gallery), "Group in Sunlight" (Tate), "Belle Darling" (Louvre), "Portraits of Three Young Men" (Boston), "Meeting of the Magi" and "Satirical Portrait" (Yokohama), etc., etc., also Loan Collection of forty works destroyed in Moscow, 1918. Cf. *The Life and Work of Lafcadio*, Vols. 1, 2, & 3, Max Fustian; *The Victorian Iconoclast*, Mrs. Betsy Fragonard; *The Moscow Tragedy*, Max Fustian; *Lafcadio the Man*, Max Fustian; *Biographie d'un maître de peinture à l'huile*, Ulysses Lafourchardière; *Weitere Bemerkungen zur Wahl der Bilder von John Lafcadio*, Gunther Wagner.

—Weber's *Who's Who in Art*

LAFCADIO, J., see *Charles Tanqueray, Letters to* (Phelps, 15/—)

—Dent's *Dictionary of Authors*

"LAFCADIO, . . . the man who saw himself the first painter in Europe and whom we who are left recognize as the last."
—K.J.R. in *The Times*, April 16, 1912

DEATH
OF A
GHOST

1
Interior with Figures

There are, fortunately, very few people who can say that they have actually attended a murder.

The assassination of another by any person of reasonable caution must, in a civilized world, tend to be a private affair.

Perhaps it is this particular which accounts for the remarkable public interest in the details of even the most sordid and unintellectual examples of this crime, suggesting that it is the secret rather than the deed which constitutes the appeal.

If only in view of the extreme rarity of the experience, therefore, it seems a pity that Brigadier General Sir Walter Fyvie, a brilliant raconteur and a man who would have genuinely appreciated so odd a distinction, should have left the reception at Little Venice at twenty minutes past six, passing his old acquaintance Bernard, bishop of Mould, in the doorway, and thus missing the extraordinary murder which took place there by a little under seven minutes.

As the general afterwards pointed out, it was all the more irritating since the bishop, a specialist upon the more subtle varieties of sin, did not appreciate his fortune in the least.

At twenty minutes past six on the preceding day, that is to say exactly twenty-four hours before the general passed the bishop in the doorway, the lights in the drawing room on the first floor of Little Venice were up and Belle herself (the original "Belle Darling" of the picture in the Louvre) was seated by the fire talking to her old friend Mr. Campion, who had come to tea.

The house of a famous man who had been dead for

any length of time, if it is still preserved in the condition in which he left it, is almost certain to have a museum-like quality if it has not achieved the withered wreaths and ragged garlands of a deserted shrine. It is perhaps the principal key to Belle's character that Little Venice in 1930 was as much John Lafcadio's home as if he were still down in the studio in the garden fighting and swearing and sweating over his pigments until he had thrashed them into another of his tempestuous pictures, which had so fascinated and annoyed his gentle and gentlemanly contemporaries.

If Belle Lafcadio was no longer the Belle of the pictures, she was still Belle Darling. She had, so she said, never had the disadvantage of being beautiful, and now, at two months off seventy, ample, creased, and startlingly reminiscent of Rembrandt's portrait of his mother, she had the bright quick smile and the vivacity of one who never has been anything but at her best.

At the moment she was wearing one of those crisp white muslin bonnets in which Normandy peasants delighted until fifty years ago. She wore it with the assurance that it was unfashionable, unconventional, and devastatingly becoming. Her black gown was finished with a little white filet round the neck, and her slippers were adorned with shameless marquisite buckles.

The room in which she sat had the same lack of conformity to any period or scheme. It was a personal room, quite evidently a part of someone's home, a place of strange curios but comfortable chairs.

L-shaped, it took up the entire first floor of the old house on the canal, and although nothing in it had been renewed since the war, it had escaped the elegant banalities of Morris and the horrors of the Edwardian convention. It was Belle's boast that she and Johnnie had never bought anything unless they had liked it, with the result that the deep Venetian red damask curtains, although faded, were still lovely, the Persian carpet had worn silky, and the immense overmantel which took up all one narrow end of the room and which was part of a reredos from a Flemish church had grown mellow and at one with the buff walls, as things do when accustomed to living together.

What was odd was that the sketch of Réjane by Fantin-Latour, the casual plaster study of a foot by Rodin and the stuffed polar bear presented to Lafcadio by Jensen after

2

the 1894 portrait should also live together in equal harmony, or for that matter the hundred and one other curios with which the room was littered: yet they did, and the effect was satisfying and curiously exciting.

Mrs. Lafcadio's visitor sat opposite her, an unexpected person to find in such a room or in such company. He was a lank, pale-faced young man with sleek fair hair and horn-rimmed spectacles. His lounge suit was a little masterpiece, and the general impression one received of him was that he was well bred and a trifle absent-minded. He sat blinking at his hostess, his elbows resting upon the arms of his chair and his long hands folded in his lap.

The two were friends of long standing, and the conversation had waned into silence for some moments when Belle looked up.

"Well," she said with the chuckle which had been famous in the 'nineties, "here we are, my dear, two celebrities. Isn't it fun?"

He glanced at her. "I'm no celebrity," he protested fervently. "Heaven forbid. I leave that to disgraceful old ladies who enjoy it."

Mrs. Lafcadio's brown eyes, whose irises were beginning to fade a little, smiled at some huge inward joke.

"Johnnie loved it," she said. "At the time of Gladstone's unpopularity after the Gordon business Johnnie was approached to make a portrait of him. He refused the commission, and he wrote to Salmon, his agent: 'I see no reason to save Mr. Gladstone's face for posterity.' "

Campion eyed her contemplatively. "There's always a new Lafcadio story about this time of year," he said. "Do you invent them?"

The old lady looked demurely at the handkerchief in her hand.

"No," she said. "But I sometimes improve on them—just a little." She became suddenly alert. "Albert," she said, "you haven't come here on business, have you? You don't think someone's going to steal the picture?"

"I sincerely hope not," he said in some alarm. "Unless, of course, that supersalesman Max is planning a sensation."

"Max!" said Mrs. Lafcadio and laughed. "Oh, my dear, I've had a sweet thought about him. His first book about Johnnie, which came out after the Loan Collection in Moscow was lost, was called *The Art of John Lafcadio*, 'by one who

3

knew him.' His eighth book on Johnnie came out yesterday. It's called *Max Fustian Looks at Art*—'a critical survey of the works of John Lafcadio by Europe's foremost critic.' "

"Do you mind?" said Mr. Campion.

"Mind? Of course not. Johnnie would have loved it. It would have struck him as being so funny. Besides, think of the compliment. Max made himself quite famous by just writing about Johnnie. I'm quite famous, just being Johnnie's wife. Poor dear Beatrice considers herself famous just being Johnnie's 'Inspiration,' and my blessed Lisa, who cares less about it than any of us, really is famous as Clytemnestra and the Girl at the Pool." She sighed. "I think that probably pleases Johnnie more than anything." She looked at her visitor with a half-apologetic grimace. "I always feel he's watching us from somewhere, you know."

Mr. Campion nodded gravely. "He had the quality of fame about him," he said. "It's amazing how persistent it is. If I may say so, regarded from the vulgar standpoint of publicity, this remarkable will of his was a stroke of genius. I mean, what other artist in the world ever produced twelve new pictures ten years after his death and persuaded half London to come and see them one after the other for twelve years?"

Belle considered his remark gravely. "I suppose it was," she agreed. "But you know, really, Johnnie didn't think of it that way. I'm perfectly certain his one idea was to fire a Parthian shot at poor Charles Tanqueray. In a way," she went on, "it was a sort of bet. Johnnie believed in his work, and he guessed that it would boom just after his death and then go completely out of favour—as of course it did. But he realized that as it was really good it would be bound to be recognized again eventually, and he guessed that ten years was about the time public opinion would take."

"It was a wonderful idea," the young man repeated.

"It wasn't in his will, you know," said the old woman. "It was a letter. Didn't you ever see it? I've got it here in the desk."

She rose with surprising agility and hurried across the room to a big serpentine escritoire, and after pulling out one untidy drawer after another, finally produced an envelope which she carried back in triumph to the fireplace. Mr. Campion took the curio reverently and spread out a sheet of flimsy paper scribbled over in Lafcadio's beautiful hand.

The old lady stood beside him and peered over his shoulder. "He wrote it some time before he died," she said. "He was always writing letters. Read it aloud. It makes me laugh."

"Belle darling," read Mr. Campion. *"When you return a sorrowing widow from the Abbey, where ten thousand cretins will (I hope) be lamenting over some marble Valentine inscribed to their hero (don't let old Ffolliot do it—I will not be commemorated by nigger-bellied putti or unibreast~d angels)— when you return, I want you to read this and help me once again as you have ever done. The oaf Tanqueray, to whom I have just been talking, is, I discover, looking forward to my death—he has the advantage of me by ten years—to bask in a clear field, to vaunt his execrable taste and milk-pudding mind unhampered by comparison with me. Not that the man can't paint; we Academicians are as good as beach photographers any day of the week. It's the mind of the man, with his train of long-drawered village children, humanized dogs, and sailors lost at sea, that I deplore. I've told him that I'll outlive him if I have to die to do it, and it has occurred to me that there is a way of making him see the point of my remark for once.*

"In the cellar I shall leave twelve canvases, boxed and sealed. In with them is a letter to old Salmon, with full particulars. You are not to let them out of your hands for five years after the date of my death. Then I want them sent to Salmon as they are. He will unpack them and frame them. One at a time. They are all numbered. And on Show Sunday in the eleventh year after my death I want you to open up the studio, send round invitations as usual, and show the first picture. And so on for twelve years. Salmon will do all the dirty work, i.e., selling, etc. My stuff will probably have gained in value by that time, so you'll get the crowd out of mere curiosity. (Should I be forgotten, my dear, have the shows for my sake and attend them yourself.)

"In any case old Tanqueray will have an extra twenty-two years of me hanging over his head, and if he outlives that, good luck to him.

"Many people will try to persuade you to open the pack-

*ages before the date appointed, urging that I was not of sound
mind when I wrote this letter. You, who know that I have
never been of sound mind in the accepted sense of the term,
will know how to treat any such suggestion.*

*"All my love, my dear. If you see a strange old lady not
at all unlike the late Queen, God bless her, mingling with the
guests on the first of these occasions—it will be my ghost in
disguise. Treat it with the respect it will deserve.*

*Your husband, Madame,
John Lafcadio.
"(Probably the greatest painter since Rembrandt.)"*

Mr. Campion refolded the letter. "Did you really see
this for the first time when you returned from his funeral?"
he demanded.

"Oh, dear me, no," said Mrs. Lafcadio, tucking the
envelope back into the drawer. "I helped him write it. We
sat up one night after Charles Tanqueray and the Meynells
had been to dinner. He did all the rest, though. I mean, I
never saw the pictures packed, and this letter was sent to
me from the bank with the rest of his papers."

"And this is the eighth year a picture has been shown,"
said Mr. Campion.

She nodded, and for the first time a hint of sadness
came into her faded brown eyes. "Yes," she said. "And of
course there were many things we couldn't foresee. Poor
old Salmon died within three years of Johnnie, and some
time later Max took over the Bond Street business from his
executors. And as for Tanqueray, he barely lasted eighteen
months longer than Johnnie."

Mr. Campion looked curious. "What sort of man was
Tanqueray?" he said.

Mrs. Lafcadio wrinkled her nose. "A clever man," she
said. "And his work sold more than anyone else's in the
'nineties. But he had no sense of humour at all. A literal-
minded person and distressingly sentimental about children. I often think that Johnnie's work was unspoilt by the
conventions of the period largely because he had a wholly
unwarrantable dislike of children. Would you like to come
down and see the picture? All's ready for the great day
tomorrow."

Mr. Campion rose to his feet.

As she tucked her arm through his and they descended

6

the staircase she looked up at him with a delightfully confidential smile.

"It's like the mantelpiece in the Andersen story, isn't it?" she whispered. "We are the china figures. We come alive on one evening of the year. Tomorrow afternoon we shall retaste our former glory. I shall be the hostess, Donna Beatrice will supply the decorative note, and Lisa will wander about looking miserable, as she always did, poor creature. And then the guests will go, the picture will be sold—Liverpool Art Gallery this time, perhaps, my dear—and we shall all go to sleep again for another year."

She sighed and stepped down onto the tiled floor of the hall a little wearily.

From where they stood they could see the half-glass door to the garden, in which stood the great studio which John Lafcadio had built in 'eighty-eight.

The door was open, and the famous view of the "master's chair," which was said to be visible to the incoming guest once he stepped inside the front door of the house, was very clear.

Belle raised her eyebrows. "A light?" she said, and added immediately, "Oh, of course, that's Tennyson Potter. You know him, don't you?"

Mr. Campion hesitated. "I've heard of him, and I've seen him at past private views, but I don't think I've ever actually met him," he said.

"Oh, well, then—" She drew him aside as she spoke, and lowered her voice although there was not the remotest chance of her being overheard. "My dear, he's *difficult*. He lives in the garden with his wife—such a *sweet* little soul. I mean, Johnnie told them they could build a studio in the garden years ago when we first came here—he was sorry for the man—and so they did. Build a studio, I mean, and they've been here ever since. He's an artist; an engraver on red sandstone. He invented the process, and of course it never caught on—the coarse-screen block is so like it—and it blighted the poor man's life." She paused for breath and then rushed on again in her soft voice, which had never lost the excited tone of youth. "He's having a little show of his engravings, as he calls them—they're really lithographs—in a corner of the studio as usual. Max is angry about it, but Johnnie always let him have that show when an opportunity occurred, and so I've put my foot down."

"I can't imagine it," said her escort.

A gleam came into Mrs. Lafcadio's eyes. "Oh, but I have," she said. "I told Max not to be greedy and to behave as though he was properly brought up. He needs his knuckles rapped occasionally."

Campion laughed. "What did he do? Hurl himself at your feet in an agony of passionate self-reproach?"

Mrs. Lafcadio smiled with a touch of the most innocent malice in the world.

"*Isn't* he affected?" she said. "I'm afraid Johnnie would have made his life unbearable for him. He reminds me of my good grandmother: so covered with frills and furbelows that there's no way of telling where they leave off. As a child I wondered if they ever did, or if she was just purple bombazine all the way through. Well, here we are. It's a darling studio, isn't it?"

They had crossed the narrow draughty strip of covered way between the garden door of the house and the studio, and now entered the huge outside room in which John Lafcadio had worked and still entertained. Like most buildings of its kind it was an unprepossessing structure from the outside, being largely composed of corrugated iron, but inside it still reflected a great deal of the magnificent personality of its owner.

It was a huge airy place with a polished wood floor, a glass roof, and two enormous fireplaces, one at either end. It was also bounded on the northern side by a low balcony, filled in below with cupboards composed of linenfold panelling rescued from a reconstructed farmhouse in the 'nineties. Above the balcony were five long windows, each about twelve feet high, through which was a magnificent view of the Regent's Canal. Behind the fireplace nearest the door was a models' room and lavatory, approached by a small archway at the extreme western corner below the balcony.

The skeleton of the room, which is always in evidence in a building of the kind, was far more massive than is usual and effectually removed the temporary air of church hall or army hut.

At the moment when Belle and Campion entered, only one of the big hanging electric lamps was lit, so that the corners of the room were in shadow. There was no fire in the grate opposite the door, but the big old-fashioned stove in the other fireplace at the near end of the room was going,

8

and the place was warm and comforting after the chilly garden.

Out of the shadows the famous portrait of Lafcadio by Sargent loomed from its place of honour over the carved mantel. Of heroic size, it had all the force, truth, and dignity of the painter's best work, but there was an unexpected element of swashbuckling which took the spectator some time to realize as a peculiarity of the sitter rather than of the artist. In his portrait John Lafcadio appeared a personage. Here was no paint-ennobled nonentity; rather the captured distinction of a man great in his time.

It is undeniably true, as many critics have pointed out, that he looked like a big brother of the Laughing Cavalier, even to the swagger. He was fifty when the portrait was painted, but there was very little grey in the dark red hair which galloped back from his forehead, and the contours of his face were youthful. He was smiling, his lips drawn back over very white teeth, and his moustache was the moustache of the Cavalier. His studio coat of white linen was unbuttoned and hung in a careless bravura of folds, and his quick dark eyes, although laughing, were arrogant. The picture has of course become almost hackneyed, and to describe it further would be superfluous.

Belle kissed her hand to it. She always did so, and her friends and acquaintances put the gesture down to affectation, sentimentality, or sweet wifely affection according to their several temperaments.

The picture of the moment, however, stood on an easel on the left of the fireplace, covered by a shawl.

Mr. Campion had taken in all this before he realized that they were not alone in the room. Over in the far corner by the stove a tall thin figure in shirt sleeves was hovering before a dozen or so whitewood frames arranged on a curtain hung over the panelling of the balcony cupboards.

He turned as Mr. Campion glanced at him, and the young man caught a glimpse of a thin red melancholy face whose wet pale eyes were set too close together above the pinched bridge of an enormous nose.

"Mr. Potter," said Belle, "here's Mr. Campion. You two know each other, don't you? I've brought him down to see the picture."

Mr. Potter put a thin cold hand in Mr. Campion's. "It's very fine this year—very fine," he said, revealing a hollow

9

voice of unutterable sadness, "and yet—I don't know: 'fine,'
perhaps, is hardly the word. 'Strong,' perhaps; 'dominat-
ing'; 'significant.' I don't know—quite. 'Fine,' I think. Art's
a hard master. I've been all the last week arranging my little
things. It's very difficult. One thing kills another, you know."
He sent a despairing glance into the corner whence he had
come.

Belle coughed softly. "This is *the* Mr. Campion, you
know, Mr. Potter," she said.

The man looked up, and his eyes livened for an instant.
"Not the— Oh, really? Indeed?" he said and shook hands
again. His interest faded immediately, however, and once
more he glanced in misery towards the corner.

Campion heard the ghost of a sigh at his elbow, and
Belle spoke.

"You must show your prints to Mr. Campion," she said.
"He's a privileged visitor, and we must take him behind the
scenes."

"Oh, they're nothing, absolutely nothing," said Mr. Potter, in agony; but he turned quite brightly and led them
over to his work.

At first sight of the array Mr. Campion began to share
Mr. Potter's depression.

Red sandstone does not lend itself to lithography, and
it seemed unfortunate that Mr. Potter, who evidently experienced great difficulty in drawing upon anything, should
have chosen so unsympathetic a medium. There was, too,
a distressing sameness about the prints, most of which appeared to be rather inaccurate and indefinite botanical
studies.

Mr. Potter pointed out one small picture depicting a
bowl of narcissi and an inverted wineglass.

"The Duke of Caith bought a copy of that, once," he
said. "It was the second year we started this posthumous-
show idea of Lafcadio's. That was 1923. It's now 1930: it
must be seven years ago. That one has never gone again.
I've put in a copy every year since. The picture business is
very bad."

"It's an interesting medium," said Mr. Campion, feeling he was called upon to say something.

"I like it," said Mr. Potter simply. "I like it. It's a strain,
though," he went on, striking his thin palms together like
cymbals. "The stones are so heavy. Difficult to print, you

know—and shifting them in and out of the acid is a strain. That one over there weighed thirty-seven pounds in the stone, and that's quite light compared with some of them. I get so tired. Well, let's go and look at Lafcadio's picture. It's very fine; perhaps a bit hot—a bit hot in tone, but very fine."

They turned and walked down the room to where Belle, who had removed the shawl from the picture, was fiddling with an indirect-lighting device round the frame.

"This is Max's idea," she said, shaking herself free from the tangle of flex. "People stay so late, and it gets so dark. Ah, here it is."

Immediately the picture sprang into prominence. It was a big canvas, the subject the trial of Joan of Arc. The foreground was taken up with the dark backs of the judges, and between their crimson sleeves one caught a vision of the girl.

"That's my wife," said Mr. Potter unexpectedly. "He often painted her, you know. Rather fine work, don't you think? All that massing of colour. That's typical. Great quantities of paint, too. I used to say to him—in joke, you know—'It's lucky you make it yourself, John, or you'd never be able to afford it.' See that blue on her scarf? That's the Lafcadio blue. No one's got that secret yet. The secret of the crimson had to go to help pay the death duties. Balmoral and Huxley bought it. Now any Tom, Dick, or Harry can get a tube for a few shillings."

Belle laughed. "Both you and Linda do so begrudge anyone having the secret of his colours. After all, the world's got his pictures; why shouldn't it have his paint? Then they'll have the copy and the materials, and if they can't do it, too, then all the more honour to Johnnie."

"Ah," said Mr. Potter, "remember Columbus and the egg. They could all make it stand up after he'd shown them how to crack it at one end. The secret was simple, you see, but Columbus thought of it first."

Belle grinned. "Albert," she said, "as one of the busiest investigators of our time, has the real significance of the Columbus story ever dawned on you?"

Mr. Campion indicated that it had not.

"That the egg was boiled, of course," said Belle and went off laughing, the white frills of her bonnet trembling.

Mr. Potter looked after her. "She doesn't change," he

remarked. "She doesn't change at all." He turned back to the picture. "I'll cover it up," he said. "Lafcadio was a chap you didn't mind waiting upon. He was a great man, a great painter. I got on with him. Some people didn't. I remember him saying to me, 'Potter, you've got more sense in your gluteus maximus than old Charles Tanqueray has in the whole of his own and his damned art committee's heads put together.' Tanqueray was more popular than Lafcadio, you know, with the public; but Lafcadio was the man. They all see it now. His work is fine—very fine. A bit hot in tone—a bit hot. But very, very fine."

He was still muttering this magic formula when Mr. Campion left him to rejoin Belle in the doorway. She took his arm again as they went into the house.

"Poor Tennyson Potter," she murmured. "He's so depressing. There's only one thing worse than an artist who can't draw and who thinks he can, and that's one who can't draw and knows he can't. No one gets anything out of it then. But Johnnie liked him. I think it was all the stones he uses. Johnnie was rather proud of his strength. He used to enjoy heaving them about."

Her remarks were brought to a sudden end, as they came into the hall, by the appearance at the top of the stairs of an apparition in what Mr. Campion at first took to be fancy dress.

"Belle!" said a feminine voice tragically. "You really must exert your authority. Lisa— Oh, is that someone with you?" The vision came down the stairs, and Campion had time to look at her. He recognized her as Donna Beatrice, a lady who had caused a certain amount of flutter in artistic circles in 1900.

In 1900, at the age of thirty, she had possessed that tall beauty which seems to have been a peculiarity of the period, and she had descended upon the coterie which surrounded Lafcadio, a widow with a small income and an infinite capacity for sitting still and looking lovely. Lafcadio, who could put up with anything provided it was really beautiful, had been vastly taken by her, and she was referred to as "his Inspiration" by those romantic feather-brained people who were loath to be uncharitable and at the same time incapable of understanding the facts.

There were two superstitions connected with Donna

Beatrice. One was that in the days when everyone was chatting about the beautiful peacock strutting so proudly about the studio, she had approached Mrs. Lafcadio and, in that sweet vacant voice of hers, had murmured: "Belle darling, you must be Big. When a man is as great as the Master, no one woman can expect to fill his life. Let us share him, dear, and work together in the immortal cause of Art." And Belle, plump and smiling, had patted one of the beautiful shoulders and whispered close to one of the lovely ears: "Of course, my dear, of course. But let us keep it a secret from Johnnie."

The other superstition was that Lafcadio had never allowed her to speak in his presence; or, rather, had persuaded her not to by the simple expedient of telling her that her pinnacle of beauty was achieved when her face was in repose.

For the rest, she was an Englishwoman with no pretension at all to the "Donna" or the "Beatrice," which she pronounced Italian fashion, sounding the final *e*. Very few knew her real name; it was a secret she guarded passionately. But if in Lafcadio's lifetime she had been content to remain beautiful but dumb, on his death she had developed an unexpected force of character inasmuch as she had shown very plainly that she had no intention of giving up the position of reflected glory which she had held so long. No one knew what arguments she had used to prevail upon Belle to permit her to take up her residence in the house, but at any rate she had succeeded, and now occupied two rooms on the second floor, where she continued her hobby of manufacturing "art" jewelry and practising various forms of semi-religious mysticism to which she had lately become addicted.

At the moment she was dressed in a long Florentine gown of old-rose brocade, strongly reminiscent of Burne-Jones but cut with a curtsey to Modernity, so that the true character of the frock was lost and it became an odd nondescript garment covering her thin figure from throat to ankle. To complete her toilet she had draped a long pink-and-silver scarf across her shoulders, and the two ends rippled behind her with the untidy grace of a nymph on the cover of *Punch*.

Her hair was frankly 1900. Its coarse gold strands had

faded, and there were wide silver ribbons amongst them, but the dressing was still that of the Gibson Girl, odd in a convention not old enough to be romantic.

An incongruous note was struck by a black cord running from beneath her hair to a battery on her chest, for her hearing, never good, had declined with the years, and she was now practically stone deaf except when equipped with this affront to her vanity.

Round her neck was a beaten-silver chain of her own making, hanging to her knees and weighted by a baroque enamel cross. She was a figure of faintly uncomfortable pathos, reminding the young man irresistibly of a pressed rose, a little brown about the edges and scarcely even of sentimental value.

"Mr. Campion?" A surprisingly hard bony hand was thrust into his. "You've been seeing the picture, of course?" The voice was soft and intentionally vibrant. "I was so thrilled when I saw it again after all these years. I remember lying on the chaise-longue in the studio while the Master painted it."

She dropped her eyes on the name, and he had the uncomfortable impression that she was about to cross herself.

"He liked to have me near whilst he was painting, you know. I know now that I always had a blue aura in those days, and that's what inspired him. I do think there's such a lot in Colour, don't you? Of course, he told me it was to be a secret—even from Belle. But Belle never minds. Dear Belle." She smiled at the other woman with a mixture of affection and contempt.

"Do you know, I was discussing Belle with Dr. Hilda Bayman, the Mystic. She says Belle must be an old soul—meaning, you understand, that she's been on the earth many times before."

Campion gave way to the embarrassment which Donna Beatrice's mystic relevations invariably produced upon her more acute acquaintances. Pampered vanity and the cult of the Higher Selfishness he found slightly nauseating.

Belle laughed. "I love to hear that," she said. "A dear old soul, I always hope. A sort of Old Queen Cole. Has Linda come in yet? She went to see Tommy Dacre," she continued, turning to Campion. "He came back from Florence last night, after three years at mural work. Isn't it

14

tragic? The students used to paint cathedral ceilings; now they paint cinema roofs."

Donna Beatrice's still beautiful face adopted a petulant expression.

"I really don't know anything about Linda," she said. "It's Lisa I'm worrying about. That's why I wanted to see you. The creature simply refuses to wear the Clytemnestra robe tomorrow. I've had it let out. She ought to defer a little to the occasion. As it is, she simply looks like an Italian cook. We always look like our minds in the end—Belle, what are you laughing at?"

Mrs. Lafcadio squeezed Mr. Campion's arm. "Poor Lisa," she said and chuckled again.

Two bright spots of colour appeared on Donna Beatrice's cheekbones.

"Really, Belle, I hardly expect you to appreciate the sacredness of the occasion," she said, "but at least don't make my task more difficult. We've got to serve the Master tomorrow. We've got to keep his name green, to keep the torch alight."

"And so poor Lisa's got to put on a tight purple dress and leave her beloved kitchen. It seems a little severe. You be careful, Beatrice. Lisa's descended from the Borgias on her mother's side. You'll get arsenic in your minestrone if you tease her."

"Belle, how can you! In front of a detective, too." The two bright spots in Donna Beatrice's cheeks deepened. "Besides, although Mr. Campion knows it, I thought we'd agreed to keep Lisa's position here a secret. It seems so terrible," she went on, "that the Master's favourite model should degenerate into a cook in his household."

Belle looked discomfited, and an awkward moment was ended by a peal on the front-door bell and the almost instantaneous appearance of Lisa herself at the kitchen door.

Lisa Capella, discovered by Lafcadio on the slopes outside Veccia one morning in 1884, had been brought by him to England, where she occupied the position of principal model until her beauty passed, when she took up the household duties for Belle, to whom she was deeply attached. Now, at the age of sixty-five, she looked much older, a withered, rather terrible old woman with a wrinkled brown face, quick, dark, angry eyes, and very white hair scraped back from her forehead. She was dressed completely in black, the dead and clinging folds which enveloped her only relieved by a gold chain and brooch.

She shot a sullen, vicious glance at Beatrice, sped past her on noiseless, felt-slippered feet over the coloured tiles, and swung the front door open.

A rush of cool air, a little dank from the canal, sped down the hall to meet them, and instantly a new personality pervaded the whole place as vividly and tangibly as if it had been an odour.

Max Fustian surged into the house, not crudely or noisily, but irresistibly, and with the same conscious power with which a successful actor-manager makes his appearance in the first act of a new play. They heard his voice, deep, drawling, impossibly affected, from the doorway.

"Lisa, you look deliriously macabre this evening. When Hecate opens the door of Hell to me she will look like you. Ah, Belle darling! Are we prepared? And Donna Beatrice! And the sleuth! My salutations, all of you."

He came up out of the shadow to lay one very white hand affectionately on Belle's arm, while the other, outstretched, suggested an embrace which included Mr. Campion, Donna Beatrice, and the stealthily retreating Lisa.

When one considered Max Fustian's appearance it was all the more extraordinary that his personality, exotic and fantastic as it was, should never have overstepped the verge into the ridiculous. He was small, dark, pale, with a blue jowl and a big nose. His eyes, which were bright and simian, peered out from cavernous sockets, so dark as to appear painted. His black hair was ungreased and cut into a conventional shock which had just sufficient length to look like a wig. He was dressed, too, with the same mixture of care and unconventionality. His double-breasted black coat was slightly loose, and his soft black tie flowed from beneath his white silk collar.

He had thrown his wide black hat and black raincoat onto the hall chest as he passed and now stood beaming at them, holding the gesture of welcome as one who realizes he has made an entrance.

He was forty, but looked younger and appreciated his good fortune.

"Is everything ready?" The indolent weariness of his voice had a soporific quality, and he swept them down to the studio again before they had realized it.

Potter had gone, and the place was in darkness. Max switched on the lights and looked round with the quick, all-seeing glance of a conjuror surveying his paraphernalia. A frown spread over his forehead, and he returned to his hostess.

"Dear Belle, why do you insist on those nauseating lithographs? It degrades the occasion into a church bazaar." He pointed contemptuously to the unfortunate Mr. Potter's display. "The fancywork stall."

"Really, Belle, I think he's right." Donna Beatrice's low singsong voice was plaintive. "There'll be my little table over here with the Guild's jewelry upon it, and really I think that's enough. I mean—other people's pictures in *his* studio—it's sacrilege, isn't it? The vibrations won't be right."

Looking back upon that evening in the light of after events, Mr. Campion frequently cursed himself for his lack of detachment. Seen in retrospect, after the tragedy, it seemed to him impossible that he could have spent so long in the very heart of the dormant volcano without hearing the rumblings of the eruption to come. But on that evening he noticed nothing save that which passed upon the surface.

Max had disregarded his ally's efforts and continued to look interrogatively at Mrs. Lafcadio.

Belle shook her head at him as though he had been a naughty dog, and glanced round the studio.

"The floor looks very nice, don't you think?" she said. "Fred Rennie scrubbed it, and Lisa polished it."

Max shrugged his shoulders, a gesture almost contortionate, but having made his protest he gave way gracefully. Next instant he was himself again, and Campion, watching him, realized how he had managed to insinuate himself into the position of Lafcadio's entrepreneur.

He strode down the room, flipped the shawl from the painting, and stood back enraptured.

"Sometimes Beauty's like the Gorgon's head. One's spirit turns to stone, beholding it," he said. His voice was startlingly unaffected, and the contrast lent the extravagant phrase a passionate sincerity which startled everyone, including, it would seem, Max Fustian. To Mr. Campion's amazement the little dark eyes suddenly suffused with tears.

"We must all vibrate to green when we think of the

17

picture," said Donna Beatrice with paralyzing idiocy. "Beautiful apple green, the colour of the earth. That shawl is so helpful, I think."

Max Fustian laughed softly. "Green is the colour for money, isn't it?" he murmured. "Suffuse the picture with a green light and it'll sell. Well, I have done my part. Tomorrow everyone will be here: soldiers, poets, fat mayors buying for their cities, the intelligentsia, diplomats—the ambassadors are coming, I heard tonight—and of course the Church." He flung out his hand. "The Church, big-bellied, purple-gowned."

"The bishop always comes," ventured Belle mildly. "Dear man, he used to come before there were any pictures."

"The press," Max Fustian swept on, "and the critics, my colleagues."

"Leashed in like hounds, no doubt," said Belle, who was growing restive. "Don't let me forget to put a shilling in the meter or the whole place will be in darkness after six. I wish we'd never had it put in for that wretched dancing class during the war."

Donna Beatrice caught her breath noisily. "Belle, you promised never to mention that again. That was almost blasphemy."

Belle sniffed quite definitely. "Johnnie's stock was down, we were very short, and the money was useful," she said. "And if I hadn't had the meter put in we should never have been able to pay the electric-light bills so soon. And now—" She broke off abruptly. "Oh, Linda! My dear, how pale you look!"

They turned round immediately as John Lafcadio's granddaughter strode down the room towards them. The daughter of Belle's only son, killed at Gallipoli in 1916, was, according to Donna Beatrice, "definitely Aries."

Upon expansion this term proved to mean something uncomplimentary, a daughter of the Sun, a young soul and pertaining to some lowly plane in the astrological cosmos. To the unenlightened eye she was a strongly made, tempestuous young woman of twenty-five who bore a notable resemblance to her grandfather.

She had the same coarse tawny hair, the same wide mouth and high cheekbones. She was beautiful only by the most modern standards, and her restless violent personality was apparent in every movement. She and Belle understood one another, and a tremendous affection existed between the two. The others were all a little afraid of her, save perhaps Mr. Campion, who had many strange friends.

At the moment her pallor was almost startling, and her eyes beneath her thick brows were burning with nothing less than ferocity. She nodded to Campion and shot a frosty, barely civil glance at Max and Donna Beatrice.

"Tom is in the hall," she said. "He's just coming. He's brought some photographs of his stuff for the Puccini library. They're very fine. I suppose you didn't think so, Max?"

The challenge was gratuitous, and Belle's old eyes flickered anxiously as they had done on private-view days long ago.

Max smiled. "Dacre has all the elements of a great man," he said. "But he should stick to his medium. In tempera he can express himself. There are times when he reminds me of Angelica Kaufmann."

"The panels for the library are in tempera."

"Oh? Really? I saw a photograph of a figure piece. I thought it was a poster for a mineral water." Max's tone had a leisurely spitefulness that was masterly. "I saw the model, too. He brought her back from Italy with him. In imitation of Lafcadio, I suppose."

The girl swung round on him, unconsciously adopting the odd angular posture, with one hip thrown out, so beloved by the moderns. Her pallor had increased. It was evident that an explosion was imminent, and Belle interposed.

"Where is the man, anyway?" she demanded. "I haven't seen him for three years, and he's a very old friend of mine. I remember when he came in here as a little boy, so prim, so solemn. He told Johnnie just what he thought of one of his pictures, and Johnnie put him across his knee and spanked him for his impudence—his mother was so angry. But Johnnie altered the picture afterwards."

Donna Beatrice tittered politely at this reminiscence of John Lafcadio's disgraceful behaviour as the victim of it came into the room.

Thomas Dacre, a man of great ability, thirty-seven years old, unrecognized and obsessed by his own shortcomings, resembled a battered, careworn edition of the Apollo Belvedere in horn-rimmed spectacles. He was one of that vast army of young men who had had five all-important years cut out of their lives by the war, and who bitterly resented the fact without altogether realizing it. Dacre's natural disbelief in himself had been enhanced by severe shell-shock, which had left him capable of making any sacrifice to the furtherance of his creature comforts. His engagement to the tempestuous Linda had surprised everyone at its announcement just before his departure for Italy, but it was supposed that these two unhappy spirits had found mutual solace in each other's charity.

He came up to Belle, who greeted him with that delight which was half her charm.

"My dear, I am glad to see you. I hear you've done so well. Have you brought the photographs? Johnnie always predicted you'd be a great man."

He flushed: Belle was irresistible. But, immediately ashamed of his pleasure, he shrugged his shoulders and spoke ungraciously.

"I'm a cinema-house decorator," he said. "Ask Max. He knows good commercial work when he sees it."

But Belle was indefatigable. She slipped her arm through the newcomer's.

"Tell me all about it," she said. "Did you stay at the old studio in San Gimignano? And is poor old Theodora still alive? Isn't her cooking atrocious? Do you know, Johnnie made one of her children eat up every bit of the omelette she once sent up for our supper. And of course the wicked old thing had to nurse the poor little mite all the next day."

This unconventional sidelight on the character of a great man was suitably received, but Max was not willing to lose command of the stage for long. With his little dark eyes flickering mischievously, he glanced at the girl, who had lit a cigarette and was surveying her grandfather's picture with the critical but unbiased gaze of a fellow craftsman, and turned again to Dacre.

"How does the lovely Rosa-Rosa take to London?" he enquired. "Such a romantic name, madame. Rosa-Rosa."

"Your new model?" said Belle, still concentrating on the younger man.

He nodded. "One of the Rosinis. Do you remember them? She's a bastard, I think, by a German. Extremely modern in shape. The Teutonic streak gives her an extra-

20

ordinary flatness. I've used her for nearly a year now. Her feet are ugly."

Belle, who had listened to this somewhat technical description with complete understanding, nodded her white headdress sagely.

"All the Rosinis have little, stubby feet. You don't remember Lucrezia? There was a great fuss about her thirty years ago. She claimed to be descended from Del Sarto's model, but she grew tired very easily and wouldn't work."

"You must have found the girl very useful," drawled Max with another glance at Linda, "since you bring her home despite the official business of permits and so on."

Dacre looked at him with lazy surprise. "Of course the girl's very useful," he said stiffly. "A reliable model who isn't hideous or temperamental is the most difficult thing in the world to get hold of. This girl sits like a rock."

"What an extraordinary addition to the ménage in Drury Lane. How does the estimable D'Urfey respond to the lady's charms?" Max seemed to be deliberately offensive, and again he shot that sidelong glance at Linda.

Suddenly she seemed to become aware of it.

"Rosa-Rosa is the most beautiful creature I ever saw," she said with dangerous quietness. "She's got the figure of a John gipsy and the face of a fiend. Both Matt and Tom are hysterical about the things she says. *And you're a nasty little sneaking, trouble-mongering mongrel.*"

She strode over to him and caught him a savage blow with the back of her hand which brought out a red mark on his sallow cheek. The attack was so sudden and unwarranted, and betrayed her so utterly, that the shocked silence in the great room lasted until she had disappeared through the doorway.

It was then and only then that Mr. Campion caught a glimpse of something dangerous beneath the surface of this odd pantomime rehearsal performed in such solemn deference to the fancy of a dead man.

Max laughed sulkily and pulled the cover over the painting so that his back was turned to the company. Dacre looked after the girl, his forehead knotted with fury. Donna Beatrice remarked "Aries, Aries" with that sublime complacency known only to those who have the happy conviction that they are not as other men, and Belle, her lips pursed into a little grimace of pity and her faded brown eyes shiny with tears, murmured deprecatingly, "My dear—oh, my *dear!*"

2
Show Sunday

In the great days of the 'nineties, when Art and the Academy were synonymous in the public mind, the Sunday before sending-in day was a festival. In every studio in the kingdom was held a solemn exhibition of those works intended for the Selection Committee's delectation. Since it was so often the first and last time that the pictures were ever exhibited anywhere, the gathering served a useful purpose, and while much tea and sherry was consumed many technical mysteries were discussed.

The death of this pleasant custom marked the end of an era, and it says much for Max Fustian's powers of showmanship that he managed to turn the annual affair at Lafcadio's studio into a minor social event and to create in it one of the little ceremonies which mark the very beginning of the Season.

To the press it was a yearly blessing, provoking the first fanfare before that hardy set piece, the opening of the Royal Academy's Summer Exhibition. Lafcadio, always in advance of his time, was still a good deal too modern for "Constant Reader" and "Paterfamilias," and the element of surprise connected with the yearly picture and its subsequent purchase by the inevitable public body or philanthropist made it one of those sure-fire newspage-column headings comparable with the arrival of the Cambridge crew at Putney or the Birthday Honours List.

On a Sunday in March 1930, therefore, the dusty windows of the dusty yellow houses of Swallow Crescent reflected some of the glories of their past in the parade of automobiles parked against the plump stone balustrade of the canal.

Little Venice ceased to look merely shabby and became interestingly Bohemian, as in its doorway Fred Rennie, magnificently unself-conscious in his leather apron and crimson shirtsleeves, stood to receive the guests.

Fred Rennie was yet another denizen of Lafcadio's remarkable garden. Rescued as a child from a fever-infested canal boat by the painter, he had been taken into the household as a colour mixer. His somewhat sketchy education he had received from Lafcadio himself, and he served the great man devotedly, grinding up the colour and experimenting with new mediums in the grand manner of centuries before. The old coach house at the end of the garden had been turned into a little laboratory, and in the room above it Fred Rennie lived and slept.

When Lafcadio died, disdaining the offers from several paint firms, he had remained with Lisa to form the domestic staff of Little Venice.

Even his service in the war had not uprooted him. For female society he depended upon the canal boats, so that his attachments were necessarily of a transitory nature. His life was peaceful, and it is probable that he enjoyed these annual ceremonies more than anyone save Max Fustian himself.

His costume was Donna Beatrice's idea, since the picturesque rags he had worn in Lafcadio's studio as a child were scarcely suitable for state occasions.

For the rest, he was a little, wiry person with thick dark hair, quick eyes, and hands stained and bitten with acid.

He greeted Mr. Campion as a friend. "We're very full now, sir," he murmured deferentially. "A good many more than last year, I should say."

Campion passed on down the wide hall and would have gone on to the studio had not someone plucked at his arm in the dark corner by the basement stairs.

"Mr. Campion. Just a minute, sir."

It was Lisa, Lisa bad-tempered and uncomfortable in a shiny purple gown only too evidently let out at the seams. In the shadow, with her dark eyes glittering at him, he caught a glimpse of her as she must have appeared that morning on the slopes of Veccia. But the next moment she was the old wrinkled Italian woman again.

"You come up to see Miss Linda?" The foreign intonation turned the remark into a question. "Mrs. Potter's with her in her room. Mrs. Lafcadio told me to look out for you and to ask you to persuade her to come down. There are not enough people to greet. Donna Beatrice cannot leave her little jewelry table."

The contempt in the last words was indescribable. Lisa's opinion of Donna Beatrice defied thought, much less print.

Mr. Campion, whose rôle of universal uncle brought him many strange commissions, accepted this one without a thought, and with a word to Lisa he hurried up the six flights of stairs to the third floor, where, in one of the little attics under the slates Linda had her studio.

The uncarpeted room with its uncurtained windows smelt vilely of oil paint, and the usual paraphernalia of a work studio as opposed to the show variety was heaped about the floor.

Linda Lafcadio was leaning on her elbows at one of the windows looking down at the canal.

Mrs. Potter stood in the centre of the disordered room. She was a little dowdy woman with iron-grey bobbed hair, capable hands, and an air of brisk practicalness which stamped her at once as one of those efficient handmaids-of-all-work to the arts who are capable of undertaking any little commission from the discovery of a Currier & Ives to the chaperoning of a party of society-girl students across Europe. She was an expert embroideress, a connoisseur of bookbinding, and supported herself and, it was said, her husband by sundry art classes at fashionable day schools and a few private students.

She looked at Mr. Campion uncertainly, and he introduced himself.

"I know what you've come to say. You want me to come down," she said, before he could get in a word of explanation. "Belle wants me. I was the model for this picture, you know—I don't like to think how many years ago. Well, I'll leave you to talk to Linda. Try and persuade her to come down. After all, we don't want to let anything spoil today, do we? So grateful to you, Mr. Campion."

She bustled off, leaving a tang of schoolmistress in the air.

As Linda did not move, Mr. Campion looked for somewhere to sit down.

Displacing a heap of paint rags, an ashtray, a bottle of glue, and a small plaster cast, he spread a handkerchief over the seat of the only chair the room contained and settled himself. He sat there for some time looking inoffensive but hopelessly out of place. As the owner of the room did not move he took a wallet from his breast pocket and extracted a newspaper cutting. Adjusting his spectacles, he began to read aloud:

"*DEAD HAND SPEAKS AGAIN. Today, in a little old forgotten corner of our wonderful London, the ghost of a great artist, thought by some to be the greatest artist of our time, entertains the glass of fashion and the mould of form for the eighth time in a twelve-year programme. Ambassadors, prelates, society matrons will all vie with one another in discussing John Lafcadio's new picture, which comes to us across the gulf of the years.*

"*Are you embarrassed when you meet a duchess? It may be your lot to rub shoulders with the nobility, or yours may be a humbler station, but, in whatever circle you move, you should be prepared at any moment to meet the most trying of social ordeals. What would you say if Royalty spoke to you, for instance? Would you stand tongue-tied, or break into hysterical laughter, thus wasting for ever a golden opportunity never to be—*Oh, I beg your pardon: I'm in the wrong column. This is all about a free booklet. Let me see; where were we? *Peeking in at a certain hotel in the Strand, I found Lady Gurney laughing heartily over her husband's adventures in the East.*"

There was still no sign from the figure in the window. He threw the cutting away disgustedly.

"There's nothing else on that," he said. "Should I sing, perhaps?"

There was a long silence after he had spoken, and presently she turned round and came towards him. He was startled by her appearance. Her pallor of the preceding night had gone, and a livid hue had taken its place. Her eyes looked dangerous, her mouth unnaturally firm, and her whole body stiffened and unnatural.

"Oh, it's you," she said. "What are you here for?"

She did not wait for his answer, but walked across the room, and, taking up a palette knife, began to chip little flecks of colour off a partially finished canvas on the easel.

25

She paid minute attention to the damage she was doing, her face very close to the knife.

Mr. Campion, who recognized this symptom, bounded to his feet and caught her by the shoulders.

"Don't be a fool," he said sharply. "And for heaven's sake don't make an exhibition of yourself."

The unexpected vigour of this attack had the desired effect. Her hands dropped to her sides.

"What's up?" he said, more kindly. "Tommy?"

She nodded, and for an instant her eyes were honestly angry and contemptuous.

Mr. Campion sat down again. "Serious?"

"It wouldn't be, if I wasn't such a fool."

She spoke savagely, and her despair was evident.

"You haven't seen her," she said, after a pause, "have you?"

"Who? The model?" Mr. Campion felt he was coming to the root of the matter.

Her next remark startled him.

"It's the hopeless interference of people who don't even understand the facts which is making me hysterical," she said. "Claire Potter has been trying to explain for the last half hour that in her opinion models are barely human and it doesn't follow that just because a man brings one back from Italy he's in love with her. As if that came into it! If Tommy had fallen in love with Rosa-Rosa the situation would be very simple, and I shouldn't feel so much like murdering him as I do now."

She walked over to a cupboard and, after rummaging in its untidy depths, returned with a sketchbook.

"Look at that," she said.

Mr. Campion turned over the pages, and his casual interest suddenly deepened. He sat up and readjusted his spectacles. "I say, these are very fine," he said. "Where did you get them?"

She jerked the book from his hand. "Tommy," she said, "before he went away. And now he's doing stuff that would disgrace a magazine cover. Do you realize he's brought that girl over here to make wrappers for patent medicines? Don't you see, he's thrown everything away. It looked like madness when he gave up oils to go in for tempera. *Now* it's just suicidal, turning to this sort of thing."

Mr. Campion, who had been impressed by the sketches,

could see this point of view, but could not work himself up into the quivering state of indignation which she had achieved. After all, in a cold world it seemed that if the fires of high art had died down in a man's heart a taste for commerce was not to be deplored. He said as much.

She turned on him, blazing. "Quite," she said. "I've got nothing against commercialism. But it puts a man on a different plane. It's insufferable of him to expect the same sacrifices. If he hadn't brought Rosa-Rosa over, the whole thing would probably never have arisen—at least, not violently."

"If I may say so," said Mr. Campion quietly, "I don't quite see how Rosa-Rosa comes into this."

"You're extraordinarily dense," said the girl. "He married her first, of course. How d'you think he got her into England for keeps otherwise? That's what Max was getting at last night. That's why I hit him. As I say, if Tommy had been in love with her it wouldn't have been so bad."

Here was a grievance that even Mr. Campion could understand.

"I see," he said weakly.

She came towards him, looking for an instant like a passionate untidy child.

"Can't you understand that if he'd gone on doing his own sort of stuff it wouldn't have mattered? I wouldn't have been insulted last night when he suggested that we should all three set up house together. The trouble of getting this girl into England permanently would have been a sufficient reason for his marriage, but if he simply needs her for commercial work he's not worth it. Oh, I wish to God he was dead!"

Campion felt that it was impossible not to sympathize with her, even if her point of view was not altogether his own. One thing remained clear: her grievance was not imagined.

"Don't mention it to Belle," she said quickly. "She'd be furious, and it wouldn't do any good. Belle's very conventional."

"So am I," said Campion, and a long pause ensued. "Look here, I'd better go down," he said at length. "I don't see that there's anything I can say about this bad business, but if there's anything I can do you've only got to point it out."

She nodded absently, and he thought she had returned to the window, but before he had reached the first landing she caught up with him, and they went down together.

As they reached the hall the constant stream of incoming visitors had thinned and was now jostled by a secondary stream coming out. Mr. Campion and the girl were held up on the staircase by two old gentlemen who had taken possession of the bottom stair for a moment of conversation.

Noticing the young people hovering behind them, the acquaintances shook hands hastily, and Brigadier General Sir Walter Fyvie hurried out while Bernard, bishop of Mould, strode down the hall into the studio.

3
Murder at the Reception

The evening mist rising up from the canal had grown perceptibly thicker, Campion noticed as he walked behind the bishop down the asphalt path, and the studio lights were blazing. Lisa had drawn the curtains over the tall windows to shut out the melancholy yellow sky, and the grateful heat and scented air of the crowded studio was comforting after the dankness of the garden.

The reception was drawing slowly to a close. The majority of the guests had gone, but the big studio was still alive with chatter and polite laughter.

Max had every reason to be satisfied with his organization. The gathering had been the most brilliant of its kind. The ambassador and his satellites were still hovering about the picture, which dominated the room, and there was a fair sprinkling of personages among the lesser social and artistic fry.

No one could doubt that the gathering was an Occasion. It seemed impossible that Lafcadio himself should not be there striding about, welcoming his friends, overwhelming in his size and magnificence.

But if it was a triumph for Max, it was also one for Belle. She stood in the centre of the studio greeting her guests, her black velvet frock severe and simple as ever, but her peasant bonnet of crisp organdie sewn with Valenciennes.

The bishop went up to her with outstretched hands. They were very old friends.

"My dear lady," he said, his famous voice rumbling like the organ in his own cathedral in his efforts to lower it a little. "My dear lady, what a triumph! What a triumph!"

Mr. Campion gazed round the room. It was evident that he would not be able to get near Belle for some time. He caught sight of Donna Beatrice, a startling vision in green and gold, talking psychomancy to a bewildered-looking old gentleman whom he recognized as a scientist of world-wide distinction.

In the background, unnoticed and forlorn, he espied the melancholy Mr. Potter, whose eyes turned ever and again with shuddering agony to the dismal display of prints upon the curtain.

He heard Linda catch her breath, and he turned to see her gazing across the room. He followed her glance and caught sight of Tommy Dacre leaning by the table where the jewelry made by Donna Beatrice's protégées, the Guild of Women Workers in Precious Metals, was displayed. He was standing with his back to the table, half sitting on the edge of it, in fact. He was carelessly dressed, but had taken the precaution of conforming to the costume permitted by popular superstition to the artist.

By his side was a girl, a girl so striking, even startling, in her appearance that Campion recognized her immediately as the cause of the passionate resentment in the breast of the elemental young woman at his side. Rosa-Rosa looked less like an Italian than one would have thought possible. She had a curious angular figure whose remarkably well-developed muscles showed through her thin grey dress.

Rosa-Rosa's frizzy yellow hair was parted in the centre and hung obliquely round her head. Her face was beautiful but fantastic. She had the dark mournful eyes and arched brows of a Florentine Madonna, but her nose was long and sharp and her lips thin and finely curled. Like all natural models she moved very little and then only to drop from one attitude into another, which she held with remarkable faithfulness.

At the moment she was listening to Dacre, who was

29

chatting to her in Italian, his head thrown back, his hands thrust deep into his pockets, and his black hat crushed under one arm.

She was leaning forward, her chin tilted slightly, her weight supported on one foot, her arms hanging at her sides. It was an arrested movement, perfect in its way and utterly unexpected and striking.

She looked, Campion thought, less like a human animal than an example of decorative art.

Linda walked across the room towards them, and Campion followed her. Dacre's smile vanished as he caught sight of the girl, but he did not look embarrassed, and as a layman Campion wondered afresh at the oddities of the artistic temperament.

He was introduced to Rosa-Rosa, and as he spoke to her he understood some of Linda's fury. Rosa-Rosa had another of the perfect model's peculiarities; she was unbelievably stupid. She had been trained not to think, lest her roving fancy should destroy the expression she was holding. For the best part of her life, therefore, her mind remained a complete blank.

"I've brought Mr. Campion to admire the exhibits," said Linda.

Dacre slipped off the table and turned round lazily to survey its display.

"I'm minding them for Donna Beatrice," he said. "She wanted to toddle off and chat to her friends. I don't know if she's afraid someone'll walk off with this junk—kleptomaniacs, and that sort of thing. Pretty terrible stuff, isn't it?"

They stood looking down at the handiwork of the industrious Guild of Women Workers in Precious Metals, and the depression induced by the contemplation of the useless and the unlovely descended upon them.

"Modern design approached from the outside by the eighteen-ninety mentality can be rather terrible, can't it?" said Dacre, indicating a pair of table-napkin rings in enamelled silver.

Rosa-Rosa pointed to a pair of lapis lazuli earrings.

"Attractif," she said.

"Don't touch," said the man, pushing her away as though she were an overeager child.

She rewarded him with a blank stare and relapsed into a pose, indicating respectful submission.

Mr. Campion felt Linda quivering at his side. The situation was very trying.

"What do you think of the pièce-de-résistance?" said the girl. She indicated a pair of scissors with slender blue blades some nine inches long and handles so encrusted with chunks of coral and cornelian that it seemed impossible they could ever be used.

"Toys," said a voice behind them. "Rather stupid toys."

Max hovered for an instant behind Campion. "You should be looking at the picture, my friend. I am afraid it is going out of the country. I cannot say any more just now—you understand? But—in your ear—the sum was fantastic."

He sped off again, and they had the satisfaction of seeing him waylaid and captured by Donna Beatrice.

"Flatulent little tuft hunter," said Dacre, looking after him.

Rosa-Rosa endorsed this remark with a gesture of startling and violent vulgarity which took them all completely by surprise.

Dacre reddened and admonished her sharply in her own language. She did not look crestfallen but merely bewildered, and stepped back a little.

Linda was still looking at the scissors. "It's a pity to waste steel like that," she said. "The blades are beautiful."

Again the young man in the horn-rimmed spectacles had an inkling of danger in the wind. It was nothing in the girl's tone—of that he was certain; but a wave of alarm passed over him for no apparent reason. Mr. Campion was not a person given to psychic experiences, and the phenomenon irritated him, so that he put it hastily from his mind. But the impression had been there, and it had been very strong.

His thoughts were diverted at this point by a guffaw from Dacre.

"Max is in the toils," he said. "Look."

The scene he indicated was amusing. Donna Beatrice was talking volubly to Max Fustian. Knowing her, Mr. Campion shuddered to think of the matter of her discourse. It was evident that her victim could not escape.

Linda, who had been watching them steadily, laughed contemptuously.

"She's telling him all about the time in the Turkish bath when she was likened to the Rokeby Venus. That's all there

31

is to it, but it goes on for hours. Once she's on the subject you can't stop her, and today Max can't even be rude to her to any good purpose because she's taken off her ear thing. She always does on state occasions, so that she's as deaf as an egg and about as intelligent."

"I think," said Rosa-Rosa with the naïveté of a child, "I shall now go to the water closet," and went off, leaving them all a little embarrassed.

Mr. Campion caught sight of Belle standing in the middle of the room unattended for the moment, and seized the opportunity to pay his respects.

"Oh, my dear," she said, clutching at his arm and speaking with that charming trick of hers which gave each newcomer the impression that he and he alone was the reason for the gathering, "I'm so glad you've come. Isn't it a crush? I'm so tired. Wouldn't Johnnie have loved it? Look at him up there, smiling all over his face." She nodded her bonnet at the Sargent portrait. "I do hope he's not tormenting Charles Tanqueray at some heavenly peephole."

She paused for breath and, leaning heavily on his arm, gazed round anxiously at the visitors.

"There's whisky and soda on the balcony," she murmured. "I think Max has got a cocktail bar there, too. I'm not supposed to approve. I don't know whether I do or not. I can't get over the feeling that gin's so vulgar. It always was when we were young. But now, since it's come into money, as it were, I suppose it's all right. Look at the dear old bishop," she continued practically in the same breath, "standing over there. Doesn't he look a dear? Don't breathe a word to a soul—but his bootmaker pads his gaiters just a little bit. I know, because he came to dinner here one night and got his feet so wet I made him take them off. He sat in front of my fire with a quilt over his knees. We talked about sin, I remember."

"John Lafcadio should be very grateful to you," said Mr. Campion. "It's a very brilliant gathering."

She sighed, a little murmur of satisfaction, and her faded brown eyes twinkled.

"It's wonderful," she said. "It makes me feel thirty-five again. Everyone here—everyone admiring Johnnie. It's all going smoothly; everyone being polite, very silly, and very flattering."

As the last word left her lips there was a faint whir over

their heads and every light in the studio went out, leaving the brilliant assembly in complete darkness save for the faint glow from each fire. Belle's grip on Mr. Campion's arm tightened involuntarily.

"The shilling in the meter!" she murmured huskily. "Oh, Albert, I forgot it!"

The immediate effect of the sudden darkness was such as is usual in such emergencies: there was the familiar pause in the conversation, the startled giggle of some half-wit female; somebody whispered and someone else stumbled over something. And then politeness reasserted itself and conversation went on only a little more quietly than before.

Mr. Campion felt in his pockets. "I've got one," he said. "Leave it to me."

He set off, crossing the room cautiously. The majority of people had the intelligence to stand still, but there were a few who moved about, aimlessly it seemed.

Campion found his way to the little doorway under the balcony with some difficulty; he also experienced some delay because Mr. Potter, who had grown tired of standing beside his "lithographs," had placed a chair for himself with its back against the door.

It was while Campion was removing this obstruction that he noticed some commotion on the far side of the room, somewhere near the jewelry table. He thought nothing of it then and hurried into the cold concrete passage within, where, with the aid of his cigarette lighter, he located the meter and inserted the shilling.

As he came up into the once more brilliantly lighted room he became aware again of the disturbance near the table, and for an instant the wild notion came to him that some sort of smash-and-grab raid had taken place. The next moment he saw that it was a case of faintness. One or two people had gathered round a figure doubled up beside the table. The rest of the guests were studiously taking no notice of the incident, and, miraculously, it seemed, a long queue had already formed to take leave of Belle.

Max, flustered a little by the incident but keeping his head admirably, was assisting the old lady, and Donna Beatrice was making her way towards the door to shake hands with her acquaintances after they had parted from Belle.

Lisa and Fred Rennie were among the group by the table, and even as Mr. Campion looked he saw Rennie bend

33

down and hoist a figure up before taking him out to the models' room through the little door from which Campion had just emerged. That young man, seeing nothing else that he could do, joined the queue.

The business of saying farewell seemed to be an interminable affair, and the queue moved very slowly.

He had allowed his attention to wander, and it must have been a good seven minutes later, when he had moved up some six feet or so in the line, that he became aware of Lisa staring at him intently as though she would force his attention by sheer personal magnetism. As soon as she caught his eye she beckoned to him furiously.

He stepped out of the line and hurried over to her. She led him over to the little door under the balcony, her bony fingers biting into his arm. Once they were out of sight he turned to her enquiringly and was startled by her appearance. The little woman in the tight purple dress was staring at him, her yellow face a mask of horror. When she spoke, her lips moved stiffly and her voice was strangled.

"It was young Mr. Dacre," she said. "He's dead. And the scissors—oh, Mr. Campion, the scissors!" The young man put his arm about her as she tottered towards him.

4
"Not I!"

The steady stream of departing guests flowed slowly out of the studio. A gloom had descended upon the gathering, although the majority had no idea at all that anything unusual had happened; much less that one of their number now lay dead in a little models' room behind the panelling, surrounded by a terrified group and guarded by a bewildered doctor.

The atmosphere was rather one of cold inhospitality than horror, as though the lights had never regained their former brilliance and the occasion had been disappointing.

Nevertheless probably everyone save the immediate members of the household and Mr. Campion might have left the house without being aware of the tragedy at all had it not been for Rosa-Rosa, who suddenly burst through the little doorway under the balcony, screaming.

The noise she made attracted everyone's attention, and her appearance did the rest.

Her training had made her face expressive, and now she presented a picture of such exquisite terror that it was impossible to disregard it. Her yellow hair, crimped like a Botticelli angel's, hung stiffly round her face; her eyes, widened to their utmost, were black pits of fear, and her wide mouth was drawn up into a blue O in her pallid face.

"*Santa Maria! Mari di Dio! È morto! Cosa posso fare? Il mio marito è morto—ucciso!*"

The shrill Italian ended and she began to shout in English: "Murdered! Murdered! Right through the stomach. They did it with the scissors."

It took Max just those three seconds to get across the room and seize the girl by the arms, while the shocked silence in the room deepened into a growing perception of horror.

Max spoke to the girl softly and volubly in her own language. She began to sob noisily, great gulping animal sounds which whipped the already jolted nerves of the company to the point of agony.

A few of the die-hard school of maners clung to their standards and talked together quietly, affecting not to have noticed this second disturbance, while they edged as unobtrusively as possible towards the exit.

But the majority forgot themselves sufficiently to stand silent and agape, watching the girl as Max led her firmly back to the door under the balcony.

These were rewarded by the unusual spectacle of Sir Gordon Woodthorpe, that eminent society physician who had been present at the reception, hurrying out of the little concrete passage, his elegant white hair dishevelled and two patches of crimson burning in the sides of his throat, while he licked his lips feverishly, a nervous habit that had persisted since childhood.

He hurried over to Belle, who was standing in her place by the door, superbly gallant and unruffled in the nightmare crisis. He spoke to her for some moments, and even the die-hards looked curiously in their direction.

After the first few moments Sir Gordon appeared to

be arguing with the old lady, offering, it appeared, to take a duty from her shoulders, but she repulsed him gently. Taking his arm, she leant heavily upon it and raised her voice, which was still clear and soft in spite of her age and emotion.

"Ladies and gentlemen," she began, and then her voice quivered and she stood looking at them, her old mouth trembling slightly.

There was silence instantly. The moment was one of drama, and those minds which had hastily dismissed Rosa-Rosa's outburst as a regrettable, hysterical, or drunken incident suddenly wheeled round to face the half-formed fear which had secretly assailed them all.

"My dears," said Belle piteously, "something very terrible has happened. There has been—well—there has been an accident."

Her voice was trembling unashamedly, and her unconscious use of the endearment made her announcement very real and her appeal very personal. She went on, still leaning heavily on the doctor's arm, while they listened to her breathlessly with that sinking of the heart and faint sense of nausea which always comes just before the worst is told.

"A young man who was with us here a few minutes ago is now dead. He died in here when the lights were out. Sir Gordon feels that—that no one should leave until the police have come."

She looked round her appealingly, as though imploring them to understand. It was odd what an impressive figure she was, this plump old lady in the high white bonnet and the long black dress.

"Of course I can't order you to stay if you want to go," she went on. "That would be absurd. In the circumstances I can only appeal to you. I can't tell you any more. This is all I know myself."

She finished, and Sir Gordon, very conscious of his responsibility and the position in which he stood as Belle's champion, escorted her to a chair on the far side of the room.

Another old woman, Lady Brain, a friend of Belle's of long standing, hurried over to her, and Sir Gordon, forgetting to excuse himself, turned with a sigh of relief to the door under the balcony, skilfully avoiding the eye of acquaintances who would have waylaid him.

There were many peculiarities about the murder at Little Venice. Not the least of these lay in the quality and variety of intelligences who shared its first shock.

There are in England an average of about one hundred and fifty murders a year. The majority of these are of a simple and sordid nature, and the aggregate brain power of those present at their discovery is as a rule something less than normal.

But here in Little Venice at the time of the crime was gathered together a collection of people all notable in varying degrees, the majority recruited from the successful professional classes. Once the existence of the tragedy had percolated and the shock had been assimilated, the reaction was ordinary enough inasmuch as the male half of the gathering formed itself into a group of grave-faced important-voiced personages anxious to cling together and protect their womenfolk, while the said womenfolk hung back and, with the natural secrecy of their kind, chattered in little groups with lowered eyes and voices.

As soon as it was established that the victim of the tragedy was a young man scarcely known, even by sight, to anyone, the peculiarities of this particular gathering began to assert themselves.

In ninety-nine cases out of a hundred Belle's hearers had taken the sense of her words rather than their literal meaning; that is to say, they realized that a murder had taken place, moreover a mysterious murder and in their own immediate proximity, and with the exception of two or three rare and somewhat unnatural souls each man and woman began to consider the affair as it most nearly touched himself.

Some were appalled by the thought of the notoriety entailed, others were shamefacedly excited by it, and immediately wires were jerked, wheels began to turn, and fifty little comedies were enacted.

The sturdy, brown-skinned, and rather stupid young equerry to the ambassador, whose eyes had snapped while Belle was speaking and whose brain was quick to seize the possibilities of any situation, permitted himself the thought that if only some foolish policeman could be persuaded to forget himself for a moment and offer an ill-advised question to His Excellency, quite a little insult could be worked up and an unpleasant incident averted only by the brilliance and tact of His Excellency's equerry.

Meanwhile, on the other side of the room a soldierly man whose unobtrusive polish and sharp intelligence had made him invaluable to the Foreign Office stood watching the ambassador's equerry and reflecting that a timely telephone call to headquarters must certainly be arranged somehow, and that meanwhile every conceivable means must be employed to get the ambassador and his equerry out of the house before any fool policeman had a chance to put his foot in it. He began therefore to move unobtrusively towards the door.

At the far end of the narrow concrete passage, standing beneath the very meter into which he had so lightheartedly dropped a shilling only fifteen minutes before, Mr. Campion hesitated. On his right was the door of the models' room from which he had just come, and the recollection of the scene within was still clear in his mind. It had been very stuffy and dusty. The dressing table was dismantled, and the green-covered couch had looked dingy, like the furniture in a secondhand shop. It was upon this couch that the body still lay.

Mr. Campion, in spite of his long association with crime, was not callous enough to be entirely unmoved by the spectacle of a young man suddenly dead.

He was human enough also to consider his own position. Very few people knew much about Mr. Campion. In the first place, that was not his name. The majority of his friends and acquaintances knew vaguely that he was the younger son of some personage, who had taken up the adventurous calling of an unofficial investigator and universal uncle at first as a hobby and finally as a career. His successes were numerous, but for the best reasons in the world he remained in the background and avoided publicity like the plague.

There were some who insisted that he was in reality a member of Scotland Yard's vast army of unobtrusive agents whose work is done entirely behind the scenes, but Mr. Campion himself would have denied this vigorously. The fact remained, however, that he had many friends at Scotland Yard.

At the moment he was in a quandary. He was in the house of friends. Obviously it was his duty to do what he could. He knew enough of English law and English justice to realize that in a case of murder the pursuit is relentless and the punishment unavoidable.

He had no doubt in his mind concerning the author of the crime. He could see Linda now in his mind's eye as she had turned from the window and come towards him. Temporary insanity, of course.

Rapidly he considered the chances of there being insufficient proof. The handles of the long narrow-bladed scissors still protruded from the grey pull-over. Sir Gordon Woodthorpe had been intelligent enough not to attempt to remove the weapon before the arrival of the official doctor.

The useless ornate handles presented no flat surface, so that the chances of their retaining fingerprints were remote. Nevertheless it would all be very difficult.

He was shocked when he thought of Linda. She was just the wild emotional type who might easily succumb to a sudden impulse. It was amazing that she had waited until the darkness.

Of course, even if the best happened and the matter were dropped for lack of evidence, she would have to be put under restraint.

He passed his hand over his forehead. It was damp, and he felt cold. God, what a terrible thing to have happened! Poor Belle. Poor Linda. Poor tragic, insufferable young blackguard lying dead in the next room.

There was the model, too, who had probably been in love with him. Lisa was quietening her now, speaking harshly in her own language, bright startled tears on her withered cheeks.

Mr. Campion checked himself. Something must be done immediately before some bobby off the beat made matters even more difficult. He remembered that the telephone was on the landing and that the door on his left led into the garden. Inspector Stanislaus Oates was the man to get hold of; the shrewdest and at the same time most kindly member of the Yard.

It was Sunday afternoon; therefore he would probably be at home. Campion remembered the number as he ran: Norwood 4380.

Within the studio the atmosphere was becoming unbearable. There were sporadic silences which hung heavily over the great room. One or two people were becoming hysterical. No one complained openly, largely out of deference to Belle, who with remarkable fortitude and typical good sense remained where she was, knowing that her presence alone prevented an open demonstration.

Mr. Campion came in so unobtrusively that his reappearance was not noticed, and he spoke to Belle for some moments unobserved.

"I've been on to Inspector Oates of Scotland Yard," he murmured. "It's quite all right. He says he's coming round right away, but that meanwhile there's no point in keeping this crowd here. After all, everybody came by invitation, and anyone who was particularly anxious to escape after—well—after the lights were turned on again could easily have done so. I saw twenty or thirty people go myself."

He did not look at her as he spoke. He could not bring himself to face her warm brown eyes swimming in tears.

She took his arm and drew herself up.

"I'll tell them," she said.

She moved over towards the door, a solitary figure, very brave and very lonely standing beneath the portrait of her smiling husband.

Gradually the whispered talk died away and all eyes were turned to her enquiringly. She opened her mouth to speak, but words failed her, and, stepping to the door, she pulled it open and stood clinging to the handle, waiting.

The steady stream began again moving a little more quickly than before.

The old woman stood erect, shaking hands mechanically, smiling wanly at the murmured words of commiseration and regret, looking exactly what she was, a very gallant old lady.

Mr. Campion conquered his impulse to remain by her side. There were other things to be done. He disappeared through the door under the balcony, slipped out into the garden by the back way, and by entering the kitchen door in the basement escaped collision with the departing guests.

He guessed there must be a back staircase, and he found it and reached the landing outside Linda's studio without encountering a soul. He stood listening outside the door. Everything within was silent.

Campion was no fool. Linda had been in an unbalanced

nervous condition that afternoon, and he had no illusions concerning her probable state of mind at the present moment. He went in prepared to meet a lunatic.

He knocked, and, receiving no response, opened the door quietly and stepped into the darkness.

"Linda," he said softly.

There was no reply, and he felt round the door for the switch. As the room leapt into sight he realized that, save for himself, it was empty.

He was just going out again when a door on the other side of the room opened and the girl came out. She was still pale, but seemed remarkably composed. She laid a finger on her lips when she saw him.

"Hush," she whispered. "Rosa-Rosa's here in my room, asleep. I've given her an enormous bromide. She won't wake for a long time."

Mr. Campion was prepared for the worst, and her words sent a thrill of horror down his spine.

"Good God, Linda! What have you done?"

The words were forced from him, and he shot past the girl into the little bedroom beyond.

Rosa-Rosa, her face red and swollen with tears, lay on the bed sleeping naturally enough. Campion went over to her, scrutinized her face, and touched her wrist as it lay upon the coverlet. When finally he straightened himself and turned, Linda was standing in the doorway regarding him, a puzzled expression gradually deepening to horror in her eyes.

When he went out into the little studio she followed him and touched his arm.

"What did you mean?" she demanded breathlessly.

Campion looked down at her, and his pale eyes behind his spectacles were troubled.

"What did you mean?" the girl insisted.

He passed his hand over his forehead. "I don't know what I thought, Linda."

She caught hold of the cupboard door to steady herself.

"Albert," she said, "you don't think that I killed Tommy, do you?"

When he did not answer she drew back from him, her eyes starting with terror.

"Albert, you don't think I'm insane!"

When he remained silent, she put her hand up to her mouth as though to stifle a cry.

"What shall I do?" she said huskily. "What shall I do?"

She suddenly stepped forward and caught him by the shoulders.

"I loved Tommy—at least I suppose I did. And I was angry with him. But not as angry as that—not mad. I'd moved away from him when the lights went out. I was at the other end of the table. I heard someone moving in the darkness, and I heard him go down, though I didn't realize what had happened then, of course. Oh, Albert, you do believe me, don't you? You do—you *do* believe me?"

Campion looked down at her. The world was reeling. This was the last development he had expected, the last eventuality for which he had been prepared. He looked down into her face, saw the agonized appeal in her eyes, and spoke truthfully.

"I do, old dear," he said. "Heaven help me, I do."

5
Inspector Oates

Inspector Oates, sitting in the library at Little Venice, a pad of scribbling paper in front of him, bore a gloomy expression upon his cold, rather weary face. He had spent a trying three hours. There may be Scotland Yard detectives who enjoy wringing secrets from unwilling witnesses and placing their fingers unerringly upon the most likely suspect late on a Sunday evening, but Stanislaus Oates was not among them. He had found the whole business very tedious, very distressing, and probably auguring a lot of trouble.

His last witness was now on his way from the drawing room, where the family had assembled, and Mr. Oates was quite anxious to see him, so that when the door opened and a uniformed constable put his head in to say that Mr. Campion was outside he pushed the pad away from him and looked up with interest.

Albert Campion wandered into the room looking his usual vacant, affable self. If there was a hint of anxiety in his eyes it was hidden by the spectacles.

The inspector regarded him solemnly, and Campion was reminded of very much the same scene in a headmaster's study many years before. There had been the same feeling of apprehension, the same air of calamity.

"Well?" said Oates, using very much the same inflection that old "Buggy" had chosen, and very nearly the same words. "How did you manage to get mixed up in all this? You've got a nose for crime. Sit down, won't you?"

The fact that Mr. Campion and Inspector Oates were old friends never obtruded itself when there were business matters at hand.

For the first two or three minutes the proceedings were positively formal, and Campion's alarm increased.

"Oates," he said, "you're behaving as though it were all over, bar the arrest. Is it?"

Oates shrugged his shoulders.

"I'm afraid so," he said. "It seems very clear, doesn't it? I'm afraid it's going to be awkward for you, a friend of the family and that sort of thing. Still," he went on more cheerfully, "we've got to collect the evidence. I don't think we've got anything conclusive enough for a conviction. No one saw her do it, you know."

Mr. Campion blinked. The sudden fulfilment of a fear, however much expected, always comes as something of a shock. He leant back in his chair and regarded the inspector gravely. "Oates," he said, "you're on the wrong horse."

The inspector looked at him incredulously.

"And you've known me all these years!" he said. "You've known me all these years, and you make a deliberate attempt to impede me in the course of my whatever it is."

"Duty," said Mr. Campion helpfully. "No. You've known me long enough," he went on, "to realize, I hope, that I have no conscience in these matters at all. Conscience doesn't come into it. If I believed that Linda Lafcadio killed her fiancé and I thought any good purpose could be served by throwing dust in your eyes, I should do so if I could."

The inspector grunted. "Well, we know where we are, don't we?" he said pleasantly. "How did you know I'd found out that the girl did it?"

43

"Well, it's the easiest theory," said Campion. "Not wishing to give offense, Stanislaus. You're always hot on the easiest scent."

"You won't offend me," said the inspector, bridling. "But because you've been lucky enough to come across a few really interesting cases you expect to have the same experience every time."

Something in Mr. Campion's manner had made him slightly uncomfortable, however. In the last case they had worked on together, Mr. Campion's fantastic theory had been correct, and the inspector, who was a superstitious man in spite of his calling, had begun to regard his friend as a sort of voodoo who by his mere presence transformed the most straightforward cases into tortuous labyrinths of unexpected events.

"Look here," he said persuasively, dropping entirely the headmaster manner, "a passionate, slightly unbalanced girl goes to meet her fiancé off a boat train. She finds he's brought a beautiful young Italian home with him and afterwards discovers that they are married. The young blackguard cheerfully proposes that they shall set up a ménage-à-trois, which she very properly refuses. The young man comes to a party. She happens to be standing by him, driven insane by jealousy, when the lights go out. Those damned scissors are near her hand. What a filthy weapon, Campion! Did you see 'em? They opened a bit in the heart itself. Killed him instantly, of course. Let me see, where was I? Oh, yes. Well, she was in the dark. She sees her weapon, sees her opportunity. Then she just loses her head and there you are. What could be plainer, what could be clearer than that? It's so simple. In France, you know, she might get off. It'll be insanity as it is, I expect."

Mr. Campion regarded his friend steadily. "You know you'd never get a conviction on that," he said. "It isn't even circumstantial. You've got a possible motive, but that's all."

The inspector looked at him uncomfortably. "I told you I didn't think there was enough evidence," he said. "I did say that, didn't I?"

Mr. Campion leant forward. "Leaving the girl out of it for the moment," he said, "what do you actually know? Have you got any fingerprints on the scissors? Could the blow have been driven home by a woman? Wasn't it very clever of the murderer to take a single shot in the dark and drive the scissors straight into the man's heart?"

Stanislaus Oates rose to his feet. "If you're going to set up as counsel for the defense—" he began.

"I should be doing you a singular service, my dear peeler. Why take an unprofitable theory to your heart just because it happens to be the first one you think of?—or you knew a case once where the same sort of thing happened? Were there any fingerprints?"

"Did you see the scissors?" countered the inspector, and as Mr. Campion nodded he shrugged his shoulders. "Oh, well, then, you know. Of course there weren't. I never saw such stupid things in my life. Absolute waste of good steel."

Mr. Campion blinked. He had heard a phrase very much like that before, and the scene when Linda and he had stood talking to Dacre and his amazing wife returned to him vividly. Just for an instant his belief in Linda wavered, but, as he recalled the episode in her little studio only a few hours before, his conviction returned.

"Well, that's disposed of," he said cheerfully. "How about the blow? Could it have been struck by a woman?"

"I've had all that out with Sir Gordon Woodthorpe and old Benson, our man." The inspector's gloom was returning. "It was a most extraordinary blow, Campion. How anybody struck it in the dark, I don't know. It's practically the only sort of knife wound that would kill a man instantly— that is, before he had time to make any sound. It entered the body just under the point of the breastbone and went straight up, skewering the heart completely. The scissors were broad enough and thick enough to destroy the organ at once. I don't see how anyone could have done it intentionally. I mean, I don't see how anyone could have been sure that it would come off just like that. Both doctors admitted they wouldn't have been anywhere near certain of bringing it off themselves. I suppose artists know a good deal about anatomy, but even so she had diabolical luck."

"Are you sure a woman could have done it?" ventured the younger man.

"Well"—the inspector spread out his hands—"my mother couldn't have done it, and I don't suppose yours could. But these modern kids are as muscular as boys. The blow was a hefty one—I admit that—but it wasn't in the kick-of-a-horse class. And you know, Campion"—he lowered his voice—"there's insanity in the family, isn't there?"

"Insanity? Certainly not. I've never heard of any. You're on the wrong tack here completely, Stanislaus."

The inspector considered a moment before continuing. He sat down at the table and rubbed his moustache the wrong way, an irritating habit he possessed.

"That woman who lives in the house, is she an aunt or something?" He consulted his notes. "Here you are: Harriet Pickering, alias Donna Beatrice. I realized she was going to keep me up half the night if I was going to get even the more ordinary facts from her, so I left it till later. Well, she's a perfectly ordinary hysterical type, there's no doubt about that. Very near the edge of mania, too, I should say. You must know the woman I mean—wears an acoustic device," he went on testily, catching sight of Campion's blank face. "I couldn't manage her, so I turned her over to the doctors. She told me a cock-and-bull story about seeing lights round my head. Seeing lights round the victim's head. Something to do with indigo and the viler emotions. She seemed to be in fancy dress, too. She may not be certifiable, but—well, she's not quite *compos mentis*, poor soul. That was one of the things I wanted to ask you. Who is she? And what is she doing here?"

Mr. Campion did his best to give the inspector a brief outline of Donna Beatrice's career as he knew it, during which Oates's eyes widened and his moustache seemed to be in danger of being rubbed off altogether.

"Really!" he said at last. "Lafcadio's Inspiration? I didn't know he was that sort of man at all."

"He wasn't," said Mr. Campion. "I doubt if he ever treated the lady with anything but the utmost propriety."

"Oh, well, then, there's your insanity," said the inspector easily. "The whole household is definitely queer. There's that cook who used to be a model, and those funny people who live in a shed in the garden. Bohemia's one thing, but this has a respectable veneer. I think you'll find that there's insanity somewhere. All round, if you ask me."

"What about Mrs. Lafcadio?" Campion ventured.

The inspector smiled. "I wasn't counting her," he said. "There's something very attractive about the real McCoy when you meet it. I told her she ought to go and lie down. It's been a shock, I'm afraid. I want you to go and prepare her for something worse soon. I think we shall have to detain the girl."

"You'll be making a very silly mistake if you do, on a par with the time when you nearly arrested Uncle William in Cambridge."

The inspector was silent for a little while.

"If you want to get rid of that moustache, why don't you shave it?" said Campion.

The inspector laughed and dropped his hand.

"Oh, well," he said, "it all falls back on routine in the end. That man Rennie seems an intelligent sort of person. I'm getting a list of the guests from him. We shall take a statement from each of them, and you never know, something may turn up. But I'm afraid there's no doubt about it this time. The girl had the motive, and she had the opportunity. I know that's not conclusive, but it's nine points out of the ten. Will you go to the old lady, Campion, while I see Rennie? Oh, by the way, you didn't see anything, did you? I haven't had a statement from you. Where were you when it happened?"

"In the passage, putting a shilling in the meter."

"Of course!" said the inspector bitterly. "Probably the one trained observer in the party out of the room at the psychological moment."

He walked over to the door with Campion.

"You see, that meter is another thing," he said. "No one could have arranged for that light to go out just then. It all points to an impulsive, insane gesture that happened to come off. You work on the line of insanity; you'll find it there somewhere."

"If you detain that girl you'll never prove anything against her," said Campion, his hand on the door knob.

"That's the trouble," said the inspector. "Without conclusive evidence we shouldn't be able to get a conviction, but the whole world would believe she's guilty."

"That's what I'm afraid of," said Mr. Campion and went out.

6
The Gesture

Mr. Campion went slowly upstairs to the drawing room reflecting that the situation was impossible. He dreaded the meeting with the family. Belle, he knew, looked to him for comfort, and in the circumstances he had very little to offer her.

The cold air of calamity had permeated the whole household. The atmosphere of the hall was chill and yet curiously stuffy.

They would have to be warned of the inspector's intention—he realized that—and there was the question of insanity, too. The longer he considered his task the less he was attracted by it.

He pushed open the door of the drawing room and went in. They were all there save Linda and Rosa-Rosa. Belle sat in her usual chair by the fire just as she had done on the evening before, when she had been chatting so happily to Campion. She was very grave now, but there was no sign of weakness on her face. Her hands were folded in her lap, and she stared down into the fire, her mouth screwed into a small grimace of pity.

Lisa was crying softly, huddled up on a low chair by Belle's side. At least it seemed that she was crying, for she dabbed her little black eyes with a big white handkerchief from time to time.

On the opposite side of the hearth, Donna Beatrice, the only one of the party who had changed her dress, sat swathed in black georgette, a silver chatelaine hanging from her girdle and a great silver cross round her neck.

Max strode up and down the room impatiently. Like Donna Beatrice he had been quick to see the dramatic possibilities of the affair, and whereas he did not actually "make copy" out of them he obviously got a modicum of satisfaction out of the drama. At worst it seemed to mean that something else was happening on the little stage which he made his life. The vital question whether the scandal would affect Lafcadio's reputation advantageously or adversely also confronted him.

As the young man came in he glanced at Campion carelessly and made him a helpless gesture. If he had said, "It's too terribly trying, isn't it? But emergencies do occur," he could not have conveyed his thought more clearly.

Donna Beatrice's greeting was more sensational, and Campion remembered with sudden satisfaction that her real name was Harriet Pickering. She rose from her chair.

"Your aura," she said. "Your aura . . . You looked like a flame coming into the room, a vigorous cosmic flame."

Lisa made some muttered protest in her own language, and Belle put out a hand to soothe her.

Donna Beatrice sank down again.

"The vibrations in this house are terrible," she continued. "The air is full of evil spirits crowding upon one another. I can feel them oppressing me, wearing me down. It's all very well for you, Lisa. They pass you by. But I'm attuned to the higher consciousness, and I know we're all in danger. The evil act has set millions of vibrations going. We must be very strong. I must be very brave."

Belle dragged her eyes from the fire and let her mild gaze rest upon the other woman.

"Harriet," she said, "*don't* enjoy it."

It was the first ill-natured remark any of them had ever heard her make, and the rebuke was all the more effective.

Max permitted a smile to pass over his face, Lisa ceased to sniff, and Donna Beatrice herself made a noise like a startled hen. Then with tremendous conscious dignity she reasserted herself.

"Belle darling, you should lie down. This terrible thing is getting on all our nerves. I can stand it because I'm an old spirit. I've probably gone through this sort of experience in other incarnations many times before."

Belle, who realized that for chronic hysteria there is no cure, ignored her and stretched out a hand to Campion.

"Come and sit down, my dear," she said. "Tell me, whom are they going to arrest?"

Campion looked at her sharply. Her shrewdness was always surprising him. He saw that they were all looking at him, waiting for his news. He realized that he was their only friend, their only personal link with that terrifying organ of justice, the Police.

Mr. Campion had faced many dangers in his time and had come unscathed through many adventures, but at this moment he was desperately uncomfortable. He cleared his throat.

"Look here, Belle," he said, still holding her hand, "this is rather an awkward question, but do you know anyone who was at the reception or—" he hesitated—"anyone in the house who is liable to uncontrollable fits of fury? I mean, have there ever been violent incidents in the past? Not verbally violent, you know, but—well, has anybody ever done anything almost dangerous?"

Whatever reply he expected, the immediate results of his question were startling in the extreme. A wail of mingled anguish and terror sounded in his very ear, and Lisa, her face ashen, rose from her seat and stumbled blindly out of the room. There was a blast of chilly air as the door swung open and the little click which the catch made as it closed to echoed forlornly in the silent room.

"Lisa also appears to be a recipient of the higher consciousness," Max drawled, nettled into impoliteness, while Donna Beatrice caught her breath sharply and Belle's hand tightened over Mr. Campion's.

Donna Beatrice shrugged her shoulders.

"So it's come out at last," she said. "When I first saw the scissors I knew there was something strange about them. Something repelled me slightly when I touched them. I might have known—I might have known!"

Campion looked at Belle. His eyes were sharp behind his spectacles, and his manner had authority.

"I think you ought to tell me," he said. "What is it?"

Belle seemed loath to speak, but Donna Beatrice sailed in with an eagerness that was frankly uncharitable.

"Some years ago," she said, "Lisa made a wholly unwarrantable attack on me down in the studio. It was the outcome of ungovernable fury."

"Beatrice!"

Belle stretched out her hand.

"Oh, nonsense! You can't hide things like that. Mr. Campion's asked for the truth, and now he shall have it. After all, it's only fair to ourselves. If you get a young, unbalanced soul to deal with, you must protect yourself in a practical manner."

Mr. Campion was listening patiently, and even Max had paused in his perambulations and now stood behind Belle's chair watching Donna Beatrice's placid face wearing its smug expression. She was very conscious of her audience and told her story with a simulation of hesitancy which they found unbearably irritating.

"It was when the Master was alive," she began, dropping her eyes as usual on the name. "Lisa was just beginning to lose her beauty—all traces of beauty, I mean. She confided to me that she was worried about it, and I tried to help her by telling her of the beauty of the spirit. Of course, I was inexperienced then or I should have recognized her as the young soul she is, incapable of benefiting in that way. Anyhow, the poor creature lost her temper and made an attack upon me. I've had to remind her of it since, several times. I made no complaint at the time because the Master was anxious that I shouldn't, but I've never forgotten it. I put up my arms to shield my face, and I had a cut quite a quarter of an inch deep right across both my forearms. I can show you the scar on my left arm now. She was trying to disfigure me, you see."

Mr. Campion looked at her in amazement. It seemed impossible that she could not realize the full gravity of the accusation she made.

"That's what she was thinking of when she ran out of the room," the woman continued. "It's understandable, isn't it?"

Belle peered at Mr. Campion anxiously.

"It's twenty-five years ago," she said. "Quite twenty-five years ago. I thought we'd all forgotten it. Johnnie was so upset at the time, and poor Lisa was so penitent. Need it all be brought up again now?"

Mr. Campion looked reassuring. "I don't think so," he said. "After all, it is rather different, isn't it?"

Donna Beatrice pointed a long, white finger at him.

"I know we must be charitable," she said. "And I realize that we must do the right thing. But there's something Belle

51

hasn't told you, something that I consider very significant. You see, Lisa happened to have attacked me with a pair of scissors. She had them in her hand at the time."

"Oh, Beatrice!" The reproach in Belle's voice was bitter. "How could you!"

Mr. Campion remained unimpressed. He thought he could imagine almost any woman in the situation which Donna Beatrice had described being moved to stop that excruciatingly stupid voice with whatever weapon came to hand. He shook his head decidedly.

"No," he said. "Inspector Oates is not particularly interested in Lisa."

"Of course he's not," said Donna Beatrice. "He's not interested in anyone, I hope. It's perfectly obvious that poor misguided Dacre committed suicide. I told the inspector there were angry dull brown and indigo rays round the boy's head last night. Read what all the authorities say about dull brown and indigo rays. I don't suppose even the inspector is going to question the authority of men like Kunst and Higgins. Dull brown and indigo rays mean violence, depression, and a lowering of the cosmic tone. A perfectly simple case of suicide. After all, that's the only charitable way to look at it."

"You saw the rays?" said Max, fixing her with a dark, unwavering eye. "Are you prepared to swear in court that you actually saw coloured rays of light encircling young Dacre's head any time in your life?"

Donna Beatrice's gaze wavered for an instant, but not for long.

"Yes," she said exasperatingly. "I can see rays round all your heads now. There are too many dark colours in your own aura, Max."

He continued to look at her with gloomy irritation. Then he bowed ironically.

"Dear lady, you are superb," he murmured and turned away with an exaggerated gesture of exasperation.

But Donna Beatrice was equal to any treatment of this sort. "Don't flounce, Max," she said.

Belle seemed to be oblivious of the exchange. Her old brown eyes had grown introspective, and her lips moved ruminatively. Suddenly she turned to Campion.

"My dear," she said, "I've got to be told some time or other, haven't I? What is it? Whom do they suspect? Linda?"

52

Mr. Campion squeezed the hand which still rested in his own.

"It's only some batty idea Stanislaus has," he said lamely. "There's nothing to worry about, of course."

Belle nodded. She was not listening to him. "Oh, dear," she said piteously. "Oh, dear."

Both Max and Donna Beatrice were startled out of their respective poses by this development.

"Linda?" ejaculated Lafcadio's Inspiration. "Oh, how wicked! How dreadful! Oh, Belle, we must do something. Oh, oh, how wicked!"

Max confronted Campion. He looked less affected and more human than the young man ever remembered seeing him before.

"Another Scotland Yard blunder?" he enquired bitterly.

Having plunged into the trouble, Mr. Campion struck out.

"Well," he said, "there's the motive, you know. It's ridiculous, of course, but Dacre having married Rosa-Rosa like that did suggest to the inspector—" He paused without finishing the sentence.

"Dacre married to the little model?" exploded Donna Beatrice. "Oh, how dreadful! Oh, poor Linda! I understand how she felt. Poor girl! Ought I to go to her?"

Both Max and Campion seemed to be moved by a single thought, for they started simultaneously as though they would detain the good woman by force if necessary.

Belle allowed a stern expression to creep into the lines of her face.

"Don't be a fool, Harriet," she said. "We must pull ourselves together and think what's best to be done. Of course, there's no question that the poor child is innocent, but not everyone knows her as well as we do. Albert, my dear, what shall we do?"

Donna Beatrice began to sob. The refined sniffing which is perhaps the most irritating sound in the world heightened the tension in the room until it was unbearable. Belle was trembling. Campion could see her struggling to keep back her tears and forcing herself to think consecutively.

Max had been temporarily forgotten, so that when he spoke, his exaggerated drawl startled them all.

"My dear people," he said, "don't disturb yourselves. I

see this matter must be cleared up immediately, and if you'll permit me to use the phone, Belle, I think everything will be satisfactorily arranged."

He moved over to the instrument, an extension from the hall, with his old self-conscious swagger, and, sitting down before it, dialled a number. They listened to him as people always do listen to telephone conversations, that half-permitted eavesdropping which is irresistible.

"Hullo, is that you, Mrs. Levy? This is Max Fustian. Could I have just a word with Isidore?"

He paused and glanced back at them with a reassuring smile.

Campion recollected that Isidore Levy was the astute, thickset gentleman who assisted in the management of Max Fustian's Bond Street business.

"Hullo, is that you, my dear boy? Listen. I haven't much time. You must send Miss Fischer to the Picasso show. She knows my views. She must do my article this week. Now listen . . ."

He went on, evidently ignoring some muffled question from the other end of the wire.

"The American—you know who I mean—will probably come in tomorrow. Show him the Degas only. You understand? Nothing else. Only the Degas. You must attend the Leamington Castle sale without me. Our top price is fifteen thousand; not a penny more. . . . We shouldn't get it back—don't argue—we shouldn't get it back."

He paused, listening, and when he spoke again his tone was so casual that the words were barely formed, and it occurred to Campion that the man was labouring under some tremendous excitement.

"Yes," said Max Fustian into the telephone. "Yes, I shall be away. For two or three days; perhaps longer. . . . What? Something important? Yes, in a way. I suppose so."

He lifted the phone and looked over it at the puzzled group round the fire. When he was satisfied that he held their attention he devoted himself once more to the instrument. His hand was shaking, and his little dark eyes danced.

"My friend, my friend, why so importunate? . . . Very well, then; I don't know when I shall come back. . . . I say my return is problematic. . . . Yes. You see, I'm just going down to a lugubrious policeman in Lafcadio's dining room."

He looked up and spoke half to the room, half to the phone. "I'm going to confess to a murder. That's all."

7
Confession

"So you killed the deceased deliberately, Mr. Fustian? Well, now, perhaps you wouldn't mind sitting down and telling us clearly and concisely in your own words just exactly how you did it and why."

The inspector's slow voice sounded startlingly matter-of-fact in the room, which still tingled and vibrated with the dramatic eloquence of Max Fustian's announcement. Oddly enough the drama became more intense, more serious, the difference between the real thing and a play, and the constable sitting at one end of the long mahogany table, his helmet placed carefully in front of him, breathed heavily as he waited, pencil poised, to take down the dictation.

Apart from the inspector and the self-accused man the room also contained Mr. Campion, lounging carelessly against the bookcase, his fair head bent and his hands thrust deep in his pockets.

The light seemed irritatingly bad and the atmosphere of the room cold and unventilated.

Max was excited, not to say exalted. There were feverish spots of colour in his sallow cheeks, and his eyes were unusually bright.

"You wish me to make a formal confession, I take it, Inspector? Well, that's perfectly in order. My name is Max Nagelblatt Fustian. I am forty years of age—"

"That's all right, Mr. Fustian."

Once again the inspector's patient, unemotional voice supplied a genuine note in Max's histrionics.

"We know all that. I shan't cast this into statement form until after we've got the facts. It's very important to take a thing like this quietly. We don't want any mistakes at the beginning. If you start off right it's easier for everybody in the end. Don't go too fast, because Bainbridge here will be taking it down. Think before you speak. What happens afterwards is nearly always based on what you said at the beginning, and a word spoken now will carry more weight than a dozen tomorrow morning. Now then, just start from where you made up your mind to kill the other gentleman."

Max regarded the grave-faced, slow-speaking policeman with contempt and exasperation. As an appreciative audience the inspector was a failure.

"I resent this official attitude," he burst out. "Can't you see I'm trying to help you? If I hadn't chosen to come forward you'd still be floundering. I made up my mind to kill young Dacre last night. I was not sure when or how, but last night when I heard that insufferable young idiot had married the girl Rosa-Rosa and had insulted Miss Lafcadio I decided that the man should be done away with. My motive was purely altruistic. I am one of those people who are blessed, or cursed, with a nature which has to interfere. If I see a thing that needs doing I do it."

He was striding up and down the room as he spoke, throwing off the short, explosive sentences with the transparent conceit of a child.

The inspector watched him gravely, and the constable scribbled without once lifting his head. Mr. Campion appeared to be lost in thought.

"I had no time to lay my plans carefully. The opportunity came and I took it. From the beginning the scissors fascinated me. When the lights went out I saw my opportunity. The rest was simple. I went quietly across the room, picked up the scissors, struck the blow. The boy grunted and went down like a pig. The dagger was still in my hand. I wiped the handle, dropped it on the body and moved away. It was really very simple. I think that's all I can tell you. Would you like me to come with you at once? There's a cab rank on the corner. Perhaps Mr. Campion would be so kind as to tell Rennie to fetch one."

The inspector grunted.

"All in good time, Mr. Fustian," he said mildly. "You must let us have our own way a little, you know. There's just one or two things we shall have to ask. Just read what the gentleman said about the actual stabbing, Bainbridge."

The constable, looking undignified and very young without his helmet, cleared his throat and read the sentences without punctuation or expression:

" 'I went quietly across the room picked up the scissors struck the blow the boy granted and went down like a pig the dagger was still in my hand I wiped the handle and dropped it on the body.' "

"Ah," said the inspector. "The word's 'grunted,' Bainbridge, in the second line. 'Grunted and went down like a pig.' "

"Thank you, sir," said the constable and made the correction.

"Yes, well," said the inspector, "that's all right as far as it goes. Now, Mr. Fustian, supposing this was the scissors. Would you hold it, please?"

He picked up a long, round ruler from the inkstand and handed it gravely to the man.

"Now you, Mr. Campion, would you come and be the deceased, please? The man Dacre was sitting on the edge of the table where the jewelry was exhibited; leaning on it, I take it, supported partly by his hands. Now would you take up that position, please, Mr. Campion?"

Mr. Campion came forward obligingly and took up the position the inspector indicated. It was some moments before the inspector was satisfied, but at length he stepped back and returned to Max.

"Now, Mr. Fustian, would you demonstrate with the ruler, please, exactly how you struck the blow?"

"But this is ridiculous—insufferable." Max's voice was high-pitched with exasperation. "I've confessed. I stand before you self-accused. What more do you want?"

"Just a matter of routine, sir. We want to do everything right. It saves a lot of trouble in the end. Now, just go over it exactly as you did it in the studio in the dark. You walked over to him. We'll assume you've picked up the scissors."

Max was staring at the man, his eyes glittering. He was trembling with excitement and uncontrolled temper, and for a moment it seemed as if he would forget himself entirely and resort to physical violence. However, he pulled himself together and with a superb shrug of his shoulders permitted himself his famous crooked smile.

"Oh, well," he said, "if you want to play games, why not? Look very closely and I'll show you just how the horrid murder was done."

He gripped the ruler, raised his arm above his head, and brought it down within an inch of Campion's waistcoat.

57

"There you are," he said. "Perfectly simple. Straight through the ribs and into the heart. Very pretty blow, really. I think I'm rather pleased with it."

The inspector's nod was noncommittal.

"Just once again, please," he said.

Max complied, all his old contemptuous amusement returning. "I raised my hand, thus, and brought it down with all my strength."

"Did you feel any resistance?" said Oates unexpectedly.

Max raised his eyebrows. "Well, I—I felt the slight resistance of the waistcoat cloth, and I think I touched a bone, but really it happened so quickly . . . I'm afraid I haven't your prosaic mind, Inspector."

"Very likely not, Mr. Fustian."

There was no underlying tartness in Oates's tone.

"What did you do then—after you felt the resistance of the bone, I mean?"

"Then I felt the man fall. Then—oh, let me see—then I wiped the handle of the scissors on my handkerchief and dropped them on the body. Then I moved away. Anything else I can tell you?"

Oates considered. "No," he said at last. "No, I think that's all, Mr. Fustian. Perhaps you will sit down."

"Really, is all this hanging about necessary?" Max's drawl was becoming plaintive. "After all, this is a nerve-racking business for me, Inspector, and I should like to get it over."

"So would we all, Mr. Fustian." Oates was gently reproving. "But then it's a serious business. Murder's a capital charge, remember, and, as I say, we don't want to make any mistakes at the beginning. Hand me that note, will you, Bainbridge? Thank you. Now, you went across the room in the dark and picked up the scissors. The failure of the lights was a complete accident. It came as a surprise to everyone. There's no question on that point. We have evidence to show that you were standing talking to Miss Harriet Pickering when the lights failed, at approximately a distance of fifteen feet from the table where the deceased was leaning. We have there separate statements to show that. According to your story you went over and picked up the scissors.

"Well, we won't question that. Wait a minute, sir," he continued, waving aside Max's excited outburst. "You then tell us—and we've been very careful over this point; you've shown us and you've described it—that you raised your hand above your head and brought the weapon down, noticing the resistance of the tough cloth of the deceased's waistcoat and a slight resistance which you thought must be caused by the blades glancing off a bone.

"Now that brings us to another point. The blow which killed Thomas Dacre was an upward thrust delivered very scientifically. As the deceased was wearing a woollen pullover and not a waistcoat, there was very little resistance offered to the blow by the clothing. The weapon entered the body just below the lower rib and went straight up into the heart, causing almost instantaneous death."

Max was sitting very stiff and white in his chair, his bright eyes fixed upon the inspector's face. Oates remained slightly preoccupied and perfectly grave.

"Now, to return to your statement, sir. You then removed the weapon, wiped the handle, and dropped it on the body. I query this because the weapon remained in Dacre's body until the police surgeon took it out. Also, the handle was not wiped.

"I think that's all, except for the matter of the motive. We have a great many murders every year, most of them committed for obvious reasons, some of them very sound reasons. The altruistic murderer is rare, and of course I couldn't say what the chances of your being one were until we have the evidence of the police doctor as to the state of your mind. But I'm prepared to forego the trouble of instituting an enquiry of that sort in the present instance. I don't think it's necessary in view of the discrepancies I've already mentioned."

Max regarded him narrowly. "Do I understand that you are refusing to accept my confession?" he said icily.

Oates folded the constable's notes and fitted them into his pocketbook before he replied. Then he glanced up. His rather tired eyes were as mild as ever.

"Yes, Mr. Fustian," he said. "That's about it."

Max said nothing, and after an interval the inspector went on speaking. He was very quiet, very friendly, and unexpectedly authoritative.

"Now look here, Mr. Fustian," he said, "you may as well understand our position. We've got to get at the truth. No doubt you did what you did for the best reasons in the world. You thought a young lady was about to be arrested, and you thought you'd do her a good turn. Very likely you thought we were making a silly mistake and didn't care what you did to stop us giving unnecessary pain. I appreciate your motives, and I think you've done a very nice thing, in a way, but you must see that you're only wasting our time and your own and not really helping things forward at all.

"Oh, I may as well mention, too, before you go, that in Miss Harriet Pickering's evidence she states that she was talking to you throughout the entire time that the lights were out, so you see your gesture was doomed to failure from the beginning. Good evening. I'm sorry this should have happened like this, but you see how it is."

There was a moment or two of silence after the inspector had finished speaking, and then Max rose slowly to his feet and went out of the room without uttering a word. They heard his brisk pattering footsteps disappearing down the corridor.

The inspector nodded to the constable, who picked up his helmet and went out.

Mr. Campion and his friend exchanged glances.

"A bad show," ventured the younger man.

The inspector grunted.

"There's one born every minute," he said. "I don't like that type, though. Exhibitionists they're called, aren't they? It leaves us with our original problem. There isn't anything to be gained from it at all. I shall give the girl twenty-four hours yet, in case something turns up. Now I think I'd better get back and make my report. A nice thing to happen in the middle of a Sunday afternoon!"

Mr. Campion lit a cigarette.

"It's an incomprehensible business," he said. "As you say, the only person in the world who could have had any conceivable reason for killing so insignificant a person as young Dacre was the girl, and I assure you she's innocent. I'd stake my last bob on it.

"Of course," he added hopefully, "the whole thing might have been an accident. I mean, there's always the possibility that Dacre was not the man the murderer intended to kill. After all, there's an element of chance about the whole affair; the blow being struck in the dark and going straight home and that sort of thing."

"Oh, it's a stunner," said the inspector gloomily. "I knew

that as soon as I heard the telephone bell going this afternoon." He spoke savagely and as one who believed in premonitions. He tapped the papers in his hand.

"From the statements here you'd think we'd come to a lunatic asylum. There's only two or three concise stories among the lot. That woman Potter was as good as anyone. She seemed to have her wits about her. But her husband was the vaguest thing on earth. D'you know, Campion, I sometimes wonder how some of these fellows manage to keep alive. God knows it's hard enough to earn a living when you've got all your wits about you. But these blokes don't die. Someone looks after 'em."

Campion accompanied the inspector to the front door, and as they passed through the hall the object of Oates's gloomy conjectures hurried out of the dining room to meet them. Mr. Potter's red unhappy face wore an even more wretched expression than usual, and his eyes were frightened.

"Oh, I say, you know, I would like to go back to my studio," he said. "I don't see any point in hanging about here any longer. It's all very sad and awkward, I know, but we must live. I mean, life's got to go on, hasn't it? I can't do any good here."

He was half in and half out of the dining-room doorway as he spoke, and twice he glanced apprehensively over his shoulder back into the room during his short speech. He was so palpably alarmed and preoccupied that both men instinctively glanced past him.

What they saw was completely unexpected. Lying upon the hearth rug and cutting into the picture made by the angle of the door was a pair of feet encased in sensible brown shoes.

The inspector walked into the room, sweeping aside Mr. Potter's tentative and ineffectual gestures of protest.

"That's all right, Mr. Potter," he said. "I see no reason why you shouldn't go back to your studio now. It's only in the garden, isn't it?"

"Yes, yes, that's right." Mr. Potter was still dancing in front of the policeman in an attempt to screen the object on the floor.

His efforts were completely fruitless, however, and Campion, who had followed Oates, found himself looking down at Mrs. Potter lying upon her back, her face crimson and her sleek hair disordered. She was breathing stertorously, and her eyes were closed.

Mr. Potter gave up all attempts at deception with a rather pathetic little shrug of his shoulders, and then, as the silence became oppressive, "It's my wife," he said apologetically. "The shock's been too much for her, you know. She feels things very deeply. These—these masterful women sometimes do."

"You'd better get her to bed," said the inspector casually. "Can you manage?"

"Oh, yes, yes. It's nothing." Mr. Potter was already motioning them towards the door. "Good night."

"Good night," said Oates. "Are you coming, Campion?"

As they walked down the steps to the street, the older man glanced at his friend.

"Did you see that?" he said. "That was a funny thing, wasn't it? Now I wonder what that means."

The younger man's friendly face wore a faintly puzzled expression. "I didn't go very near her," he said, "but it looked to me as if—"

"Oh, she was drunk, all right," said Oates. "Didn't you see the decanter on the sideboard? She must have taken pretty well a tumblerful neat to put her out like that. Some people do, you know. It's a form of drugging. But what for, I'd like to know? What's she got on her mind that she can't bear to think about? There's something very odd about all this, Campion. Well, well, I wonder now."

8
Little Things

The affair at Little Venice might have lingered on at this stage in its development until it became a tabooed subject at Scotland Yard and a worn-out scandal in Bayswater, had it not been for the conversation which the grave-faced man from the Foreign Office held with his department.

The dictates of diplomacy being of considerable importance in those days of conferences, the Home Secretary took action, and the press became oddly disinterested in the murder. A discreet inquest was followed by a quiet funeral, and the remains of Thomas Dacre were deposited in Willesden Cemetery without further attention from the police.

Lafcadio's household quietened down and might never again have emerged from its seclusion had it not been for the startling, utterly unexpected tragedy which was the second murder.

A little over three weeks after Dacre's death, when Inspector Oates had ceased to sigh with relief for the intervention of the powers that be, Mr. Campion was seated in his own room in the flat at Bottle Street when Linda called.

She came in hurriedly, her coat clinging to her lean young figure. She looked modern and distinctive, and once again he was reminded that the tempestuous Lafcadio was her grandfather. There was the same faint air of rebellion about her, the same nonchalance, the same frank consciousness that she was a privileged person.

She was not alone. Her companion was a young man of her own age. Campion found himself liking him even before the introductions had been effected.

He was not unlike the girl herself, loosely but strongly built, wide of shoulder and narrow of hip, with faded hair, a big characterful nose, and shy dancing blue eyes.

He seemed delighted to see Campion and favoured the room with the frankly approving stare of a friendly child.

"This is Matt D'Urfey," said Linda. "He used to share a hovel with Tommy."

"Yes, of course. I've seen your pen drawings about, haven't I?" Campion turned to the visitor.

"Very likely," said D'Urfey without pride. "I must live. I say, I like your flat."

He wandered across the room to look at a small Cameron over the bookshelf, leaving Linda to continue the conversation. She did this at once, plunging immediately into the matter on her mind with her usual directness.

"Look here, Albert," she said, "about Tommy. There's something very queer going on."

Campion glanced up at her shrewdly, his pale eyes suddenly grave behind his spectacles.

"Still?" he enquired, adding, "I mean, anything fresh?"

"Well, I think so." Linda's tone kept a touch of its old defiance. "Of course you may pooh-pooh the whole thing, but you can't get away from the facts. That's why I've brought Matt along. I mean, look at Matt; he's not the person to imagine anything."

The recipient of this somewhat doubtful compliment glanced over his shoulder and smiled delightfully, returning immediately to the etching, which he evidently enjoyed.

"My dear girl,"—Campion's tone was soothing—"I haven't heard the facts yet. What's up?"

"There aren't any actual facts. That's what's so infuriating." Her big grey-green eyes above the wide cheekbones were suddenly suffused with helpless tears.

Campion sat down. "Suppose you tell the sleuth all about it," he suggested.

"I want to. That's why I've come. Albert, whoever killed Tommy is not content with stealing his life. They're just obliterating him as well, that's all."

Mr. Campion had a gentle, kindly personality and was possessed of infinite patience. Gradually he calmed the girl and got her to tell her rather curious story.

"The first things that disappeared were those drawings of Tommy's that I showed you on the day of the private view," she said. "You remember them. They were in that cupboard in the studio. About a dozen or fourteen. Just sketches, most of them, but I'd kept them because they were good. I went to get them out last week because I wanted to have a little show of Tommy's work somewhere—nothing ambitious, you know, just a few things of his in one of the small galleries. I didn't want him to just fade away utterly, you see, because he—he—well, he had *something*, didn't he?"

Her voice, never very steady, threatened to break, but she controlled herself and went on:

"First of all I found my drawings had gone. I turned the place out and raised hell generally, but they'd just vanished. They've gone as completely as if they'd never existed. And then, of course, I couldn't get a gallery."

She paused and regarded Campion earnestly.

"Can you believe that there isn't a single small gallery in London to be had for love or money to exhibit Tommy's work? It isn't even as though times were good and money was floating around. It's a conspiracy, Albert, a wretched, measly, mean effort to stamp Tommy out of the public mind for ever."

Mr. Campion looked uncomfortable.

"My dear girl," he said at last, "don't you think the— well, the unfortunate circumstances of young Dacre's death may have something to do with it? After all, I know the good gallery folk aren't all renowned for good taste, but don't you think they feel they don't want to lay themselves open to any accusation of sensation-mongering? Why not leave it for a year or so and let him burst on the world without any unpleasant associations?"

The girl shrugged her shoulders.

"Perhaps so," she said. "That's what that little beast Max says. Still, that's only a half, only a quarter, of the whole thing. You see, Albert, it isn't only my drawings that have vanished. All his work, everything he ever did, is going. Someone hated him so much that they don't want anything he possessed to remain."

Matt, who had given up contemplating the walls, lounged back to Linda's side.

"I thought it was rather odd that anyone should burgle the hovel," he remarked. "I mean, what had Tommy got? Nothing but his paints and a spare shirt. Nothing of mine was touched. Thank God," he added piously.

"Burglary?" enquired Campion.

"Good Lord, yes. Hasn't Linda told you? I thought that's why we came." Mr. D'Urfey seemed astonished. "The night before last, when I was down at the Fitzroy, some lunatic walked into the hovel and removed every single thing Tommy possessed. His clothes, one or two old canvases, all his paints, brushes, and other paraphernalia. Rather queer, wasn't it? I was glad to get rid of the stuff in a way— other people's junk, you know—but I thought it was odd, so I mentioned it to Linda, and since all the poor chap's stuff is vanishing she thought we'd better come along."

Mr. Campion listened to this somewhat extraordinary announcement with interest. "When you say all his stuff is vanishing, what do you mean?" he enquired.

"Just that," said Linda. "Seigal's in Duke Street had a few of his drawings, and just after he died they displayed them in that small box case on the left of the door. You know they haven't much window space. Well, the whole box was taken, stolen, some time in the lunch hour when the street was pretty well deserted. No one saw them go. Then there were the contents of his studio in Florence. Someone bought the lot within twenty-four hours of his death. I wrote the people last week and got their reply yesterday."

She hesitated and went on awkwardly:

"He owed quite a lot, and they were glad to accept any offer for the stuff he left behind. They didn't seem to know who the man was. I've wired them for full particulars, but I haven't had any reply yet."

Mr. Campion sat on the arm of his chair, his long, thin legs stretched out in front of him.

"This is very odd," he said. "About the—er—hovel burglary. You say nothing but Dacre's stuff was taken?"

"Oh, well, they lifted an old overall of mine," said D'Urfey casually, "but the rest was all his. That wasn't so difficult, as a matter of fact," he went on frankly. "Dacre was a tidy bloke anyway, and he'd only just returned, so most of his stuff was stacked up in a corner of the studio, hardly any of it unpacked. What made me think it was a bit queer," he continued, evidently making a much longer speech than was his wont, "was why anyone should come to the hovel. It's perfectly simple to walk into, of course, but why should anyone do it?"

"Where," enquired Mr. Campion, "is the hovel?"

"Christian Street. It turns off the wrong end of Shaftesbury Avenue," said D'Urfey promptly. "It's that smelly little road on the right, opposite the Princess Theatre and parallel with Drury Lane. The hovel is two top rooms in the house over the rag-and-bone shop. The stink has worn off by the time you get to the top, or you've grown used to it— I've never been sure which," he added frankly. "It's not bad. No sanitation, but central and all that. Anyone could walk in and move out my entire estate at any time, of course, but no one ever does. Why should they?"

"No one saw any stranger go up, I suppose, on the day of your burglary? The people underneath, for instance?"

"No. Mrs. Stiff lives on the floor below. She's a flower girl in Piccadilly, and she was out all the evening. The rag-and-bone shop closes at five, and the place is pitch dark after eight. We're not very hot on street lamps in our district—the kids smash 'em—so anyone could have come in. Still, it doesn't matter, but it's funny, isn't it?"

Mr. Campion considered. Linda was regarding him sombrely, but Mr. D'Urfey's dancing eyes had already strayed to a Currier & Ives which had taken his fancy, and he moved over to get a closer view.

Campion framed a delicate question.

"There is Dacre's wife," he ventured at last. "Might not she have felt that his things were her property?"

"Wife?" Matt left his print unwillingly. "Oh, Rosa-Rosa. I forgot. Yes, we thought of her at once. I looked her up, but she doesn't know a thing about it. In fact she's livid about his trunk going. Apparently there's a pair of stays in it that he refused to let her wear. She was very fond of them. She's very dense, you know, but these things were heirlooms as far as I could make out. Did you understand her, Linda?"

"Rosa-Rosa did not take Tommy's things." The girl spoke with the quiet conviction which quenches all argument. There was a pause. "I don't know why I've come to you, Albert. I don't know what I expect you to do," she burst out suddenly. "But something queer is happening; something I don't understand."

Her strong brown hands fluttered in an odd, helpless gesture. "Do you know, I can't think of anything in the world I can lay my fingers on that he ever possessed—not a scrap of drawing, not a paintbrush."

Campion rose to his feet and patted her shoulder.

"I think I can alter that for you," he said, a tinge of satisfaction in his voice. "I've got a drawing of Dacre's in the next room. You can have it if you like."

He hurried out, to return almost immediately with a big flat brown-paper parcel which he set down on the desk.

"I'm afraid I ought to confess that I did a bit of sharp buying myself," he said, snipping the string. "I phoned Max Fustian at his office on the date after the—er—private view and told him that I'd seen some of Dacre's work and was very impressed with it. He went round to Seigal's, I suppose, for when I got to his gallery he had half a dozen to show me. I bought one, and as I was off to Paris that afternoon they kept it and didn't send it round until yesterday. I haven't opened it yet. I like it immensely. It's the head of a boy, a Spaniard, I think."

On the last word he brushed back the brown paper and revealed a strip of plywood packing within.

"Here we are," he went on, lifting it up and removing the layers of tissue, "all mounted and everything—"

His voice trailed away on the last word, and a startled exclamation escaped the girl, for the pristine mount was empty, and, although they searched the parcel again and again, of the "Head of a Boy" by Thomas Dacre there was no sign whatever.

9
Salesmanship

"My dear fellow, fantastic! Positively fantastic!"

Max Fustian strode up and down the luxurious carpet which covered the floor of the principal salon of his exquisite little gallery and offered this opinion with a wealth of gesture.

The Salmon Galleries in Bond Street had been redecorated when he took them over, and now they were a fitting tribute to his taste and his business acumen. Save for a few carefully displayed pictures, Mr. Fustian's stock-in-trade was kept delicately in the background, and the unwary visitor might imagine that he had inadvertently strayed into the private house of some fabulously wealthy personage whose taste was so elegantly refined that it had almost reached the point of negation.

The soundproof walls shut out all noise from the street, and, in the hushed atmosphere common to art galleries, cathedrals, and banks, Max's melodious drawl sounded less out of place than it had done in Belle's drawing room.

Mr. Campion leant upon his stick and watched the man with interest.

"Well, I thought I'd tell you, you know," he said half apologetically, since it seemed to be committing sacrilege to mention anything so vulgar as the contents of a brown-paper parcel in such a rarefied atmosphere.

"My dear Campion, of course." Max was magnificently condescending. "I've sent for the man who does our packing. No drawing in the mount, you say? It's fantastic. But then, you know, extraordinary things are happening in connection with that wretched boy's death; the wildest things. I had an amazing experience myself. I'll tell you about it. If you've seen Linda—poor child! how decorative she is in her grief—you know about Seigal's case of drawings. Really, until this morning I thought you were the last man in London, possibly in the world, to have a specimen of Dacre's work."

With the movement of a ballet dancer he swooped down upon a beautifully chased steel box, the only object on an exquisitely figured walnut table, which in turn shared with two William and Mary chairs the privilege of being the only furniture in the room.

Mr. Campion refused an Egyptian cigarette which looked odd, unpleasant, and possibly of enormous value.

"You agree with Linda, then, that someone's trying to stamp Dacre's work out of existence?" he ventured.

Max raised his eyebrows and spread out his long white hands.

"Who can tell?" he said. "Nothing's impossible, you know, Campion. Personally, I'm not inclined to bother about it. Dacre had talent, you know, but then who hasn't in these days? He was one of thousands—thousands! Talent is not enough, Campion. The modern connoisseur wants genius. Poor Dacre! Poor, mediocre Dacre! Only his death made him interesting."

Mr. Campion grinned. "That's a distinction he shares with quite a lot of painters," he ventured.

The other man's little bright black eyes flickered for an instant.

"How exquisitely true," he said. "But I suppose we ought to be grateful to Dacre that at least his death was genuinely interesting. All his work vanishing like this, it's quite romantic. My own experience was interesting. I didn't admire Dacre's work, you know, but there was a little thing—just a study of a hand—a little thing of no value at all, but it pleased me. There was something in the line, something—how shall I say?—enlightened, you understand. I had it framed rather charmingly. A new idea of my own: the moulding was carved from stone. It's exceptionally right for certain pencil drawings. The greys blend. I had it hanging in my dining room just above a rather lovely stripped Stuart bread cupboard."

He paused and held a gesture which Mr. Campion took to indicate that he was visualizing a pleasing scene.

"It was a conceit of mine," he went on, sublimely unconscious of any impression but the one he intended, "to keep a certain coloured rose in a pewter jar a little to the left of the picture. It formed a little group, broke the line, and pleased me. The other night when I came into my flat I realized at once that someone had been there. Just little things altered, you know—a chair not quite in alignment, a cushion on the wrong end of the sofa—just little things that offend one's eye. Although nothing was actually in disorder, you understand, I knew at once that someone had been through the place, and I hurried into my bedroom.

"There was the same story. Just little things altered. The moment I entered the dining room the thing hit me in the eye. The pewter jar with the rose was set directly beneath the picture. I hurried over, and there was the empty frame. The drawing had been taken out quite skilfully.

"I don't mind admitting to you, Campion, that at first I was inclined to suspect Linda, although how she could have got into my flat, I don't know. But after seeing her and talking to her I realized, of course, that she didn't know anything and was just as puzzled as I was. The whole thing's absurd, isn't it?"

"The drawing had gone?" said Mr. Campion, who seemed to be afflicted with a sudden stupidity.

"Completely." Max waved his hands in the air. "Just like that. Ridiculous, isn't it?"

"Amazing," said Campion bluntly.

The conversation was interrupted by the arrival of a sallow, somewhat scared-looking child in a travesty of one of Max's own suits.

"This is Mr. Green, who packs our pictures," said Max with the air of one introducing a rare and privileged creature. "You've heard of our difficulty, Mr. Green?"

The boy looked bewildered. "I can't understand it, Mr. Fustian. The drawing was all right when I packed it."

"You're sure it was there?" Max fixed the young man with a bright, beady eye.

"There, sir? Where, sir?"

"I mean," said Max with gentle force, "I mean, my dear

Mr. Green, that you're certain there was a drawing in the mount which you so carefully packed and sent to Mr. Campion?"

The boy's sallow cheeks flushed. "Well, naturally, sir. I'm not barm—I mean, I'm sure it was there, Mr. Fustian."

"There you are, Mr. Campion." Max turned to his visitor with the gesture of a conjuror removing the black cloth.

Campion turned to the boy.

"What happened to the parcel after you had packed it? Was it delivered straightway?"

"No, sir. I understood you didn't want it delivered at once, and so it stood on the rack in the room downstairs where we make tea for about a week."

"The room where you make tea, Mr. Green?" asked Max coldly.

The child, who Campion decided, could not be more than fourteen, wriggled painfully. "Well, the room where we wash our hands, sir," he muttered.

"In the staff cloakroom?" said Max in cold astonishment. "Mr. Campion's beautiful drawing stood on the rack in the staff cloakroom for almost a week? Surely, Mr. Green, that was a mistake?"

"Well, it had to stand somewhere," said the wretched Mr. Green, goaded into revolt by this mixture of injustice and the inexplicable.

"I see," said Max coldly. "Then at any time during the week anyone could have tampered with Mr. Campion's beautiful drawing. That will do, Mr. Green."

Mr. Green departed miserably, and Max returned to Mr. Campion with a rueful gesture.

"One's staff!" he said. "One's staff!"

Mr. Campion smiled politely, but his pale eyes behind his spectacles were thoughtful. On the face of it this new development in the affair at Little Venice was frankly bewildering. At first he had been inclined to suspect Linda of a disordered imagination. Then the thought had occurred to him that some price-forcing conspiracy might be afoot. But although there are many collectors who will buy up all the pictures of a painter tragically dead, there were surely few who would go to the lengths of committing burglary and appropriating old clothes.

On the other hand, in his own surroundings Max was

inclined to be a more comprehensible person than he had appeared in Lafcadio's home. His somewhat extraordinary line of conversation sounded less bizarre in the gallery.

Mr. Campion, who had the wit to make a study of men without considering himself a connoisseur of humanity, began to regard him with new interest. The inspector, he felt, had not done him justice.

It was at this point in his reflections that Mr. Isidore Levy, plump and intelligent, came hurrying up to murmur a few words to Max.

Campion saw the little black eyes light up.

"He's come, has he?" he said. "I'll be with you immediately."

Mr. Campion hurried to make his excuses. In the past few moments he had become aware of a suppressed excitement in the gallery, an air of momentous happening.

"I'll come back later," he said. "Or perhaps you'd phone me?"

"My dear fellow, don't go." Max's tone was obviously genuine. "I have a client." He lowered his voice. "Sir Edgar Berwick—yes, the politician. He rather fancies himself as an authority on Flemish art."

He slipped his arm through Campion's and led him down the room away from the door, talking softly.

"It's really rather amusing. He wants to make a presentation to his local art gallery, and I think I have something that will interest him. Come along; you must hear it. It's part of your education. I insist. And besides," he added with sudden naïveté, "I'm better with an audience. You're a student of psychology, aren't you? Here's an interesting example for you."

When he followed Max into the smaller salon which formed the other showroom of the gallery, Campion saw at once that salesmanship had already begun. The high narrow room with its top lights and stripped-pine panelling had been prepared for the contest. The picture stood at the far end of the room on an easel, and the only other touch of pure colour was provided by a long velvet curtain draped graciously over a second doorway. By happy chance or ingenious design, the vivid blue in the picture was echoed in this hanging. The effect was very pleasant.

When Mr. Campion entered unobtrusively behind Max,

Sir Edgar was already standing before the picture, his grey head bent. He was an oldish man, large and remarkably dignified. His skin was pink and his natural expression belligerent. At the moment he looked important and extremely wise. He also appeared to be aware of the fact.

Mr. Campion, while feigning interest in a screenful of early German engravings, had leisure to observe the greeting. Max, he reflected, was superb. He approached his somewhat pompous client with just the right mixture of deference and friendliness and then stood beside him in silence, looking at the picture with somewhat self-conscious satisfaction, patently aware that he saw it as an expert and as no ordinary man.

Sir Edgar remained so long in contemplation that Mr. Campion had time to get a glimpse of the picture itself and all the others in the gallery before the interview continued.

He was not a judge of oils, but he could see from where he stood that the piece was a Flemish interior in the Jan Steen manner. It represented a christening party in a pleasant, clean-looking room where many little comedies were taking place. The painting seemed to be in good condition apart from a rather serious crack straggling across one corner.

At length, when Mr. Campion had completed his circle of the gallery and was back again at the colour prints, Sir Edgar stirred and turned to Max.

"Interesting," he pronounced. "Definitely interesting."

Max seemed to shake himself out of a trance. He dragged his eyes away from the canvas and permitted a faint enigmatic smile to pass over his countenance.

"Yes," he said softly. "Yes."

The superb noncommittal of this opening gambit over, silence again ensued. Sir Edgar squatted down on his august heels and peered through a small glass at the texture of the paint on the very bottom of the canvas.

Presently he rose to his feet and spoke brusquely:

"Can we have it out of the frame?"

"Of course." Max raised a hand, and magically two assistants in baize aprons, one of them the ubiquitous Mr. Green, appeared, the beautiful old frame was removed, and the picture, looking surprisingly less important, relinquished naked to Sir Edgar's little glass.

Then followed a minute examination of the canvas, back and front, interspersed by little grunts and muttered technicalities from the two combatants.

Presently the frame was restored and they took up their old positions in front of the easel, Sir Edgar a little pinker and a trifle dishevelled from his exertions, Max quieter, more enigmatic, than ever.

"No signature and no date," said the amateur.

"No," said Max. "Only internal evidence."

"Of course," the other agreed hastily. "Of course."

And once again there was silence.

"There's no mention of this christening piece in the catalogue of Steen's work," Sir Edgar ventured at last.

Max shrugged his shoulders. "In that case there'd hardly be a question," he said and laughed a little.

Sir Edgar echoed his laugh. "Quite," he agreed. "It's indubitably the right period."

Max nodded. "We have only the picture to go upon," he said, "and of course doubts naturally crowd into the mind. But there are little touches which you as an expert must recognize, Sir Edgar; that curious cross-grained canvas, that sitting figure in the foreground. Very like Steen himself. Interesting how those men went in for self-portraiture.

"Of course," he added, shrugging his shoulders, "I know no more than you. As I told you, it came into my hands in a perfectly orthodox way. I bought it at Theobald's in January. I paid fourteen hundred and fifty for it. I bought it after examining it very closely, you understand, and I backed my own judgment. I can't tell you whether it's a genuine Steen. I don't know. I'm inclined to think not. After all, a piece of luck like that doesn't happen these days. Not to me, at any rate. A signed Steen was sold in the same sale for two thousand seven hundred pounds, and A. T. Johnson, who bought that picture, ran me up to fourteen-fifty for this.

"But of course," he went on with a sudden gesture which swept aside anything so uninteresting as money, "there's the picture itself. This little group here, for instance"—his long fingers described an airy circle—"there's spirit and jollity there. There's something quite indescribable. Don't you notice it?"

"Oh, I do." Sir Edgar was plainly impressed. "I do. In

fact I'm inclined to go further than you, Fustian. You were always overcautious. The drawing of the child, that little piece of drapery, that suggests Steen to me."

"Yes," said Max casually. "Yes. Or a pupil."

"A pupil?" Sir Edgar considered this contingency and shook his head. "But," he went on, feeling perhaps that he had gone too far, "as you say, we can't be sure."

"No," said Max. "No. There's a mention in the first catalogue of a picture called 'The First Birthday.' If the child were older—but no. Even supposing the early chroniclers had not been too accurate, I fancy the production of a new find of that name would call into question a picture of that name in the Viennese collection."

Sir Edgar produced his glass once again and peered long and thoughtfully at the child.

"Well, Fustian," he said, "I'll let you know definitely. Fifteen hundred, you say? In the meantime I'll get you to put it on one side for me."

Max hesitated and then, with the air of one making a decision, produced what Mr. Campion suddenly felt must be the master stroke of this ordeal by innuendo.

"Sir Edgar," he said, "I'm sorry to disappoint you, but I've been thinking this matter over while we've been standing here, and I tell you frankly that I do not think it is a Steen. On the face of it I can't sell it with any kind of guarantee. It's charming, it's like—it's very like—but in the absence of external evidence I don't think I can commit myself to such a pronouncement. No, no. Leave it at that. I don't think it is a Steen."

Sir Edgar's bright, rather greedy blue eyes smiled.

"Officially," he murmured.

Max permitted himself a deprecatory grimace.

"No, I won't even say that," he said. "I'm afraid you must let me make it quite definite. I don't think it is a Steen. But I shall sell it to you for fifteen hundred, or I shall put it back in the sale room with that reserve."

Sir Edgar laughed and polished his glass carefully with his handkerchief before replacing it in his pocket.

"Cautious," he said. "Too cautious, Fustian. You ought to stand for Parliament. Put it on one side for me."

Mr. Campion drifted into the other salon. The interview, he understood, was at an end.

Max returned after some minutes, quietly elated. His

small black eyes were supremely happy, and although he did not directly refer to the interview which had passed, Campion felt that he was to understand that it had been a triumph.

They parted with many protestations of regret on Max's part and a reckless promise that the "Head of a Boy" should be recovered though it lay at the end of the earth.

Mr. Campion wandered off down Bond Street. His mind was uneasy. The affair of the Dacre drawings was odd and irritating, but he was aware that the root of the uncomfortable impression chipping at his mind lay not here. Rather, it was something that had happened during the last few minutes, something which his unconscious mind had seized and was trying to point out to him.

In sheer annoyance he forced himself to think of something else.

10
The Key

When Mr. Campion went to call on Belle three days after his visit to the Salmon Galleries his interest in the murder was still mainly academic.

The police, embodied by the inspector and his sergeant, had their own cut-and-dried views of the case. These had become crystallized in their minds by the cessation of the investigation, and their curiosity was appeased.

Campion, on the other hand, was convinced afresh every time he saw Linda that she had had nothing to do with the killing of Dacre and also that she was not hiding anything.

For him the question remained, and as he walked up the staircase to the drawing room he felt strange in the old house. It was as though he were visiting it for the first time and noticing something uncanny about it, something inhospitable, as though the very walls were hugging themselves away from him with jealous secrecy.

The drawing room looked much the same as usual,

however. A fire had been lighted against the chilly spring weather, and Belle sat in her low chair beside it, her plump hands held out to the blaze. As soon as Campion saw her he experienced his first feeling of animosity towards the murderer.

In the few weeks since the affair Belle had aged. She looked thinner and more fragile than before. There was a droop in the muslin of her bonnet and another at the corner of her mouth. Her brown eyes were more faded, and her welcome, although warm, was a trifle tremulous.

They were careful not to mention the business in those first minutes when they sat together by the hearth and waited for Lisa to bring tea, but its presence was very obvious, and even the grand bravura of John Lafcadio's trophies scattered round the room seemed to have lost its magic beside the piece of violent, sordid reality which had invaded their fastness.

When Lisa, the tea, and the inevitable Donna Beatrice arrived together, the skeleton could be kept decently in the cupboard no longer. Indeed, Donna Beatrice drew it forth with a flourish and the same air of self-righteous courage with which some people disclose the more disgusting details of their ailments.

"Mr. Campion," she said, thrusting her surprisingly strong hand into his own, "you don't regard us as social lepers, at any rate. As soon as I came into the room I was aware of a strong blue aura over here in the corner by Belle, and I said to myself, 'Well, here's a *friend* at any rate.' "

Mr. Campion, who had forgotten her rainbow complex, was taken aback.

"Not at all," he murmured unsuitably and rose to assist Lisa in the matter of the tea table. The old Italian woman shot him a sly, grateful smile from under her yellow lids, an expression immediately followed by a most expressive glare of hatred directed at the unsuspecting "Inspiration," who had seated herself in the high Stuart chair across the hearth.

Donna Beatrice was still dramatizing the situation on National Theatre lines. Her heavy black velvet, chased silver cross, and fine lace handkerchief were almost traditional. Belle's kind brown eyes rested on her a little wearily.

"No news, no developments. The secret grows oppressive," Donna Beatrice remarked with relish as she accepted a cup of tea. "Tell me, Mr. Campion, have the police really dropped the case, or are they just crouching, watching, waiting to spring?"

Mr. Campion glanced at Belle for support, which she gave him generously.

"I don't want to talk about it, Beatrice, if you don't mind," she said plaintively. "I'm growing old. I don't want to think of unpleasant things."

"Always a weakness, Belle dear," said the irrepressible Inspiration with intentional gentleness. "But if you say so, we'll change the subject. Tell me, Mr. Campion, do you think the trend of modern art shows degeneracy or a leaning towards the primitive?"

Half an hour later, when Campion was wondering why, with a murderer at large in Little Venice, Donna Beatrice should have escaped killing, Max arrived.

He made his usual entrance, kissed Belle's hand, bowed to the younger lady, all but chucked Lisa under the chin, and seemed a little put out to see Campion.

"Tea, Lisa," he said. "Tea, that vulgar little stimulant we sip to soothe our afternoons. Bring me tea."

With his arrival the talk steered onto more general subjects, and Donna Beatrice was eclipsed.

"Linda spends a great deal of her time with the boy D'Urfey," Max remarked suddenly. "I met them going out together just now when I came in from my call on Claire Potter."

"He seems a nice boy," said Belle. "He reminds me of poor Will Fitzsimmons before he became famous."

Donna Beatrice made a gesture. "Isn't that typical of Belle?" she said. "I'm afraid I'm more squeamish. Linda's infatuation for the friend of her murdered fiancé seems too much like morbidity for me."

Belle's eyes hardened.

"My granddaughter is neither morbid nor infatuated," she said with sudden vigour, and Max, who had opened his mouth, shut it again with the words unspoken.

Mr. Campion found himself growing more interested in Max. The man was not merely an empty poseur, and he felt he could begin to understand how he had carved a niche for himself in contemporary letters without having any especial gift. His was a tortuous, subtle brain, unexpectedly mobile and adroit.

Glancing at him now, lounging gracefully on a settee, his small dark face with its blue jowl and lively eyes turned towards the fire, Campion found him a most arresting personality.

"I trust the outcome of your masterly piece of salesmanship was successful the other afternoon?" he enquired.

Max turned to him lazily, but his smile showed him to be pleased.

"Eminently, thank you," he said. "The deal went through without another word."

Campion turned to Belle. "I had the privilege of seeing Fustian sell an old master the other afternoon," he said. "A most exciting experience. Tell me," he added, glancing back at the indolent figure on the settee, "how much doubt was there about the authenticity of that thing?"

"None whatever." The drawl was very pronounced. "None in the world."

Belle looked up sharply.

"What picture was it?" she enquired.

"Nothing to interest you, dear lady." Max seemed anxious to let the question drop. "A conversation piece in the Steen manner, that's all."

His casualness had not deceived the old woman, however. She leant forward, her eyes fixed upon him.

"Not a christening scene?"

Max avoided her glance at first, but presently he laughed and looked into her eyes.

"There was a child in it," he admitted.

"And a lot of blue and a kneeling figure in the foreground?" Belle persisted.

Max shot a glance at Campion.

"I confess to all of these," he said, laughing.

Mrs. Lafcadio sat back in her chair, her eyes round and reproachful, a flush in her wrinkled cheeks.

"Max, that's very disgraceful," she said. "Very disgraceful indeed. Poor old Salmon would turn in his grave if he knew about it—he's probably doing it now. Really, my dear, that's dishonest!"

"But my adorable Mrs. Lafcadio,"—Max was still smiling—"you don't understand. I never for one moment suggested that the christening scene was a genuine Steen. Campion must bear me out—I told my client very definitely that in my opinion it was not a Steen. I sold it on the strict understanding that I could give no guarantee of any kind. I said that in front of witnesses, didn't I, Campion?"

Mr. Campion was spared replying by Belle, who continued in the same impulsive way.

"That picture," she said, "as you must know very well, Max, was painted by old Cornelius van Pipjer. Surely you remember his widow? She used to live in the Cromwell Road. Johnnie and I were so sorry for her. I remember her dying quite well. It's some years ago, of course, because Linda's father wasn't born."

Max smiled faintly. "It's an old picture, then, anyway," he said.

For a moment Belle's eyes clouded and then she too smiled.

"I forget how old I am," she said. "Yes, of course, poor Hester van Pipjer was before any of your time. But I remember that picture. There were half a dozen of them, and Johnnie made Salmon buy them. Van Pipjer was a copyist, but that one picture was an original in the Steen manner. Van Pipjer himself would never part with it, but when he died and his widow was so desperately poor, Johnnie made Salmon buy the pictures. I remember, poor dear, he was very cross at having to pay as much for the original as the copies. He could sell the copies, you see, for what they were, but a single picture by an unknown artist in the manner of a master was hardly worth anything at all. Still, Mrs. van Pipjer was very glad of the money. I remember how she cried when she saw it, poor thing."

Max continued to smile, mischievously now, his eyes dancing.

"Dear Belle—what a gift!" he said. "You touch everything with the fairy finger of Romance. Can't you see her, Campion? The old Dutch widow weeping, the corner of her apron held to her eye, while my portly predecessor in the frock coat of munificence slips the golden guineas into the bosom of her dress!"

"Max, you won't get out of it that way." Belle shook her head at him angrily. "Besides, old Salmon would never think of slipping guineas into anyone's dress, although he certainly did wear a frock coat. But Mrs. van Pipjer never wore an apron, and if she had and was weeping into it, it would have been impossible to put money down her chest. But that's not the point. How much did you get for that picture?"

Mr. Campion looked the other way.

Max closed his eyes. "Fifteen," he said.

"Guineas?" demanded Belle, a little mollified.

"Hundreds," said Max.

"Fifteen hundred? Oh, Max, I won't have you here. I'm disgusted."

Donna Beatrice laughed a little enviously. "Very clever of Max, I think," she said.

"Don't encourage him." Belle was furious. "Oh," she added inconsequentially, "what a boon that money would have been to Hester! She had such a pretty daughter—in consumption, I remember."

Max burst out laughing. "Belle, you exquisite period piece," he said. "You do me wrong. I told my client that in my opinion the picture was not a Steen."

"Then why did he pay fifteen hundred pounds for it?"

"Because," said Max superbly, "the man was a pompous imbecile who imagined that I could be wrong."

"I suppose you suggested that it was a contemporary picture?" persisted Belle.

"I suggested nothing," said Max. "He did all the talking. Isn't that so, Campion? He certainly said it was painted on canvas contemporary with Steen, and I agreed with him. So it was. Your friend Van Pipjer must have had a stock of old canvases. Very useful."

Belle's muslin bonnet quivered in the warm air.

"You're very clever, Max," she said, "but you're not good."

Max's reply to this summing up of his character was typical. He slipped onto one knee at her side and burst into a torrent of words.

"Let me explain, dear lady. You're judging me unheard. If you had seen the man, you'd have agreed with me. You would have been my ally. You'd have convinced him it was a Steen, sold it for three thousand pounds, and spent the money on Hester van Pipjer's descendants. And you'd have been right."

He threw out his arm.

"There was this man, an overfed, self-important ignoramus with a ridiculous little glass—the sort of thing the detective in a farce might use—crawling about on my floor talking about the texture and the pigment as though he knew what the words meant. Why was he doing it?"

He sprang to his feet and strode down the room, working himself into a passion of eloquence, his eyes blazing with righteous fire.

"He was attempting to get an important picture cheap to present to the Art Gallery in a beastly town whose underfed millions he hopes to represent in Parliament. By this ostentatious gift he intends to impress the undereducated snobs on the local town council while the shivering children of the poor who subscribe to the rates and taxes are not interested in pictures at all. They want food. Do you know what I intend to do with that fifteen hundred pounds, Belle? I shall buy a motorcar. This fellow's rival candidate owns a factory which employs hundreds and thousands of men. I shall buy one of his cars, and the money which my idiot client should have spent on the poor children of his constituency will go back to them after all, with the picture thrown in."

He finished his peroration, one hand thrown out expressively.

The silence which followed this somewhat extraordinary argument was broken by a ladylike and ridiculous "Hear, hear, Max!" from Donna Beatrice.

"I agree with Max entirely," she said. "Too many people imagine they know something about Art."

Belle raised her eyebrows. "It seems to me," she said, "that two blacks make a white and there's a very expensive motorcar thrown in somewhere."

Mr. Campion alone was silent. He was assimilating the facts he had just heard and comparing them with the interview he had witnessed in the Salmon Gallery. It seemed to him that he was on the verge of a very startling and important idea.

He and Max left together soon afterwards and walked through the Crescent to a taxi rank on the railway bridge. It was raining and unusually dark for the time of year. Max appeared to be in high spirits. He strode along jauntily, his immense black hat set at an angle. Its brim was so wide that Campion, who towered above him, could not see his face beneath its shadow.

"The memory of the old!" Max remarked. "The coincidence, too! Extraordinary, wasn't it? Quite an instructive afternoon."

Campion was thinking furiously. The idea which had been nibbling at the back of his mind ever since he had turned out of the Salmon Gallery and walked down Bond Street suddenly became clear, and its significance sent an unaccustomed thrill down his spine.

What he had noticed subconsciously at the Salmon Gallery was an unmistakable family likeness between Max's story to the politician and his confession to Inspector Oates.

Apart from the obvious difference of emotional tone, the points of resemblance were striking: the apparent frankness, the flamboyancy, the whole-hearted courage, the completeness of the job. The other side of the picture-selling episode he had heard, and now a thought seized and bewildered him. What if there was another side to the confession? What if that, too, had been an essay in the second degree of subtlety?

He glanced down at the figure at his side, walking down the deserted London street, and experienced the odd physical phenomenon so aptly described as "the blood running cold." The more he thought about it the more clear it became. Max's confession had been altogether too easily discounted by the inspector. It was the confession of the hysterical and affected egotist Max appeared to be at first sight, and which the inspector still supposed him.

Mr. Campion now knew more than the inspector. He knew that Max was not a negligible idiot; moreover there seemed a reasonable chance that he was one of those strange, slightly crooked brains who not only take the courageous path but blind themselves to danger and truth alike. As Campion saw it now, Max's confession might very well have been a doubly ingenious lie, and if so the truth was terrifying.

He was aroused at this point in his reflections by a taxi pulling up beside them and Fustian's solicitous enquiry if he desired a lift.

Campion made his excuses, and Max entered the vehicle and was driven away. Mr. Campion stood in the rain looking after the cab until it disappeared from sight, momentarily stricken by what he could only regard as a species of revelation.

In the taxi Max removed his hat and lay back and laughed a little.

For some time he remained content in the contemplation of his own cleverness, but after a while he frowned and his bright black eyes narrowed. He was thinking of Mrs. Potter.

11
Before the Fact

On the morning of the Thursday on which she died, Mrs. Potter rose a trifle earlier than was her wont because there was so much to do.

She climbed out of the bed, which was a divan by day, and stood for a moment thinking. Her nightdress, copied from a figure on a Grecian plate, was surmounted by a pathetically warm and ugly bed jacket, comforting her throat and arms which the linen draperies neglected.

Her iron-grey hair was tousled and her face very pale. She had slept badly.

Mr. Potter had already risen and had retired to the lean-to shed behind the scullery in which he bit and printed his lithographs. He was safe for another hour at least.

His wife dressed mechanically, nervous lines wrinkling her forehead.

The studio was draughty and not very comfortable, so that its air of careful unconventionality was a little sad. The Chianti-bottle and Roman-shawl school of decoration now suggested less of the *vie-de-bohème* than the set for an amateur production of *Trilby*, and the romantic makeshifts and picturesque squalor so brave in youth were in the middle aged merely disheartening.

Claire Potter hurried, arraying herself in a Russian overall for housework. It was William's day at Blakenham, the school in Chelmsford which was optimistic enough to employ him as a visiting art master. He had to be "got off" in time.

In her efforts to set aside the one vital and terrible thought which had haunted her nights and days for the

84

past three weeks, Mrs. Potter forced herself to consider the duties of the day. There were the tickets for the Roman Guild's water-colour show to be sent up to the committee for distribution. Then the efforts of the Gipsy Sketch Club had to be marked and a hurried criticism scribbled on the back of each; arch little criticisms they would be: "Tone values! Careful!"—or "That broken wash again! Avoid viridian."

Claire Potter took them very seriously, which, since she was paid for them, was to her credit and very nearly constituted an excuse.

When the bed had been draped into its striped homespun blanket and the pillows thrust into their daytime slips and piled into one corner to give a "touch of colour" to the room, Mrs. Potter made her toilet at the scullery sink.

She had never identified herself with the unwashed movement and performed her ablutions carefully, finishing off her face with rice powder, which she packed herself and sometimes sold in pretty, hand-painted boxes.

She moved deftly and methodically, the only way of doing anything in the face of so many domestic inconveniences, although on this particular morning much of her wonted brisk efficiency was absent.

She paused for a time, a wave of sudden heat sweeping up her backbone and over her head, leaving her scalp tingling and her eyes feeling sticky and uncomfortable. She had lived in a world of small things for so long that the intrusion of something really large hardly registered on her conscious mind, but it had a curious physical effect upon her.

She took her brushes out of the turpentine, cleaned them carefully before preparing breakfast, but she dropped the whole handful of them and upset the jar at the sound of a footstep outside the studio door.

She was angry when she remembered it was probably Lisa or Fred Rennie leaving the *Morning Post*, which came to the Lafcadio front door.

It was some time before she could bring herself to look at the paper. She was the last person in the world to indulge in premonitions, but the restless, terrified feeling which had been slowly increasing all through the week seemed to have become insupportable this morning. It was as though she felt the breath of disaster on her cheek.

She snatched up the paper at last and scanned the news columns, an ever-growing sense of relief spreading over her as no familiar name caught her eye.

She turned back resolutely to the work of the day. There was so much to do and so little time. It was a terrible life. When one was really artistic, it did seem a pity that one should have to spend one's whole time working.

She began to think of Italy, of a little village up in the hills behind San Remo, where one could prop up one's easel beside the church and sit in the shadow and enjoy the lighting. It was all so clean and clear and courageous; the colours straight out of the tube.

She repeated this to herself aloud as though she found a particular comfort in it. If it weren't for William, and their dreadful poverty, and the never-ending round of things to do, she would go back to that village.

Just for an instant, when she was spreading the peasant cloth over the old English gate-legged table, an impulse seized her to go, to go at once, to leave everything and fly precipitately. But this outcome of an instinct for self-preservation was unfortunately hastily set aside.

She would think about it, perhaps. If her nerve failed her she might try it in the autumn. As it was, she must see Fred Rennie about some paint. And there was Miss Cunninghame coming at half past three for her lesson. The day was going to be a rush.

There had been times when Mrs. Potter had enjoyed Thursday. She liked being busy, she liked the air of importance which being secretary to the Roman Guild gave her, and she enjoyed pointing out to the refined and wealthy Miss Cunninghame exactly where that good lady's rather dated taste had let her down.

But today it was different.

Mr. Potter returned from the shed at the moment when the kippers were set on the table.

Mrs. Potter looked at him as though she were seeing him for the first time as he came in at the doorway, and it occurred to her forcibly that he was of no possible help to her in her terrible situation. She had never had a great opinion of him and, looking at him now in this new cold light, she wondered how on earth they had ever come to marry. Surely it must have been obvious in those halcyon days thirty years ago at St. Ives that the burden which that sad-faced youth had carried in his soul was not genius but a gloomy conviction of his lack of it.

All this was particularly sad because Mr. Potter was very happy. He was collarless, his old canvas trousers bagged at knee and seat, and his feet thrust into heelless Turkish slippers were bare. But he was joyful. The wretchedness had almost completely vanished from his face, and he waved a damp piece of jap paper at his wife in something akin to triumph.

"A beauty," he said. "A beauty. Claire, my dear, that last stone is a corker. I'm afraid I'm a little dirty. The ink, you know. But look at it! You couldn't get that feeling on ordinary stone. Sandstone's a new and important medium. I've always said so, and this is going to prove it."

He pushed the crockery out of the way and set the print down upon the tablecloth, leaving an inky thumb smear upon the linen.

The sight of this blemish was the first blot on Mr. Potter's morning, and he dropped his hand over it hastily, glancing at his wife out of the corners of his eyes.

Somewhat to his relief, she was not looking at him but staring out of the window, an expression on her face that he did not remember having seen there before. She looked almost afraid, almost gentle.

For some reason which he did not understand, this phenomenon delighted him. He plucked at her sleeve.

"Look," he said. "It's good, isn't it? I was going to call it 'A Bit of Old Bayswater,' but I think I might have something a bit more modern than that, since it's come off. There's the railway bridge, you see. It's come out beautifully, hasn't it? Those nice shadows there."

She still did not speak, and he continued to gloat over the lithograph.

"I thought I'd frame it and hang it over there, instead of the Medici print. After all, an original's better than a reproduction any day."

"Oh, William, don't be silly. Get on with your breakfast. I've got such a lot to do."

Mrs. Potter flicked the print onto the divan and put the food back in front of her husband.

"Oh, be careful, my dear. It's not dry. Such a beautiful print. It's taken me all the morning."

Despair was creeping back into Mr. Potter's tone, and

as he sat down meekly now and pecked at his kipper, which had grown cold and unappetizing, he looked old and neglected and rather dirty.

Mrs. Potter ate her breakfast as though she would have disliked it had she thought about it. Once again the frightened expression which made her look gentle deceived her husband, and, after a sly glance to see that his print was all right, he leant forward.

"Are you well, Claire? You've seemed nervous and not quite the thing ever since the reception."

To his surprise she turned on him with quite unwarranted vigour.

"That's not true. I'm perfectly all right. The reception has got nothing to do with it, anyway. Hurry. You've got to catch the ten-thirty at Liverpool Street."

"All right." Mr. Potter's gloom had completely returned. "I'm sorry I've got to go today," he said. "I would have liked to make one or two more prints. Mrs. Lafcadio would like one, I know. It's deadly work, teaching," he went on. "It's difficult enough teaching people who want to learn, but those boys aren't a bit keen. It makes it very difficult."

Mrs. Potter made no reply, but sipped her coffee from the *filtre* glasses they had brought from Belgium and quite evidently did not think of him at all.

Mr. Potter's glance stole round again to the lithograph.

"It'd look very nice over there," he said. "The light's good and it's interesting. I think I shall frame it and hang it up if you don't mind, my dear."

"I don't want it there, William. I've taken a lot of trouble over this room. I receive my pupils here, and it's important to me that it should be kept just so."

Mrs. Potter found that it relieved her feelings to be so definite. Moreover, this question of the decoration of the room was an old bone of contention between them, and she always prided herself upon never permitting her personality to be overshadowed by her husband's. The fact that this was a rather superfluous precaution never seemed to occur to her.

In the ordinary way Mr. Potter gave up without a struggle, but today he was flushed with triumph, emboldened by success.

"But, my dear," he said gently, "there *are* people who

like my pictures. Someone might come in and see it and want to buy a copy. The Duke of Caith bought one once, remember. He liked it."

"William, be quiet. I can't stand it."

Mrs. Potter's tone was so hysterical and so unlike herself that her husband was silenced and sat regarding her in open-mouthed bewilderment.

The rest of the meal passed in silence, and after it Mr. Potter shambled back to his shed with his precious print, his old despondent self again.

At a quarter to ten he departed for his school and as his wife saw his untidy, unhappy figure wandering out of the garden gate, his lank hair tufting under his hat and his brown-paper parcels of drawings flapping under his arm, she knew that she would not see him again until seven o'clock. She waved to him perfunctorily.

Had she realized that she would never see him again it is doubtful whether her adieu would have been much more cordial. From his wife's point of view, Mr. Potter was an impossible person.

The Roman Guild tickets and the Gipsy sketches combined with a modicum of housework, kept Mrs. Potter busy until just on one o'clock, when she went over to Fred Rennie's for a tube of flake white.

The lower part of the converted coach house, where the Lafcadio secret colours were still prepared, had much of the alchemist's laboratory about it. Fred Rennie was no chemist, and he did his work in the curious elementary fashion which he had learnt from the painter.

The whole place was indescribably untidy, and the chances of any thief stealing the process were ludicrous. Only Rennie knew his way about the littered benches where poisons, food, and quite valuable pure colour were littered in small screws of dirty brown paper. Rows of old jam jars contained valuable mixtures, and the smell of medium was overpowering.

Fred Rennie was at work, and he looked up and smiled at her as she came in.

Rennie did not like Mrs. Potter. He considered her nosy and officious and suspected her of trying to buy paint from him at less than cost price, which was in point of fact quite justified. He had an elementary sense of humour, and

Mrs. Potter disliked him because he had no deference as far as she was concerned and was inclined to treat her as an equal.

Getting out the flake white entailed a certain amount of furniture-shifting before he could reach the great press at the far end of the room where his completed products were kept.

While his back was turned, Mrs. Potter moved to the bench on which he had been working and peered at the paraphernalia spread out upon it, not because she was particularly interested but because it was her habit to peer at other people's work. Indeed, the movement was mechanical and her mind very far away, still obsessed by its stupefying secret, so that she came to herself with a start to find Fred Rennie holding out a great brown-paper bag full of white powder. She saw his leering cockney face behind it.

"Take a pinch," he said.

Somewhat taken aback by this familiarity, she spoke sharply: "What is it?"

"Arsenic," said Fred Rennie and laughed till he was nearly sick. He was an uncouth person.

He gave her the flake white, was firm in their usual argument about the price, and when she went off he congratulated himself for having snubbed her for her curiosity.

Mrs. Potter had very little time for lunch. The shop in Church Street which sold her pen paintings phoned her when she came in from Rennie's shed, and she spent a busy hour packing up, pricing, and getting off a consignment of table centres.

When she came in again and took in the parcel of wood blocks from Salmon's which had been left with Rennie, there were only fifteen minutes to spare before Miss Cunninghame was due. She made herself a cup of Bovril in the scullery and settled down by the window in the studio to drink it. It was the first quiet time she had had since breakfast. Yet she found herself thinking it was too long.

In the ordinary way she could keep her mind happily occupied by thinking of little things, but lately she had been forced not to think at all. Whenever she let her mind loose it reverted to the one subject which was taboo, the one thing she dared not consider, this impossible and awful thing which had descended upon her and made everything in which she was interested seem negligible by comparison.

It was with a sense of relief that she heard the latch of the garden gate and Miss Florence Cunninghame's soft heavy feet on the brick.

She thrust the empty cup out of sight and rose to meet her visitor with a travesty of her bright professional smile.

Miss Cunninghame was a very fair specimen of her type. She was plump, ladylike, elderly, and quite remarkably without talent. Her tweed coat and skirt, silk blouse and pull-on hat might have belonged to any provincial schoolmistress. She had money of her own and an insatiable passion for painting water-colours.

As a person she was not very nice. Her blue eyes were set a little too closely together, and her mouth had small vertical creases round it which made it look as though it drew up on a string. It was her habit to bring her sketches every fortnight to Mrs. Potter for criticism and advice. She had a great portfolio of them now, having just returned from an orgy of painting near Rye.

"Glorious weather," she said in a faint, rather affected voice. "I painted the whole time. The colouring is so beautiful down there. There was quite a crowd of us."

Mrs. Potter felt suddenly helpless, an experience she never remembered knowing before in a similar situation, but the fine weather and colour near Rye and Miss Cunninghame's sketches seemed to have become inexplicably silly.

Her visitor stripped off her brown kid gloves and set about unpacking the portfolio with the eagerness of a child preparing a surprise.

Mrs. Potter felt her eyes glazing as she watched, and when the dozen or so green landscapes, horrible in their wet similarity, were spread out in front of her on the table she could hardly force herself to say the right things, to remember the well-worn words and phrases, the right inflections of surprise and gratification for which her visitor waited and would eventually pay her.

When the first excitement of showing her drawings had passed, Miss Cunninghame's blue eyes took on a more determined light and she sat down, quite frankly preparing to gossip.

"No more *news*?" she said, lowering her voice and leaning forward confidentially. "I mean," she went on hastily, "last time I was here it was just after the—the affair. Don't you remember? You were very upset, and I only stayed for ten minutes or so. You poor thing, you did look ill. You don't look very much better now," she went on, eyeing her victim appraisingly. "I've been away, so I haven't heard much. The newspapers have been very quiet, haven't they? But my friend Miss Richards, whose brother is in the Foreign Office, tells me that the police have dropped the whole affair. Is that true?"

Mrs. Potter sank down in a chair opposite Miss Cunninghame, not because she wanted to talk but because her knees would no longer support her. She knew her forehead was damp under her fringe, and wondered how long this dreadful physical reaction to the thoughts she would not permit herself to face would last.

Miss Cunninghame went on with the dreadful eagerness of one who has broken the ice of a difficult subject.

"You haven't heard, I suppose? The police are very inconsiderate, aren't they? I've always understood that. It must have been very terrible for you," she added in a blatant attempt to flatter her hearer into a confidence. "You knew him quite well, didn't you? Was he ever a pupil of yours?"

"Dacre?" said Mrs. Potter. "Oh, no. No, I never taught him anything." She might have added that that would have been impossible, but her instinct was to keep very quiet, to say nothing. It was as though she were standing in the middle of a stream of traffic and her only hope was to remain still.

Something that was almost a smile of satisfaction broke through Mrs. Cunninghame's imperfect mask of sympathy.

"I mean, the inquest was so *funny*, wasn't it?" she said. "I didn't go, of course, but the reports in the newspapers were so vague. There was one thing I was going to ask you. They said he was married. *I* always understood that he was engaged to Miss Lafcadio. But perhaps I was mistaken."

Mrs. Potter forced herself to speak. "They were engaged once," she said, "but it all blew over. Before he went to Italy, you know."

"Oh, I see." Miss Cunninghame nodded and pursed the lips which pursed so easily. "Of course," she went on suddenly, her mild blue eyes widening alarmingly, "he *was* murdered, wasn't he? Oh, forgive me for using that word, but I mean he was stabbed. But I see that perhaps you don't want to talk about it. Perhaps it's too painful."

The mild eyes seemed to have become positively devilish. Mrs. Potter wondered if the beads of sweat had rolled down under her fringe. The chattering old gossip seemed to have become a fiend possessed of superhuman insight in the power to wrest truth from its well.

Mrs. Potter defended herself weakly. "It was a great shock," she said. "I know nothing about it."

"But of course you don't," laughed Miss Cunninghame, a little nettled. "Of course you don't, my dear, or else you wouldn't be sitting here, would you? I only wondered. Of course I did hear—or at least I gathered from something Miss Richards let slip—that there was some business about an ambassador.

"Not that he had done it, you know, but that—well, that he was there. Miss Richards thought," she went on, lowering her voice, "that it might be—well, Bolshevists, you know. Not quite intentionally, you know, but for propaganda, like the suffragettes. One does hear such extraordinary things.

"I suppose," she went on in a last attempt to get something intelligent out of her informant, who had become wooden-faced and dumb with sheer, unmixed, stultifying fear, "I suppose you haven't any idea?"

"No," said Mrs. Potter dully. "I haven't any idea."

When Miss Cunninghame had packed up her drawings and stood ready to go, having already stayed a little over her time she made a final effort.

"Poor Mrs. Lafcadio!" she said. "She's so old. What a shock for her! It's so terrible, it being left like this with nobody really knowing."

Mrs. Potter gripped the door handle.

"Yes," she said unsteadily. "Nobody *really* knowing. That's the awful part."

"That's what I say," said Miss Cunninghame brightly and went.

Left to herself, Mrs. Potter glanced at the clock. It was half past four. William would not return until seven, and until then she was free. There was no need to prepare a meal. At a quarter to seven Belle would come down the garden path and ask them both to dinner: "As you're so busy on Thursdays, my dear, I'm sure you haven't had time to get anything ready."

Belle had done this every Thursday for nearly six years

now. The invitation sounded spontaneous every time, but it had become a tradition, and there was no reason to suppose that this day would be unlike any of the others, were it not for that awful feeling of impending danger pressing down upon her.

As she stood irresolute, her eyes wandered across the room and rested on something standing there, but she drew them away from it. That was not the way. She must pull herself together and not think.

Suddenly everything in the room became startlingly clear. She saw it as though she had never seen any of it before. The fact that it was the last time that she would ever stand and look round this little room, so full of its pathetic mementos of past affections, was, of course, unknown to her, but the fact remained that she saw it all in relief. Every piece of furniture, every picture, every drapery stood out clear from its neighbour.

It was while she remained there wondering at this phenomenon that the telephone bell began to ring.

12
What Shall We Do?

It was Belle who found the body; sweet, friendly old Belle with her white Breton cap aflutter from the breeze in the garden and her skirts held up a little to escape the dewy grasses on the sides of the path.

She paused for a moment on the Potter step to break off a dead rose hip left over from the autumn on the rather straggly seven-sister tree which grew over the porch.

Then, mildly surprised at receiving no answer to her knock, she went round to the scullery door, which stood open. "Claire, my dear," she called. "Claire, are you busy? May I come in?"

Her voice fluttered round the little building and was silent, and after waiting expectantly for a moment or so she went in and passed through to the studio.

Claire Potter lay face downward on the divan, her arms limp and her features mercifully covered by the cushions. Her small compact figure in its art overall mingled so well with the homespun blanket that for a moment Belle's eyes failed to distinguish it, and she stood looking round the room, faintly disappointed to find it deserted.

She had decided to sit down to wait, avoiding the exertion of a second visit, when the body on the divan caught her eye, and her whole attention was focused upon it, as if its shape had been defined by thick black lines.

A quick intake of breath preceded her sharp exclamation: "Claire! I didn't see you, my dear. What's the matter?"

Claire Potter's body lay limp and flat, like a heap of clothes. Belle went over to it, her puckered face colouring with motherly concern.

"Aren't you well, child? Claire!"

She laid a hand upon the flaccid, unresisting shoulder and attempted to rouse the piteous thing in the art overall.

"Come, dear. Come, Claire. Sit up."

Beneath the old woman's frail strength the body lifted a little, and for an instant the face which had once been Mrs. Potter's was exposed. Blue skin, distended eyes, and terrible, parted lips, they all showed clearly against the raucous orange of the cushions.

Belle's old fingers released their hold, and the face disappeared again in the pillows.

The woman standing in the studio straightened herself. The movement was very slow. Her face was pale and her gentle brown eyes oddly expressionless. For some seconds she remained irresolute. Then she began to move with remarkable determination and agility.

She glanced round the studio, noted that the place seemed to be in normal good order, and then, stepping gently out of deference to that odd superstition that the dead sleep lightly and so must be preserved from noise, she went out into the scullery again.

The small mirror over the sink shocked her with its reflection of a tottering, white-lipped old woman in a dishevelled bonnet of lawn, and she stopped resolutely to compose herself.

At all costs, for everyone's sake, there must be no fuss,

no painful scene. No one else must be subjected to the shock of seeing unexpectedly that terrible, terrible face. Poor Claire! Poor, clever, practical Claire!

In a moment or so she imagined she had forced herself to look more or less normal and she continued steadily about the things she had to do.

From the scullery door she could see down the path to Rennie's shed.

"Fred," she called softly. "Fred, come here a moment."

She had fancied that her voice was normal, but the man shot up from his bench and came hurrying towards her, the liveliest concern in his face.

"Why, ma'am, what is it?" he demanded, catching her arm to support her.

Belle looked up at him and remembered disconcertingly in the midst of the crowding fears and sorrows in her mind that the first time she had seen him he had been a ragged, dirty child of five crying for his mother at her knee.

"What is it, ma'am?" he repeated urgently. "Are you ill at all?"

His concern for herself at such a time irritated the old lady, and she became briskly practical.

"Come in here, where we can't be seen from the house," she said, stepping back into the scullery, and continued as he followed her in wonderingly, "Mrs. Potter is in the studio. I've just found her. She's dead."

"Dead?" said the man, his jaw dropping open. "Are you sure, ma'am?"

Belle shuddered and was ashamed of herself for the reaction. "Yes," she said simply. "Go in, but don't disturb her, poor soul."

Fred Rennie returned, his dark face grave and his forehead puckered.

"You must come into the house, ma'am," he said. "It's not right for you to have had to see that. Not at all right. You must lie down. Put your feet up," he added rather helplessly.

"Rennie, don't be a fool." Belle's authority returned. "There are several things to be done. Poor Potter will be home at seven, and we can't let him go in there. First of all we must get a doctor."

"That's right, ma'am. We must tell someone. No need for Miss Beatrice to know at once."

"Certainly not," said Belle, adding involuntarily, "Fred, I'm glad your master's not alive."

The man nodded gravely. "It would have worried him," he said and went on after a pause. "Better have her own doctor. He lives down in the Crescent. Shall I phone him?"

Belle hesitated. "No, I don't think so. Donna Beatrice might hear you, and I don't want the household alarmed."

"There's Mrs. Potter's own phone in the studio."

Belle shook her head. "No. It's not quite respectful in front of the dead. Besides, I think nothing in that room ought to be disturbed, not even in the slightest."

"Not disturbed?" he began and broke off abruptly as the significance of her words sank into his mind. "Why, ma'am, you don't mean to say that you think she . . . that is, you don't mean that her death wasn't natural, that there's been another . . ."

He stopped, not caring to use the word.

"I don't know what I think," said Belle. "You'd better go and fetch the doctor. Bring him back with you."

"But I can't leave you here, ma'am."

"Rubbish!" she said. "Do as you're told."

But when Rennie had departed, walking with suspicious nonchalance until he was once past the garden gate and then taking to his heels like the proverbial bringer of bad news, Belle thought of Mr. Campion.

She went quietly down the garden path and called to Lisa.

"Lisa," she said, "I want you to stand on Mrs. Potter's doorstep. Don't let anyone go in until I come back."

On the phone in her own house Belle was studiously noncommittal, but to Mr. Campion, sitting up in his flat in Bottle Street, her message came like a frantic appeal for help.

"Albert," she said, "is that you, my dear? I've had such trouble getting on to you. I wonder if you could come over and see me? Yes, now. At once. No, no, nothing is exactly wrong. Nothing to get alarmed about, actually. But I should be very grateful if you could come soon. Albert, listen. Take a taxi."

It was the last three words which convinced Mr. Campion that something was seriously amiss. Like many people of her generation, Belle regarded taxicabs as telegrams, measures of emergency.

"I'll be over right away," he said and heard her gentle sigh of relief.

As Belle hung up the receiver, Donna Beatrice came to the top of the stairs.

"Whom were you talking to?" she asked suspiciously.

"Campion," said Belle truthfully. "He's coming over to talk to me."

Miraculously, Donna Beatrice was satisfied, and Belle went down the staircase to the garden again.

Lisa came out of the porch as her mistress appeared. Her skin was very yellow, and her bright black eyes looked scared. "I went in," she said without preamble.

"Oh, Lisa!"

One old woman eyed the other.

"How did she die?"

"I don't know. I'm waiting for the doctor."

"I will wait also," said Lisa, and they were both in the little scullery when Rennie returned with assistance.

Young Dr. Fettes was a quiet, square young man with bushy black hair growing low down over his forehead and the gift of looking blank without appearing foolish. During his seven or eight years of general practice he had not quite grown used to the amazing complacency with which the relations of his patients put their responsibilities gratefully onto his shoulders, as if his medical degrees carried with them a species of omnipotence together with a thorough knowledge of the world.

He surveyed the three anxious people in the scullery now, their frightened eyes resting on him trustingly, and wondered regretfully what past generation of supermedicos had engendered the superstition. Mercifully they saw nothing on his face but the comforting stamp of authority. He was a doctor.

He knew them all slightly, which made it easier, and when Belle explained that Potter was down at his school and would not return until seven he went in to see that which had once been Mrs. Potter.

Lisa accompanied him. She was firm on this point, and Belle relinquished the unpleasant duty gratefully.

Rennie brought a chair from the shed for his mistress and stood by her side like a sentinel throughout the gruesome business.

From the scullery doorway a bright corner of the studio

was visible. Its brightness was intentional, with heaped shawls and Chianti bottles and painted poppy heads. Belle could not look at it, but sat like a girl and twisted her wedding ring round and round to keep herself from crying.

Campion found her like that, sitting on the kitchen chair, her head bent and her old fingers turning in her lap. She lifted her head as he came up, and he stopped and kissed her involuntarily and slipped his hand over hers.

"What is it?"

She told him in a soft hushed voice which sounded old and pathetic, and he listened with horror creeping up his backbone.

"You found her first?"

"Yes."

"You're sure she was dead?"

"Oh—oh, yes. Yes, my dear. Quite dead. Poor, poor, busy Claire!" She swayed forward a little as she spoke, and he caught her.

She refused to go into the house, however.

"The doctor will want to see me," she said. "He told me to stay."

Dr. Fettes came into the scullery at last, was introduced to Campion, whose name he recognized, and began to ask questions.

"Mrs. Lafcadio," he said, betraying a very faint Scots accent, "when you went into the studio and found the—the lady, did you move anything at all?"

"No." The old woman spoke unhesitatingly. "Nothing at all, except—her. I lifted her up, saw her face, and came out here."

"I see. You didn't by any chance open the windows? Or the doors maybe?"

"No." Belle was puzzled. "No, I didn't."

"How long would it be after you found Mrs. Potter that this fellow here came round for me?"

"Five minutes . . . ten at the outside."

"Really!" The young doctor frowned and finally gave up the indirect method of enquiry for one better suited to his temperament.

"I'll be frank with you, Mrs. Lafcadio. You didn't notice a smell of gas when you came in?"

Belle looked bewildered.

"Gas? Why, Doctor, you don't think that she . . . I mean . . ."

"You didn't notice a smell of gas in the room, did you?"

"No." She shook her head. "No. I didn't notice anything in the least unusual. The windows were just like they are now, I think; I didn't notice."

The young doctor sighed.

"Well," he said at last, "it's half after six now. Maybe I'd better wait and see Mr. Potter."

Belle touched his sleeve. "That poor man won't be able to help you much," she said. "He's been out all day, and this shock will unnerve him terribly."

Dr. Fettes considered. He knew Mr. Potter and had no illusions concerning that gentleman's capabilities whether under nervous strain or no. He also knew that the Potters lived as it were under Lafcadio patronage, and being uncertain of the exact path which etiquette dictated wisely chose the easier.

"Frankly, Mrs. Lafcadio," he said, "I can't give a certificate in this case. There'll have to be an inquest."

Belle nodded. She made no other comment.

Campion took the situation in hand, and Fettes, who knew his name and had heard all the gossip concerning the first mysterious death at Little Venice, was glad enough to permit him to do so.

Belle was persuaded to return to the house with Lisa to look after her, and Campion phoned Inspector Oates.

He made the call from the house, leaving the doctor to keep an eye on the studio where the body lay.

"The room is practically untouched," he said. "I thought you'd probably like to come along right away. Yes, I've got the doctor here. . . . He doesn't seem to know . . . talks about gas."

Stanislaus's usually weary voice sounded brisk, almost excited.

"Good for you, Campion. Hold everything till I get there. I knew something like this would happen. Is the girl about?"

Mr. Campion passed a hand over his forehead.

"Look here," he said, "I can't argue over the phone."

"You don't have to," said Oates, who seemed to be positively elated by the gruesome news. "I'll be over in ten minutes."

He rang off.

13
Police Work

While the discovery that Linda was away in Paris and had been there for several days pursuing her own line of investigation shook the inspector's conviction of her guilt in the second outrage at Little Venice, it did not completely dispel it by any means. He was set back rather than defeated, and retained an official reticence until the facts should be assembled and his theory triumphantly proved.

Dr. Fettes repeated his opinion that Mrs. Potter's death was due to asphyxia and refused to say more until after the post-mortem.

Belle retired to the house with Lisa, and the forlorn little studio was left in charge of the police.

Mr. Campion was there, silent, observant, and marvellously unobtrusive, while the dreadful formalities were accomplished.

In the beginning Oates was nearly as cheerful as his personality permitted. Here, experience told him, was an example of premeditated crime, which was nearly always handled successfully by police machinery.

The murder—for he had already made up his mind it was a murder—was going to be subjected to the fullest floodlight of police scrutiny, and Inspector Oates considered that without undue optimism he could count on its success.

As the details sorted themselves out, however, there was born in his mind the faint beginnings of that bewilderment and irritation which so exasperated him afterwards.

He was compelled to agree with the doctor that Mrs. Potter had been asphyxiated without signs of violence, without a foreign body in the throat, and apparently without gas.

For perhaps half an hour, while the photographers and fingerprint experts were at work, things were at a deadlock.

Into the inspector's optimism crept a note of truculence, and as each ordinary avenue of enquiry proved barren in turn, his expression of hearty self-assurance became more rigidly fixed and less convincing.

Fred Rennie came in for a careful cross-examination as one of the last people to have seen Mrs. Potter alive, but beyond a careful and fairly accurate account of the purchase of the flake white they could get nothing from him.

The first light on what was fast becoming the inexplicable arrived when plain-clothesman Downing, who had been left on guard outside the studio, caught Lisa in the act of rinsing out the cup from which Mrs. Potter had drunk her midday Bovril, after he had observed the old Italian woman retrieve it surreptitiously from a clump of spear grass in the flower bed.

He brought the woman and the suspected vessel, now practically clean and of no use whatever as evidence, triumphantly before the inspector.

Lisa stood just inside the doorway, the light from the hanging bulbs shining on her face. She made an extraordinary, unforgettable picture, the flushed policeman standing at her side. Her bright black eyes glowed from out of the network of yellow wrinkles which formed her face and succeeded in giving her the appearance of incalculable guile, whereas acute alarm was probably her only emotion.

The inspector surveyed her black-clad funereal figure with mistrust. When he spoke, however, his tone was friendly.

"Miss Capella and I know one another," he said. "We met before—some weeks back."

Lisa nodded, and her misleading black eyes flickered with something which might have been malignant satisfaction but which was in point of fact mere recognition.

"Yes," she said. "At the other murder."

"Murder?" Oates pounced on the word. But Lisa seemed unaware of any admission. She stood looking at him, helplessness and stupidity alike masked by that baffling exterior.

"What makes you think Mrs. Potter was murdered?"

"I saw her face. She did not die naturally. Dead people do not look like that when they die naturally."

"Oh, you saw her face, did you?" said the inspector, sighing. "That was when you came in for the cup, I suppose? That cup."

He pointed to the rather ridiculous pottery mug which P. C. Downing still held so confidently, but if he hoped for any dramatic collapse from the old woman, Lisa was a disappointment.

"Yes, when I got the cup," she agreed, moistening her lips with the tip of her tongue, her eyes flickering maddeningly.

"Ah!" The inspector was almost embarrassed by such a wealth of admission. "You don't deny, then, that you took the cup from this room after Mrs. Potter was dead and attempted to wash it out?"

The triumphant note in his voice seemed suddenly to warn Lisa that the conversation was not merely an idle chat. She shut her mouth hard, and her eyes became dull and completely expressionless.

The inspector repeated his question.

Lisa threw out her hands expressively.

"I do not talk any more," she said.

After several hopeless attempts to make this statement untrue, Oates turned to Campion.

"You know her," he said. "Make her understand she can't go as far as this without explaining more fully."

But, once alarmed, Lisa was not easily soothed, and it was not until fifteen minutes later that she showed any further signs of being able to speak at all.

At last, however, she conceded a few hesitating replies:

"I came in when Mrs. Lafcadio went indoors to phone. It was then I saw Claire Potter's face. . . . Yes, I saw the cup, too. . . . Yes, it was then I put it in the flower bed."

"Why?" the inspector demanded.

"Because I did not wish to go into the house then. Mrs. Lafcadio had told me to wait by the studio. I did not want anyone else to go in the studio."

"Why?"

"Because Mrs. Potter was dead."

Inspector Oates sighed. Campion intervened.

"Why did you take the cup away, Lisa?"

The old woman hesitated. Her eyes were alive again, darting painfully from side to side.

"I saw it there," she said unexpectedly, pointing to the

occasional table beneath the window on the lower shelf of which Claire had thrust her cup when Miss Cunninghame arrived. "And I took it to clean."

"But why, Lisa? You must have had a reason for doing such a thing at such an extraordinary time."

The old woman turned upon him.

"I had," she said with totally unexpected vigour. "I thought perhaps there was poison in the cup and that she had died from it and that there would be trouble. So I washed the cup that there might not be any more unhappiness in the house."

The inspector was regarding her with fascinated eyes, while upon the face of P. C. Downing there was something approaching wonderment and joy.

Mr. Campion persisted anxiously.

"You must explain."

"I do not talk any more."

"But you must. Don't you see, if you don't explain, these gentlemen will naturally think it was you who put the poison in the cup if any was there?"

"I?" Lisa was plainly horrified. "Why should I?"

Oates took a step forward.

"That's what we want to know."

Lisa began to cry. She sank down on the nearest chair and wept unrestrainedly. It was all very uncomfortable.

The task of persuading the truth out of her seemed to have devolved upon Campion, and he tried again.

"Who do you think would poison Mrs. Potter, Lisa?"

"No one. No one. I only washed out the cup in case."

"Oh, but come, Lisa, that's not true. You were fond of Mrs. Potter—"

"I was not." The tearful vehemence was alarming. "She was a fool. A domineering woman. A great fool."

"Well, then,"—Mr. Campion mopped his forehead—"you liked her, you knew her well. If any—any outsider had poisoned her, you would like him to be caught. Is that true?"

"Yes,"—grudgingly.

"Well, then, you must tell us who you thought had poisoned the cup."

"I didn't think he had done it . . . I didn't . . . I didn't . . . I only washed out the cup in case. When I saw her dead I remembered him coming in and I thought . . ." Her sobs increased, and she became speechless.

Campion and Oates exchanged glances, and the inspector snorted with relief. It was coming at last, then.

"There, there," he said foolishly, patting her shoulder. "You'd better tell us the truth, you know. There's no use hiding anything in a business like this. Whom did you see coming in?"

Lisa's sobbing became hysterical.

"I don't know. I didn't see anyone. I won't speak."

Oates's grip on her shoulder tightened, and he shook her gently. "You pull yourself together. Come on, out with it. Whom did you see coming into this studio?"

The voice of authority had its effect. Lisa began to mutter tearfully:

"I don't know anything. I only saw him come in and go out again, and afterwards when I saw her dead I wondered . . ."

"Yes, yes, we know." The inspector spoke impatiently. "But who?"

Lisa raised her drowned eyes to his.

"Mr.—Mr. Potter," she said. "Her husband. For six years now he's caught the five-thirty from Chelmsford, arrived at Liverpool Street at a little before half past six and come home by seven, and so when today I saw him come in at five and go out again in a minute or two I guessed something was going to happen."

The inspector, who had been jotting down facts in a small, untidy notebook, nodded to his subordinate.

"Get on to Enquiries, and find out the number of the school at Chelmsford, and ask if Mr. Potter left early today. Don't say who you are, of course."

While this operation was in progress, Lisa was questioned closely in the matter of times. She was inclined to be sullen and unhelpful at first, but Oates revealed himself the soul of tact and patience and presently almost succeeded in pinning her down.

"It was a quarter to five by the kitchen clock when I saw Miss Cunninghame go," she said slowly. "The clock is fifteen minutes fast, so that would be half past four. Then I heard the gate go again, and I looked out to see if it was the fishmonger, and I saw that it was Mr. Potter. It was five o'clock then, because I looked at the clock. I was afraid for a moment, you see, that it was seven o'clock and I had got muddled with the time."

"Then if the clock said five it was really a quarter to, since the clock was fast?" said Oates, writing.

"No. It was five then, because when Miss Cunninghame went I knew it must be half past four, so I altered the clock. It was then I might have got muddled in the time."

"Quite," said Oates dryly and altered his notes. "How long was Mr. Potter in the studio here?"

"I don't know. I didn't look at the clock again, but I think about ten minutes."

"Ten minutes. How did he go out? Was he in a hurry?"

Lisa began to weep again. Finally, however, she nodded.

"Yes," she said. "That was what I noticed. He crept like he was afraid of being seen. That's why I washed the cup."

Downing returned from the telephone, his manner betraying respectfully suppressed excitement.

"Mr. Potter has not been at Blakenham all today, sir," he said. "They received a telegram at ten o'clock this morning to say he was confined to his bed."

The inspector grimaced.

"I see," he said slowly. "I see."

There was a silence after he had spoken, and it was in that silence that Mr. Potter opened the garden gate and, striving to step naturally and with carefree decision, crossed the path and entered the studio.

He stood in the doorway and blinked at the astonishing sight of so many people in his home, as yet not distinguishing the separate personalities and the possible significance of their presence.

He looked much as Mr. Campion first remembered seeing him. His thin red face with its enormous nose and watery eyes was melancholy even in its surprise. Also he was quite startlingly untidy. His tufty hair burst from beneath his hat, his hastily gathered papers were in painful imminence of descending to his feet in chaos, and one long refractory shoelace straggled behind him dangerously.

Yet, Campion noticed with growing concern, there was a new note in the general air of frustration and despair which was his general atmosphere: the high thin note of alarm.

It became more and more insistent as he looked from one face to another: the weeping Lisa, staring at him like a dog beseeching forgiveness, the stolid doctor, the excited plain-clothesman, Campion, and the curious inspector.

They waited for him to make the first movement, and when it came it was so natural, so utterly typical and in character, but at the same time so horrible in the circumstances, that they all felt the chill.

Mr. Potter, having taken in each face, looked beyond them to the scullery.

"Claire," he called. "Claire, we have visitors." He returned to the stricken company. "Sorry no one here," he said, relapsing into his habitual helpless mumble. "Very awkward for you . . . awkward all round. I suppose you want to see my wife? She'll be here in a moment . . ."

The plain-clothesman shifted his position, and as his bulk moved, the sheet-covered form on the bed came into view.

Mr. Potter stared at it. All the watery redness of his face seemed to rush into his huge nose, making it grotesque and absurd. His small eyes, which were set so closely beside the pinched bridge, grew round and foolish like a frightened child's.

He started across the room towards it, and Campion caught his arm. "No," he said. "No, not yet. Wait."

Mr. Potter turned to him, the incredulity in his eyes growing until it seemed they must become blank.

"Is that my wife?"

The words were whispered. Campion felt some of the choking horror of nightmare.

Is that my wife?

He had not repeated the question, but the piteous, affected little room seemed to vibrate with it.

Campion nodded.

Mr. Potter glanced at the others. Lisa's unbridled weeping was the only sound.

"Claire?" said Mr. Potter in a voice in which amazement, disbelief, and despair were all inextricably mingled. "Claire?"

He broke away from Campion and went to the divan. To their unutterable relief he did not try to pull back the sheet. He bent down and felt the cold arm through the linen.

"Dead," he said suddenly and stepped back. "Claire dead."

He moved round the room and stood with his back to them. They saw him tall and oddly held in the yellow light.

"Dead," he said again in the most matter-of-fact tone they had ever heard him use.

Then the mass of papers and his battered hat slipped to the ground, and Dr. Fettes leapt forward to catch the man as he toppled over.

"It's the shock," said the young doctor, tugging at the limp collar. "It's the shock."

14
Ravellings

"I really don't know when I've been so upset."

Miss Cunninghame, pink with excitement and an underlying sense of outrage at tragedy treading so near, made the announcement as though it were an important confidence.

"I really don't know when."

Inspector Oates sat forward on the broad Chippendale chair, his head on one side like a terrier at a rabbit hole. Mr. Campion was stationed a little behind him. The inspector never knew quite why he always invited the pale young man to accompany him on this sort of expedition in defiance of edict and etiquette alike, but the fact remained and so did Mr. Campion.

The small front suburban room in which they talked was a reflection of Miss Cunninghame's gentility and modestly sufficient means. Its white paint, shining brass, Morris chintz, and good furniture were tasteful, old-maidish, and intensely ordinary. Only the appalling water-colours in the narrow gilt frames were individual.

Miss Cunninghame went on talking.

"Of course," she said, the light of self-preservation creeping into her eyes, "Mrs. Potter was not a *friend* of mine.

I mean, we were never *intimate*, we never *talked*. I took a few lessons from her from time to time because she seemed such a capable person, and then her *background* attracted me. John Lafcadio still lives in that little colony—or did," she added dubiously, as though even that eminent ghost would hardly survive this last upheaval.

The inspector remained quiet and alert, and Miss Cunninghame was shamed into further speech.

"So you see," she finished lamely, "I hardly knew her. . . . Poor soul!"

"She didn't confide in you?" Oates seemed disappointed.

"Oh, no . . ." It seemed for a moment that Miss Cunninghame would leave well enough alone, but the inspector's air of expectancy had its reward. "I thought she seemed very odd this afternoon," she said suddenly. "But if she was going to meet her death so soon afterwards, poor creature, that's hardly to be wondered at."

"Odd?" enquired Oates, ignoring his informant's somewhat confused deductions.

Having committed herself, Miss Cunninghame did not draw back.

"Definitely odd," she declared. "I told her she looked ill, and she was almost angry. Also she was stupid."

The inspector's head straightened. It almost seemed to Campion that his ears pricked forward.

"When you say stupid, did it seem to you that she was dazed—drugged, I mean?"

Miss Cunninghame's eyes opened very wide.

"Drugs?" she said. "You don't say that she . . . Well, really, if I had ever guessed—"

"Oh, no, no." The inspector was very patient. "No, I'm only trying to get at the probable cause of Mrs. Potter's death. The doctors have not yet decided the actual cause, and as you were the last person to see her alive, as far as we know, we are naturally anxious to hear how she seemed to you."

"I was the *last* person? Was I really? Oh!" Miss Cunninghame's momentary thrill of importance was suddenly damped by a new and disturbing thought. "An inquest! I shan't be called—oh, Inspector, I shan't be called to give evidence? I couldn't—I didn't know her—"

"We're not sure of anything yet," said Oates mendaciously. "Suppose you tell me all you can now."

"Yes, yes, of course. Anything." Campion found Miss Cunninghame's pathetic terror a little nauseating. "Well, she was odd. Distinctly vague. Not herself at all. I tried to get her to talk to me about the—the other trouble—crime, I mean. I was sorry for her, and I thought she might be comforted."

Miss Cunninghame glanced guiltily at the inspector, but the omnipotent, all-seeing powers with which she credited the police were not evinced, and she hurried on:

"It was then that she seemed stupid. She heard what I said—just a few leading, quite kindly questions, but she was quite, quite blank. I left her at half past four. She didn't come to the door. I went out alone, but she was all right because I heard the phone ring."

The inspector, who had relapsed into melancholy as he realized there was nothing really definite here, suddenly revived.

"You heard her phone ring at half past four?" he said, getting out his notebook.

At the sight of this evidence of officialdom Miss Cunninghame grew visibly flustered, but she repeated the fact slowly, as though she were dictating to a spelling bee.

"I heard her phone bell ring at half past four as I was going out. . . . I also had the impression that she went to answer it," she went on more quickly, "but I couldn't be sure. I didn't stop to listen, of course."

"Of course," agreed the inspector.

"But I would have done," said Miss Cunninghame with deliberate moral courage, "had I known what was going to happen." Oates, rather nonplussed at this announcement, paused awkwardly.

"But there, I couldn't know, could I?" said Miss Cunninghame. "I only saw she was worried. And now, Inspector, I needn't give evidence, need I? I'm really very upset. After all, if we weren't friends I've visited her for several years, and I was only talking to her about my paintings this afternoon. Death," she added, with the satisfaction of one who knows herself to be right, "is a very dreadful thing."

"Yes," said the inspector. "Yes, it is."

Mr. Campion and the policeman walked back together

through the dusty squares of stolid mansions now reduced to tenements which streak their dreary way from Maida Vale to Bayswater. Oates seemed anxious to talk, a most unusual circumstance, and Campion was more than ready to listen.

"Funny type, that old woman," he remarked. "I only seem to meet 'em in murder cases. They manage to wriggle out of everything else. The world's full of uncharitable people," he said irrelevantly.

"She has told us two things," said Campion.

Oates nodded. "(A) Mrs. Potter was worried to the point of being uninterested in the old cat, and (B) she had a telephone call about half past four. The first may or may not mean a thing. The other we may be able to follow up, which may lead us a step further."

He turned to Campion. "It's funny, isn't it?"

"What's funny?"

"The whole darn thing. The two cases one after the other like this. When you phoned me this afternoon I thought we should have it straight in an hour. Homicidal mania on the girl's part. These descendants of famous men are often a bit unbalanced. But now, d'you know, I'm not so sure."

Campion forbore to comment, and the inspector went on, his grey face with its shrewd, kindly eyes grave and absorbed: "Did that woman strike you as an exaggerator or the reverse? I mean, how worried do you think Mrs. Potter was?"

"Suicide?" enquired Campion dubiously.

"Well, I wondered. There's no evidence either way yet, of course. We don't even know the cause of death. I hate theorizing. It's always silly. Still, it's as well to keep an open mind."

"Ah," said Mr. Campion, and his eyes became foolish as the idea which had been rankling in the back of his head ever since the tragedy stood out in all its absurdity.

"Of course," muttered the inspector, striking viciously at some railings with his folded evening paper, "there's that chap Potter. It was nice of Mrs. Lafcadio to take him in and pop him into bed like that. He'll be ready to talk in the morning. We ought not to think, even, until we've heard what he has to say."

"Both Lisa and the school can't be lying," said Campion.

"No," said Oates. "No, that's right. I'm not losing sight of that. He was up to something." He paused and eyed his friend. "If that first remark of his when he came in was fake," he said, "I'll resign."

This promise, as it happened, was never carried out because, of course, Mr. Potter had been acting at the time, which was certainly remarkable.

The inspector idled on.

"That Italian woman Lisa," he said. "A bad witness, but honest, I should say, although you can't ever be sure. She's probably right when she talks of poison. If the P.M. doesn't tell us about that, though, the Home Office analyst will. Amazing chaps, Campion. They bob up in court and swear to the millionth of a grain. Often right, too."

Campion shrugged with distaste.

"Poison," he said. "Bad method at the best."

"Um," said the inspector, eyeing him. "A knifing and maybe a poisoning. Italians about. It's worth considering."

"Lisa?" Mr. Campion's expression was one of complete incredulity.

"No, no. I'm not saying anything. I'm not even thinking. I'm just letting my mind run on. I find it pays sometimes. There's that wife of Dacre's—an extraordinary kid. D'you know who she is?"

"Who? Rosa-Rosa?"

"Yes. One of the Rosinis, my body. She's a niece or something of old Guido himself. She's staying at the store now in Saffron Hill. What do you know about that!"

"I don't see how being first cousin to a race gang connects one with the death of a respectable lady in Bayswater," said Campion.

"Nor do I," said the inspector, sniffing, "but it's worth bearing in mind."

Mr. Campion opened his mouth to speak, changed his mind, sighed, and walked on in silence.

"Out with it," said the inspector without looking round.

Campion shook his head.

"It's wild," he said, "and yet—"

"Oh, let's have it. We're having an orgy of idiocy, anyway. We're here, or rather I'm here, to investigate facts, not to daydream, yet we've been happily speculating for the last half hour like a couple of amateurs. So why not go the whole hog? What's on your mind?"

Mr. Campion considered Max Fustian and the ideas which had crossed his mind concerning him.

"No," he said at last. "It's too vague for anything. It was a sort of odour of an idea I had concerning the murder of Dacre, but it doesn't fit in with this new affair at all."

"Motive," said Oates vehemently. "That's the only way to connect these two affairs. Find the motive and you find the man—or woman."

"Murder and suicide, then?" suggested Campion.

Oates shrugged.

"Maybe. I hardly think so, though. Then again, what's the motive for the murder? I tell you what, though," he went on, brightening suddenly. "If this is a poisoning we'll get our bird. The Dacre business was spontaneous—impulsive. Anyone could or might have done it. But this is a different caper. This, if it is murder, is premeditated and thought out. It's not natural for there to be two killers running loose in one family at a time, therefore the odds are on it being the same person, and I don't believe there's a man alive to pull off the two."

That was the inspector's second mistake.

Campion said nothing, and Oates strode on faster.

"Motive," he repeated. "We'll get at her—or him—whoever it is, that way."

They reached the canal and turned into the Crescent. The mock stone planes of Little Venice looked sad and shabby in the lamplight. The splendours of Show Sunday had gone, leaving it melancholy. The blinds were drawn, contrary to custom, and the front door was closed. The house was in trouble.

A flashy little car outside gleaming expensively enhanced the shabbiness of the house.

"Whose?" enquired the inspector, nodding towards the shining toy.

"Max Fustian's." Campion's tone was wondering.

Oates laughed shortly. "Come to confess again, no doubt."

"I . . . I wonder," said Mr. Campion.

15
As It Happened

Mr. Campion knew that Max Fustian had killed Mrs. Potter as soon as he saw him that evening.

He did not arrive at this conclusion by the decent process of quiet, logical deduction, nor yet by the blinding flash of glorious intuition, but by the shoddy, untidy process halfway between the two by which one usually gets to know things.

When he saw the man standing on Belle's hearth rug, his swarthy face pale to blueness, his quick eye exultant and his breath a little short, Campion regarded him and thought, "Well, he did it." And afterwards, "God knows why . . . or how."

The other occupant of the room at the moment was Donna Beatrice. The inspector was conferring with the harassed Dr. Fettes downstairs while Belle was in the kitchen comforting the conscience-stricken Lisa.

The Chosen Apostle of the Higher Urge was dramatizing this new situation but halfheartedly. She sat far back in her chair, her shoulders hunched and her cold eyes stupid.

"Claire!" she repeated to herself. "Claire!" And at intervals, "So practical. So utterly the *last* person."

Max met Campion's eyes and nodded to him with superb condescension.

"How extremely lucky you were able to come to Belle's assistance so soon, my dear Campion," he said.

The liquid affectation in his voice sounded a little more pronounced to the young man's sensitive ear.

"When I dropped in myself about an hour ago she told me you had been very kind," Max continued with the same new, insufferable superiority. "I've been congratulating myself that I obeyed the impulse to come on here from Meyer's. One dare not ignore these presentiments."

For the first time Campion noticed that Max was in gala dress. His morning clothes were miraculously cut; the broadcloth gleamed with silky elegance.

"Meyer's?" he enquired.

"Private view of the Duchess of Swayne's pastels," said Max briefly. "Delicate, you know. Genuine feeling. Selling like hot cakes."

Campion sat down and looked at him. For the first time in his life he felt unequal to the situation and afraid of giving himself away.

Max was more than merely confident; he was elated. Triumph and something that was surely satisfaction glowed beneath his decent veil of sympathetic grief. Campion felt at a loss.

"He's got away with it. He knows he's safe." The thought which was no more than a nebulous irritant at first grew to a certainty in his mind.

Max went on to talk about the tragedy.

"Terrible," he said. "Terrible. One of the most useful of women. One cannot assimilate it somehow."

He sighed with genuine regret.

Campion raised his eyes to find the man regarding him impudently. There was no hiding it; Max was the master of the hour.

"Useful!" said Donna Beatrice, sitting up. "Through all the horror, that's the word I've been searching for. Claire was useful."

"Poor Potter," said Campion lamely. "He's badly cut up, I'm afraid."

He broke off awkwardly. Max was looking at him and smiling. His head was a little on one side, and his heavily drawn mouth drooped at one end with what was, unmistakably, tolerant amusement.

Outrage, combining as it does shock, anger, reproach, and helplessness, is perhaps the most unmanageable, the most demoralizing, of all the emotions. Campion pulled himself together with difficulty and strove consciously to survey the man in front of him with true impartiality, but the thought which stuck most obstinately in his mind was that Max was very sure of himself and must consider himself absolutely safe.

Donna Beatrice copied Max's smile, but without meaning, and the effect was rather horrible.

Voices on the stairs ended the nightmare, and Campion rose as the inspector and Belle came in.

It was a tottery little old woman who peered round the room from under her white bonnet. The Belle Darling whom Lafcadio had loved, protected, and leant upon was beaten to her knees by the deluge of horror poured down upon her. Campion looked at her, and there rose up in his heart genuine ruthless hatred which took possession of him and gave him back the poise and confidence which had temporarily deserted him. Belle was leaning on the inspector, who looked as nearly humanly concerned as Campion had ever seen him.

"Sit down, ma'am," he said, using the old-fashioned form of address. "Don't worry. Leave that to us. We'll see to everything."

He caught sight of his friend with relief.

"I've got to go down to the mor—I've got to go with Dr. Fettes," he said. "He's waiting for me. I'll leave Mrs. Lafcadio with you. See you tomorrow."

He nodded casually to Max, ignored Donna Beatrice, and was gone.

Belle permitted herself to be led to her chair by the fire. Max did not move from the hearth, and Campion was shocked to find that it required an absurdly vigorous effort to prevent himself from kicking the exquisite little figure out of the way. From that moment, however, Belle required all his attention.

"Albert," she whispered, beckoning him to come closer, "listen."

He dropped down beside her chair, and she laid a little plump hand on his shoulder.

"I'm worried for Linda. If that child comes home to—to *this*, after the other shock—you see what I mean? See she stays in Paris or else is told before she comes to the house."

He put up his hand and held hers where it was on his shoulder. "I will," he said. "Leave everything to us. You heard what the inspector said. Leave everything to us."

Belle's brown eyes grew slowly blurred, and the tears rolled down her cheeks.

"Oh, my dear, if I could. If only I could."

"Well, why not, Belle?" Campion was as earnest as he

had ever been. The vacuity had vanished from his face, leaving him unexpectedly capable.

Her grip on his shoulder tightened.

"Albert," she whispered. "Oh, my dear, for pity's sake find out and *stop it*."

His eyes met hers through her tears.

"I will," he said quietly. "I will. I promise, Belle."

Max did not seem to hear this conversation, or if he did he was not interested. He had moved over to the corner cupboard and was examining the useless ivory baton once presented to Wagner.

The following morning, when the inspector came, Campion was still in the house, having taken up his quarters in Linda's little suite.

Oates sat down on the window ledge, gathering the skirts of his raincoat about him. He was brisk and practical.

"The inquest is fixed for twelve o'clock," he said. "Only formal evidence, and a postponement. There's no need for either of us to turn up. I'm waiting for Fettes to see Potter before I put him through it. Care to come?"

Campion signified his grateful acceptance of the favour and enquired after Belle.

"In bed, I hope," said the inspector. "I got Fettes to insist on it. Then he can trot down to the court and swear that neither she nor Potter is in a fit state to give evidence. There's no point in dragging that poor old lady through the tiresome business again. What's the matter with you, by the way? You look all het up."

To Campion the night had brought no counsel. He was still undecided on his course of action and never remembered finding himself in a similar quandary. The situation in which he was at once so certain in his mind and so utterly devoid of concrete evidence was mercifully new. Of one thing alone he was sure: the time to confide in the inspector had not yet arrived.

"I'm all right," he said. "A bit puzzled, that's all."

"You should worry!" Oates spoke grimly. "There's hell blowing up in the department. Orders are to get it all cleared up and over quickly. Imagination is a wonderful thing. I wish that darn doctor would turn up."

In the end Dr. Fettes phoned to say that the P.M. had taken him all night and if he was to get to the inquest on time he could not visit Little Venice first. However, his assistant, Dr. Derrick, a sandy-haired young man with a blue suspicious eye, arrived and pronounced Mr. Potter fit for examination.

Campion and the inspector went into the faded spare bedroom which had housed so many famous folk in the great days when Lafcadio was a lion.

Campion was prepared for a painful experience, but even so the sight which Mr. Potter presented as he sat up in the big Italian bed, propped by the glistening pillows, had in it that element of the unexpectedly shocking which is the very essence of embarrassment.

The natural redness of his face had gone, leaving it a network of tiny red veins, so that his skin looked like crackle-ware. His eyes had shrunk and become paler, as if they threatened to disappear altogether, and his mouth was loose and piteous. He looked old and frightened to stupidity.

The inspector stood regarding him gravely, and for some seconds it seemed that the man in the bed had not noticed the intrusion. Suddenly he glanced up.

"The suggestion that I killed my wife is absurd," he said. He spoke without vehemence or, it seemed, much personal feeling.

Oates cleared his throat. "What put such an idea into your head, Mr. Potter?" he began cautiously.

For a moment the washed-out eyes rested on the policeman's grey face with contempt.

"I've been listening to Lisa," he said shortly. "No point now in beating about the bush. No time for conventions, manners, affectations. Too many affectations in my life, anyway. Too many in everybody's life. It's all no good—rotten stuff."

The inspector shot a sidelong glance at Campion.

"It's very unfortunate that Miss Capella should have been able to get to you," he said sternly. "She will probably get into serious trouble."

If he had hoped to shake the man in the bed out of his uncompromising mood by this threat he was disappointed. Mr. Potter, normally the kindest of men, shrugged his shoulders. "I really can't help it," he said. "I can't help anything. I should like to be left alone."

"Now, Mr. Potter,"—Oates's tone became conciliatory—"I do realize that it must be most painful for you to talk now, but the matter is urgent. There are several questions I want to put to you and an explanation I must have. In trying to help you yesterday Miss Capella raised a question which must be cleared up—do you understand?"

The question was an afterthought, for Mr. Potter had turned away and was staring out of the window at the speeding sky.

Oates repeated the words, and the figure in the bed moved. He looked at his tormentors and with an obvious effort strove to concentrate.

"I am alone," he said suddenly. "I am quite free. I can go where I like, do what I like. I wish I were dead."

There was complete silence after he had spoken. Campion felt breathless, and the inspector's eyes contracted. It was very terrible.

Oates deliberated. Finally he shook his head.

"I must know," he said. "Why did you send a telegram yesterday morning to the headmaster of Blakenham to say you were in bed, ill?"

Mr. Potter looked at him vaguely for a full minute before replying.

"Other things were important," he said at last, and then very painstakingly, as though he were treading on new ground: "Nothing that was important then is important now. Nothing at all is very important now. It was for some trifling reason—I had a lithograph print I was pleased about." Mr. Potter seemed astonished as he remembered. "I wanted to show it to someone. I was mad."

"Where did you go?" Oates prompted.

"To Bill Fenner's studio in Putney. We spent all day talking and looking at stuff. I was playing truant, like a child. As if it mattered!"

"When did you come back?" demanded Oates, making a mental note of the name and district. "When you saw me—all of us?"

"Yes—yes, I think so." The effort of recollection was clearly difficult, and Mr. Potter's forehead was furrowed for a moment until his eyes suddenly widened and he looked at the inspector blankly.

"No, of course," he said. "Of course, it was yesterday. I came back before, that's how it happened. I understand now."

"You came back before?"

"Yes. About five o'clock. Does it matter?"

The inspector sat down on the edge of the bed.

"Try to remember it exactly, sir," he said. "I know it's difficult."

"No," said Mr. Potter unexpectedly. "No, it's very clear, although it seems a long time ago." He sat very still, and his face worked helplessly. "I saw her and I didn't know," he said. "My poor Claire, I didn't know."

"You saw her?" The inspector's quiet voice gently forced the man to keep to the story.

"She must have been dead then," whispered Mr. Potter. "When I came in the first time, I saw her lying there, the glass at her feet, and I didn't know. Even then . . ." His voice trailed away.

The inspector's eyes snapped.

"The glass at her feet? We found no glass."

"I washed it out and put it back in the cupboard," said Mr. Potter simply.

"Why?" There was something very like stupefaction in the inspector's face.

"More affectation," said Mr. Potter. "Another thing that didn't matter. Polite fiction. It's all silly trumpery stuff . . . no real point in it."

"Why did you wash out the glass?" the inspector persisted.

"It was Thursday," said Mr. Potter. "At a quarter to seven on Thursdays, Mrs. Lafcadio always comes . . . came . . . down to the studio to ask my wife and me to dinner. I knew it was no use trying to rouse poor Claire, but I thought if Mrs. Lafcadio did not see the glass the evidences of—of my wife's condition would not be so apparent. So I sluiced it out and replaced it in the cupboard. Then, as there seemed nothing else I could do, I hurried out, hoping no one had seen me. I see now how idiotic it was. It didn't matter what I did."

The inspector, who had taken out his notebook now, sat, his pencil poised and an odd expression in his eyes. Campion caught his thought, and the recollection of the curious scene in the dining room after the reception came back to him.

He saw the bright interior, the straight brown legs in the sensible shoes sticking out across the picture framed by the doorway, and Mr. Potter's nervous attempts to keep the inspector and himself outside. The whole mystery concerning the man's early visit to the studio became suddenly clear.

The inspector braced himself. To officials facts are facts and must be treated as such.

"When you saw Mrs. Potter how did she look? Where was she?"

"She was lying face downward on the divan, half sitting, her body twisted so that her face was hidden." Mr. Potter spoke with a sort of wonder, as though his mind were concerned with essential things far removed from the trivial matters he related.

"Weren't you surprised to see her like that?"

Mr. Potter roused himself with an effort.

"I couldn't have told you this yesterday," he said, "because yesterday it seemed a serious matter, but now it seems so small. My wife frequently drank enough alcohol in one draught to render her completely unconscious for some time. I think it took effect very quickly. It was a form of drugging, I suppose. If anything upset her too much . . . I mean, if she suddenly found she could not bear anything . . . she used to do that. I remember it worried me. I was frightened by it and . . . God forgive me . . . shocked. It seems ridiculous now. Why shouldn't she?"

"So when you saw Mrs. Potter lying on the divan you thought she was . . . you thought that was what had happened and were not alarmed?"

Oates was speaking with unexpected gentleness, and it occurred to Campion that he must share his own curious feeling that Mr. Potter was living in a new stark world in which there were very few familiar landmarks.

"Yes," said Mr. Potter. "I thought she was drunk."

"So you took the glass away so that Mrs. Lafcadio should not see it, possibly examine it, and guess what was the matter?"

The man in the bed laughed. It was a strange sound, having in it nothing of the melodramatic but a percentage of pure derision.

"Yes. Asinine."

"Why did you wash the glass?"

"I—" Mr. Potter looked at his persecutor, and unexpectedly his eyes brimmed over with tears. "We had an arrangement about the incidental housework. We each

121

washed up and tidied up as it occurred. I rinsed out the glass naturally and stood it on the shelf to drain. I couldn't put it away dirty."

"I see," said the inspector hastily and busied himself with his notebook.

"Well," he said at last, "where was the bottle?"

"I don't know."

"Oh, come, Mr. Potter, where was it usually kept?"

"I don't know." The inspector's victim had the disconcerting air of speaking the literal truth about something in which he was not interested. "I never found out. It used to worry me. Good God, the things that used to worry me! I've been mad. I used to hunt when she was out. It was all so tidy—it should have been easy. I never found anything. Yet whenever she wanted it I used to find her like that. It's gone on for years."

"Years?" Campion and the inspector felt they were peering in at a secret. The vision of the tragic, ineffectual husband protecting his masterful wife in his small, worried way seemed indecent, sad, and to be covered.

"Not so much at first, of course, but often lately."

"She did it only when she was upset?"

"Oh, yes. She was very strong. She never let it take hold of her. It was only when things got too bad."

"I see." The inspector rose. "Thank you for your information, Mr. Potter. It has been very valuable. I shall try not to bother you any more than I can help. By the way, did your wife ever consult a doctor about this—er—habit of hers?"

"A doctor? No, I don't think so." Mr. Potter seemed mildly surprised. "She and I were the only people who knew about it, I think, although the others must have guessed, and she did not consider it important at all. I used to worry."

"What was it?" enquired Oates. "Whisky?"

"I don't know, I never saw it. I told you."

"Most extraordinary," commented the inspector. "Where did she buy it?"

"I don't think she did buy it."

Mr. Potter made this extraordinary announcement with the same air of detachment which had characterized him throughout the interview.

Inspector Oates paused halfway across the room.

"Where did it come from then?"

"I told you, I don't know," said Mr. Potter with patient disinterest. "Lately, whenever my wife was distressed I used to find her unconscious, usually with a glass by her side, but although I hunted everywhere I never found any supply. On one occasion I found her in the dining room at this house—you were there, I remember—but that was the only time. Apart from that it was always in the studio. I don't think she bought any alcohol, because it is expensive, you know, and our resources were so very small that it would have been impossible for her to spend even a few shillings without my knowing. We were impossibly poor. That seemed to matter very much, too. Oh, dear God, I am tired." He lay back and closed his eyes.

Campion and the inspector went out. The younger man wiped his forehead and stretched as though his clothes had become tight.

The inspector sighed.

"It's things like that that make me believe in capital punishment," he said briefly. "We'll get this bird, Campion, and we'll string him up."

16
That Was on the Sunday

"Nicotine," said the inspector, displaying his copy of the analyst's report, "one of the most pernickety poisons in the world, specially prepared by Providence, no doubt, to delay police officers in the execution of their duty."

Campion and the inspector were in the library at Little Venice. It was the morning of the Sunday following the Friday on which they had interviewed Mr. Potter.

In the circumstances it seemed to Mr. Campion that the Home Office chemists had been unusually expeditious, and he said so.

"I thought they were liable to take six weeks on a job like this," he remarked.

"Not when the whole department is up in the air." The

inspector spoke succinctly. "We all want this thing cleared up before the press decides to scream itself into a fit. Unfortunately all we seem to be able to do is to create a lot of excitement all round. In this instance it's done a bit of good. Those beggars can do with a bit of hustling. Still, it's interesting, isn't it? The nicotine, I mean. It's getting fashionable just now, yet up to a few years ago there was only one known instance of it being used criminally.* Know anything about it?"

"Not much," said Campion. "A small dose is fatal, isn't it?"

"Ten to twenty milligrams of the alkaloid does the trick in three to five minutes—paralyzes the respiratory system among other things." Oates spoke savagely. "I saw the stuff in the lab last night—I always sweat these things up as I go along. You'd be surprised how much I know about arsenic," he added with apparent irrelevance. "Criminals ought to stick to arsenic. These fancy poisons let us in for no end of trouble. Still, this nicotine is colourless, volatile stuff which goes yellow if you leave the cork out, and if you keep it long enough it goes solid. That's practically all I learnt on the subject from our boys."

Campion was looking at the report.

"By applying the Stas-Otto process to the contents of the stomach we isolated 14.80 milligrams Alkaloid Nicotiana Tabacum," he read. "Yes, well, that's clear enough. It ought to be simple to trace the source, once you get your lists of suspects. You can't go and buy this muck by the pint, I take it."

The inspector glanced at the younger man curiously, and when he spoke his voice was weary.

"Anyone can buy a box of cigars," he said.

"A box of cigars?" Mr. Campion's pale eyes widened. "Can the alkaloid be extracted easily?"

"As far as I can see." Oates was very grave. "In fact, I gather that either of us with very little knowledge and practically no unusual paraphernalia could get enough trouble out of a box of Havanas to keep the analysts busy for months, so, although we shall consider the question of source with our customary thoroughness, I don't expect much help in

---

*Tardieu records a case in which Count Bocarmé and his wife were convicted of murdering M. Fougnies by administering the alkaloid which Bocarmé manufactured himself. *Vide: L'Étude Méd. Lect. sur l'Empoisonment.*

that direction. We're up against brains, Campion. It may make it more interesting, but it's putting years on my age."

Mr. Campion hesitated and opened his mouth as though to speak, but thought better of it, and Oates did not notice him.

"Come on," he said. "We'll go down to that damn studio. We've got no business here, anyway. I seem to have been using this room as an office ever since the crime. Mrs. Lafcadio doesn't resent it, either. Bless her! Now and again she sends me a cup of tea!"

The two men went through the hall and down the staircase to the garden door.

The Potter studio was forlorn and deserted save for the plain-clothesman encamped in the tiny porch.

The inspector unlocked the door and they went in.

Without the dignity of tragedy the room looked smaller than when Campion had first seen it. The atmosphere was close and smelt abominably of damp, although the place had been unoccupied so short a time. While it was not actually untidy, the bookshelves and the side tables had a slightly ruffled appearance, betraying a recent search amongst their contents.

Oates stood looking round him in mild exasperation.

"There you are," he said. "Nothing at all. Not a sign of a bottle or a flask in the whole outfit. Not a trace of alcohol in the place."

"Could she have got it from the house in a glass?" Campion spoke without much enthusiasm, and the elder man shrugged his shoulders.

"And put the stuff in herself? Well, she might, but I don't think so. Hang it all, what did she get the nicotine out of? There's not a phial, not a pill bottle, nothing that might have contained it. Besides, someone must have seen her go into the house—Lisa, for instance, whose window looks straight out on this doorway."

Campion nodded absently. "You've made a thorough job of it, I suppose?"

"Well, I had Richardson and Miss Peters. You know 'em, don't you?"

Campion had a vision of the stout, lazy-looking man with the delicate hands and the sharp, inquisitive eyes, followed by the tiny, birdlike woman whose hands moved so quickly yet so methodically through drawers and tableloads

125

of litter. The legend concerning them was that they were relations of the Recording Angel whom nothing ever escapes.

"That settles it, then," he said. "There's nothing here."

"I know that."

"They found no alcohol and no poison?"

"Poison!" The inspector spoke explosively. "My good boy, this garden is lousy with poison. Rennie has about two stone of pure white arsenic to start with. There's a quart and a half of dilute hydrochloric acid in the shed behind the scullery—Dutch mordant. Potter used it in his lithography. Then we found spirits of salt over the sink, to say nothing of a small chemist's shop of patent medicines, all of which seemed pretty dangerous to me. But not a sign of the sort of stuff we were looking for."

"It's the choice of poisons that makes it so obviously murder, I suppose?" said Campion slowly. "Now you've spotted it."

"Exactly," Oates cut in. "If that young doctor hadn't been particularly honest, or even if he hadn't had his suspicions aroused by the Dacre business, it's a hundred to one he'd have called it heart failure—which is always true up to a point, when you come to think of it—issued a certificate and left it at that. Someone was being clever, darn clever, let's hope a bit too clever by half."

Campion sat down in the chair by the window table. He was so much more thoughtful than usual that Oates glanced at him sharply. He did not press confidences, however, but contented himself by observing that the fingerprint people had nothing of interest.

"The deceased's own prints are all over the phone," he observed. "By the way, that woman Cunninghame stuck to her tale about the phone bell she heard as she left that afternoon, so as a matter of routine I traced the call. It's hardly evidence. These exchange folks aren't reliable. How can they be? But apparently this number was called from a public box somewhere about that time. There was some hitch in the connection at first, and the supervisor was called. She got through to this exchange—that's how I was able to trace it at all. I saw both girls, but they couldn't help me much. They fixed the time, though. Four thirty-one. It bears out Miss Cunninghame but gets us no further."

"Where was the callbox?"

"Clifford Street.—What's the matter? Tell you anything?"

Campion was sitting up in his chair staring ahead of him. Presently he took off his spectacles. "Look here, Stanislaus," he said, "I'd better tell you. Max Fustian killed Mrs. Potter."

The inspector regarded him for a full twenty seconds. "Think so?" he said at last.

"I'm sure of it."

"Got any proof?"

"Not a trace."

Oates hurled his cigarette stub into the empty fireplace. "What's the good of that?" he demanded.

"It's a comfort to me," said Mr. Campion.

The inspector lit another cigarette. "Let's have the whole thing," he said. "It's mainly second sight, I suppose?"

Campion rose to his feet and, without hesitating to lay himself open to a charge of disordered imagination, related to the listening policeman all the little details and scraps of suspicion which have been here set down. When he had finished, Oates rubbed his moustache dubiously.

"I like you, Campion," he said at last. "You've got nerve. I follow you, all right, but if I may say so it's rather a case of an angel treading where even the fools fear to rush in. You've got no evidence at all."

"I know."

"Precious little in the way of definite suspicion."

Mr. Campion paused halfway across the room.

"That's what's so infuriating, Oates. Yet I'm sure. Don't you see it's only the cold facts themselves which point away from him?"

"I don't know what more you want," said the inspector glumly. "Still, I see what you mean. There's nothing more deceptive than facts. You find that out in the witness box, God knows. However, let's consider your yarn about the first murder. I concede your point that for an intelligent man Max Fustian's confession was suspiciously ridiculous if he wanted it to be believed. But the facts, my boy, the facts! What about his alibi?"

Campion glanced shrewdly at his friend.

"I wonder," he said. "When you interviewed Donna Beatrice did you ask her what they were talking about when the lights went out?"

Oates scowled. "I did, and I got a full account for my pains. Some awful interminable anecdote about a loony in a Turkish bath who mistook Miss Beatrice for a picture—that woman's mental, Campion."

"It was a long story?" the young man suggested.

"It was."

"Did Donna Beatrice strike you as a person who would let anyone else get a word in edgeways?"

The inspector shook his head.

"It's no good, Campion," he said. "If you're trying to tell me that Fustian slipped off as soon as the lights went out and left the woman talking, and came back again without her twigging, you're wasting your time and mine."

"Why?"

"Because it's not possible. Think of it. You're holding forth to me in the dark. Wouldn't you know if I was there or not?"

"How could I tell?"

"Well, damn it, man, you'd hear me breathing for one thing, shifting about, coughing perhaps or grunting as I tried to get a word in. If I moved off, even if I crept away, you'd hear me. Of course you would."

Campion nodded. "I know," he said awkwardly. "But she wouldn't. I only remembered the other day. She's as deaf as an egg without that contraption she wears, and she took it off for the party. Don't you see, she wouldn't hear a thing and it was very dark."

The inspector sat up. "Took it off? What for?"

"Vanity, I suppose."

"Well, I'm damned!" Oates leant back in his chair, and for a moment he was silent.

"There's no solid evidence, though," he said at last. "No case—nothing we could have taken to court even if that business was reopened. As I said at the time, it was the impulsive, spontaneous nature of that knifing which licked us at the outset. The luck was all on his side. This, thank God, is premeditated. That gives us an equal chance."

"You agree with me, then?"

"I? Good heavens, no. I've got an open mind. I suspect everyone and no one until I get proof." Oates grinned as he spoke. "The old official attitude is a great stand-by. Got any more revelations up your sleeve?"

Campion remained serious.

"I can't guess at the motive," he said slowly. "In Max Fustian's life young Dacre and Mrs. Potter were surely the most unimportant people on earth."

"To get back to facts," said Oates without rudeness, "where was Fus—this suspect of yours between four-thirty and five o'clock last Thursday?"

"Where he took the trouble to tell me he was," said Campion. "At Meyer's Art Gallery, enthusing over a duchess's pastels. Old Meyer is by way of being a friend of mine, and I dropped in to see him yesterday. He was very full of his private view and told me all I wanted to know without any prompting. Max came into the gallery about five-and-twenty to five. Meyer noticed the time because it was so late. He'd been expecting him all the afternoon. The exhibition shut at half past six, but Max stayed on chatting to Meyer until nearly seven. Then they both went out and had a drink. Meyer was very gratified but a trifle surprised by the great man's condescension, I fancy. Max does not usually behave so graciously."

"Miss Cunninghame left here at four-thirty," observed the inspector. "Fustian entered Meyer's at five-and-twenty to five and stayed there for a couple of hours, by which time Mrs. Potter was dead, discovered, and we had arrived. That only gives him the five minutes between four-thirty and four thirty-five to get busy in. Not long enough to do anything, my boy."

"Long enough to phone," said Campion.

"How d'you mean?"

Campion sat forward in the chair he had resumed.

"When Miss Cunninghame left here at four-thirty she head the phone bell ring. You traced that call and found that it came from a box in Clifford Street. Max entered Meyer's gallery at four thirty-five. Meyer's gallery is in Clifford Street, and there's a callbox twenty yards down the road—the only one in the street."

"That's not evidence."

"I know it's not, but it's suspicion. Dozens of people may have seen him in the callbox. He was looking pretty conspicuous, you remember. Besides, practically everyone round there knows him by sight. It ought not to be difficult to find witnesses."

"What's this leading to?" The inspector's interest was genuinely aroused. "Suppose we do prove that the phone call she had came from him—which won't be easy, by the way—what then? Did he poison her over the telephone? You've been reading thrillers again."

The pale young man in the horn-rimmed spectacles remained unusually serious.

"This bit is pure theory," he said, "but I'm open to bet anything you like it's true. Look here, we know from our own observation and from Potter himself that when Mrs. Potter was suddenly confronted by a crisis she used to pour a tumblerful of neat whisky down her throat and pass out. We know that Potter thought that had happened this time. He said so. Suppose it had happened."

"But her usual supply of liquor had the addition of a small quantity of alkaloid nicotine?"

"Yes."

"It's worth thinking about," Oates conceded cautiously. "She received her shock, or whatever it was, over the phone, the telephoner relying upon her to react to it in the usual way and so fix the moment of the murder at a time when the murderer had a watertight alibi. It's not bad, Campion."

"I think that's how it happened." Campion spoke softly. "After all, think of it. It all worked out so neatly. Mrs. Potter was bound to be in at four-thirty because Miss Cunninghame was due to leave at four-fifteen and always stayed over her time by ten minutes or so. Then Potter was away— the only day in the week he was always out—so the woman could take the stuff and die alone. Of course he couldn't hope for Potter to come in early and wash out the glass, but he could expect that Fettes would diagnose heart failure or acute alcohol poisoning."

"It's neat," said the inspector. "Very neat. And it sounds feasible. But it's too full of holes, and pure hypothesis anyway. How did he get the nicotine into the spirit, or, having done so, how did he know that she wouldn't take the stuff before he rang up?"

Campion considered.

"I think the answer to that last question is that the poisoned spirit had not been in her possession very long," he said at last. "Even Max, who's the most optimistic soul on earth, wouldn't risk her taking it too soon. Therefore the answer to the first question is that he got the stuff here some time on Thursday."

"Was he here on Thursday?"

"No."

"Or during the week?"

"No. I admit all this, but after all she was a secretive woman. It might have come by post. He might almost have given it to her in town. There are so many possibilities here that we can't work 'em all out. That's why I join with you in feeling that our only hope is to find the container, the thing that originally held the stuff."

The inspector glanced round the little room.

"We'll find it," he said with sudden decision. "We'll find it. Until then I reserve judgment. But it's a glimmer, my boy, it's a definite glimmer. Come on. We'll search this darn place ourselves."

The inspector revealed a thoroughness which surprised Campion, although he had not the neatness of the trained police searchers. Every piece of furniture in the overcrowded room was carefully examined, every loose floorboard prized up, every conceivable corner where a hidden cupboard might have been concealed laid bare.

The living room, the scullery, and the shed without all went through this gruelling examination by turns. Again and again Campion found himself confronted by little domestic secrets of the Potter household, little economies, little slovenlinesses which he felt were private and which brought home unbearably the pathos of the tragedy. However unlovable a character Mrs. Potter had been, her destroyer had also annihilated a home which without her became a desolate collection of rubbish.

They refused Belle's kindly offer of lunch and worked on until half past three in the afternoon, when their work ended. Hot, dishevelled, and defeated, they smoked a cigarette in the untidy room.

"We're sunk," said the inspector. "I'm glad I made sure myself, though. You can see for yourself that Richardson and Miss Peters were right. There's nothing here."

Regretfully Campion agreed, and they were still sitting in despairing silence when Lisa knocked at the door.

"Mrs. Lafcadio says you must have some tea," she said, planting a tray on the table. "As you wouldn't come in, I've brought it down."

She stayed to pour out for them, and Campion was acutely aware of her bright inquisitive eyes peering first at the disordered room and then at themselves.

Idly he went over ground already explored.

"After Mrs. Potter died and before I arrived, no one but you and Mrs. Lafcadio and Fred Rennie came in here at all?" he enquired.

"I have told you, no," said Lisa with some dignity. "I have also told *you*," she added, nodding to the inspector.

He smiled at her wearily as he returned his teacup to the tray. "You have, Miss Capella," he said. "Until you're tired, I'm afraid."

Campion frowned. "Someone must have come," he said. "Someone must have come—to the door only, perhaps. That's it, Lisa. Did someone come to fetch anything at that time? Anything at all?"

"I have told you," the old woman began brusquely. "No one came except the boy from the art gallery."

Both men sat staring at her. The inspector's hand was halfway to his lips, the cigarette hanging from his fingers, while Campion sat up stiffly, his face completely expressionless. Not unnaturally Lisa was taken aback by the sensation she had created. Two spots of colour appeared in her yellow cheeks.

"It was nothing," she said. "He often comes at that time. I gave him the blocks and he went. I didn't let him see inside the studio, of course. It was when Mrs. Lafcadio had gone to the telephone."

The inspector pulled himself together. His eyes were hard and concentrated on the woman's face.

"I ought to have heard of this before," he said. "But it doesn't matter. When exactly did the boy come?"

Lisa's dark eyes were frightened.

"Mrs. Lafcadio had gone to telephone," she repeated. "I had just come in here and seen Mrs. Potter. There was a knock. I was startled, I think. I went to the door. When I saw who it was I was glad it was only the boy. I told him to wait. I shut the door so he wouldn't see anything. Then I got the blocks. They were wrapped up in their cloth, and I gave them to him and he went away. That is all."

"All right," said Oates soothingly. "All right. What were the blocks?"

"Wood blocks—wood engravings." Lisa found the inspector's ignorance very disconcerting. She began to speak very clearly, as though to a foreigner, which indeed he was.

132

"Big heavy squares of wood. She cleaned and printed them for him."

"For whom?"

"For Mr. Max. I am telling you. His boy came for them. I gave them to him."

The inspector looked at Campion, his face twisted into a travesty of a smile. "She gave them to him," he said.

17
The Slack Cord

"Sebastiano Quirini? Why, my dear, his engravings were quite lovely."

Belle looked up as she spoke, and for a moment her eyes lost the dull, weary expression which Campion had grown to dread in them.

They were in the drawing room again, sitting by the fire, whose comfort had become a necessity since the second tragedy although the spring was not a cold one.

Campion and the inspector, having decided that Mr. Potter was better not disturbed unless it became absolutely necessary, had come to Belle for information.

"I believe it was a sort of secret," she said, "so you mustn't let anyone know. Max discovered nearly fifty of Quirini's old wood blocks in Paris when the Société des Arts Anciens was sold up. It was a very old business, you know. They dealt in antiques as well as pictures, and their warehouse in the Centre had not been cleared for years. When they started to turn it out before the building was pulled down, they found all sorts of things, I believe. Anyway, there was quite a sensation at the time. It's very long ago.

"However, that's all beside the point. Max picked up these Quirinis, all quite black and clotted with ink, some of them nearly ruined. He had one or two cleaned and found out what they were."

Oates was still looking puzzled, and Campion explained. "They're the solid chunks of boxwood on which the artist engraved the picture," he said. "They'd vary in size and thickness considerably. The picture was made by pressing a piece of fine paper, or silk sometimes, on the inky surface of the graved wood. Mrs. Potter melted the old ink out and reprinted them, I suppose, Belle?"

The old lady nodded. "Claire was very clever at that sort of thing," she said, her eyes softening. "Very patient and painstaking. Wood engraving is not difficult to print, you know, but it takes time and a lot of care. Max will miss poor Claire."

The inspector's eyelids flickered.

"Did she do much for him, ma'am?"

"Oh, so many things." Belle shook her head at the recollection of Claire Potter's many activities. "She worked much too hard. There are quite a number of little confidential jobs in the picture world," she went on, smiling faintly at the inspector. "Little things like this that require absolute integrity as well as skill. You see, Max wanted to get the Quirinis all ready at once, so that he could have a show of them all together and perhaps start a little fashion for them. So much depends on fashion: it seems very silly, but there it is.

"Claire had nearly finished them. She had been at work for two years."

"Two years?" The inspector was startled.

"Oh, yes. It was a long job, you know, and some of the blocks were in very bad condition. She did so many other things, too."

Oates glanced at Campion.

"She didn't keep these things in the studio, then?"

"All of them?" said Belle. "Oh, dear, no. They were much too bulky and too precious. Max used to send them down to her—one or two at a time—his boy would fetch one lot and bring another. I remember seeing him often—such a funny little grown-up boy. I wish children never had to work. The blocks were always wrapped up in a green cloth. Claire always had the second lot waiting for him, all packed and ready. She was most particular about them. No one was allowed to touch them except herself. I remember once being in the studio when they arrived, and I offered to unpack them for her, but she quite snapped at me. Poor Claire! It was so unlike her that I was quite surprised. She was most conscientious. The blocks were always kept packed up. They used to stand on the bookshelf in their cloth. Max paid her very badly, I'm afraid, but she never complained."

She sighed and looked down at her plump little hands. "She was very kind to me always," she said, and added unexpectedly, "that poor, helpless, silly man, too. No one to look after him now. She took care of him. The pity of it! The dreadful, wasteful pity of it!"

They were silent, and the moment was relieved by the arrival of Lisa with a message from Donna Beatrice.

That good lady, finding herself temporarily eclipsed by other, more important matters, had promptly taken to her bed on the ancient principle that if one cannot command attention by one's admirable qualities at least one can be a nuisance.

Somewhat grudgingly Lisa announced that Donna Beatrice was asking for Belle.

"She has not eaten," she said. "She refuses to take anything unless you are there. Shall I leave her until tonight?"

"Oh, no," said Belle, getting up. "I'll come. Poor soul," she remarked apologetically to Campion, "she's hysterical. It's very naughty of her. She makes herself so unpopular."

She went out, and Lisa followed. Campion and the inspector were left alone.

"She never let anyone unpack those wood blocks except herself," said Oates, taking out his notebook. "Max paid her very badly but she never complained. She did a great deal for him, confidential work. What are you thinking?"

"I was thinking," said Campion slowly, "that it is more than possible that Max had been in the habit of aiding and abetting Mrs. Potter in her unfortunate weakness for some time—months, perhaps even years. Underpaying her and keeping her happy that way. When the occasion arose, it was simplicity itself to poison her. It was probably so easy that he couldn't resist the temptation."

Oates sighed. "It looks like it," he agreed, "and if so we'll never get him. If the corpse conspires to shield the murderer, where are you? A couple of these wood blocks wrapped in tissue and baize would make a parcel large enough to hold, say, a flat half pint, I take it?"

"Oh, quite, I should say. It's ingenious, Oates."

"Darn ingenious," agreed the inspector. "But all conjecture, Campion. Based on strong suspicion, but all conjecture. Not a hap'orth of evidence in the lot. I'll see the boy, of course. That reminds me: Rennie says that when Mrs. Potter was out on the afternoon of the crime he took in a green-baize parcel secured by a strap from Salmon's and left it in her porch. Why did the boy call again in the evening? There's a chance I may get something out of the kid without disturbing Fustian, which is the last thing to be done at this juncture. Come on, Campion, we'll get on with it. Nothing more here at the moment."

Campion next saw the inspector at noon on the following day in his own chilly room at Scotland Yard.

Oates looked up as the young man came in, and he hailed Campion with even more enthusiasm than usual.

"I've seen the boy," he said, plunging into the business without preamble. "Caught him at the gallery first thing before anyone else arrived. He's an odd little object—name of Green."

"I think I've seen him at the shop."

"Have you? Oh, well, then, you know him. That's him—funny kid. Not too happy in his job, I fancy. Still, he didn't say so, Campion . . ."

"Yes?"

"I think you're right."

"Really? What did you get?"

Oates flipped over the pages of the ragged little book in which he kept his notes.

"The boy bears out all the other evidence, of course. He used to take those green-baize parcels backwards and forwards at irregular intervals. He usually got out to Bayswater in the evening because it was the last thing he had to do and it was a long way. There were two of them, by the way—two bits of baize and two straps, I mean—so that one parcel was always waiting for him when he brought the other."

"Did he ever see them packed at the gallery end?" said Campion.

"No. I particularly enquired about that. He was not even sure what they contained. Apparently Fustian has a habit of cooking up minor mysteries in the firm. He seems to have impressed the kid with the idea that he's a sort of art-world genius, a great financier pulling strings and starting hares and all the rest of it. These parcels were simply given to Green by Fustian, who packed them himself and who told him that they were very valuable and to be treated with great care. The boy seems to have felt that he was a privileged person to be allowed to touch the things at all. He's a simple-minded little beggar."

"Is that all?" Campion sounded disappointed.

"No, not quite. I explained to him, of course, that I was just checking up on all the people who had been to the studio during the day—you must tell 'em something, you know—and he volunteered the information that it was most unusual for him to call at the studio twice on one day and that it had happened because of a mistake of Fustian's. Apparently Green came down with one parcel on the lunch hour, and collected the other, which had been left with Rennie. This alteration in the usual time was because that evening he had to meet the five fifty-eight train at Victoria to collect some prints from Paris. The prints were on silk, and they had to be seen through the customs.

"When he arrived back at the gallery after the lunch hour, Max sent for him and explained that he had put the wrong contents in the parcel, and therefore when the kid had completed his mission at Victoria he was to go straight on to the studio and ask for the parcel back. Are you following?"

Campion nodded. His eyes were half closed behind his spectacles.

"When the kid got to Victoria the prints had not come. It took him some little time to discover this—about twenty minutes in all, he thinks. Then he went to the studio, arriving there about seven. Lisa gave him the parcel and he took it back to the gallery."

The inspector paused and regarded his friend.

"When he got there Max was waiting for him. The boy was surprised to see him and more surprised still when, after enquiring if he saw Mrs. Potter and receiving the reply that he had not but that Lisa had given him what he wanted, Max gave him a couple of bob. Then the kid went home, and that's all he knows."

"Extraordinary," said Campion.

"Interesting," said the inspector, still consulting his notes. "Oh, by the way, one other little thing: I asked the kid if he knew what was in the parcels. He said no, but after a while, as we got matey, I could see there was something on his mind, and presently he came out with it. About three weeks ago he dropped one of those darn parcels he was taking to Mrs. Potter on the tube stairs. He didn't like to open it to see if any damage was done, and in fear and trembling he took it on. He said he didn't get into any trouble, as he expected to, but when he handed the thing in he noticed the green cloth was quite wet. I pressed him, but he hadn't noticed anything else."

Campion sat up. "So we were right," he said.

"Yes," said Oates. "As far as we're concerned, the mystery's solved, but we can't say so. Exasperating, isn't it?"

"There's not enough evidence for an arrest?"

"Enough! There's none at all."

The inspector rose to his feet and stood looking out of the window.

"Another unsolved mystery, that's what the papers say," he remarked. "In all my experience I remember only one murder case in which the police didn't know whom they wanted. We haven't got enough here even to have him up and question him. He's licked us. While we were deciding if the corpse was poisoned or not, he was downstairs in the cloakroom of his gallery washing out the bottle."

"If only Potter hadn't washed out the glass," said Campion.

Oates considered. "I'm not sure about that," he said at last. "On the face of it I admit it looks as though that were the intervention of Providence on the wrong side, but was it? Suppose Potter had behaved like any ordinary sane person on finding his wife. Had a look at her, found she was dead, sent for the doctor and told him the whole story about the whisky drugging. It's ninety-nine to a hundred he'd have diagnosed heart failure and alcohol poisoning and we shouldn't have come into it. It was only the mystery at the beginning that put us onto it at all."

Mr. Campion was still digesting these reflections when Oates spoke again.

"Nothing," he said. "Not a thing on him. He's got away with it."

"What are you going to do? Drop it?"

"Good Lord, no!" The inspector looked shocked. "You ought to know more about police procedure than that. We shall go on snuffling about like an old terrier on a stale scent. We shall write each other coldly disapproving letters from department to department. We shall tell each other the facts in confidence and go on worrying round a little less week by week. Then something else will turn up and we shall all be very busy and this will get crowded out."

The young unhappy face of Dacre as he lay in the little robing room in Lafcadio's studio; Mr. Potter standing with his back to the shrouded figure of his wife; Belle sitting in the scullery twisting her fingers; these things passed in front of Mr. Campion's eyes, and he looked up.

"At least you can find the motive," he said bitterly. "Couldn't you get him on that?"

"Motive and doubtful circumstantial evidence isn't enough," said the inspector gloomily, "much less the mixture of conjecture and suspicion we've cooked up. Besides, there may not be a motive."

"What d'you mean?" The words had crystallized a fear which Campion had been fiercely refusing to recognize.

The inspector met his eyes for an instant. "You know what I mean. Nothing sufficient, not a *sane* motive."

Mr. Campion studied the carpet. "You suggest—"

"Look here," cut in the inspector, "I admit it's a disturbing thought, but you know as well as I do that when a chap of that age and type suddenly becomes a killer it means something's gone radically wrong with his sense of proportion. The cleverer he is the later we get him."

"Then you don't think we can do anything now?" Campion's tone was lifeless.

"No," said the inspector. "No, my boy, he's been too neat. We must wait."

"Wait? Good God, what for?"

"Next time," said Oates. "He won't stop at this. They never do. The question is, who is going to annoy him next?"

18
Dangerous Business

The coroner was an honourable man, but he was also sensible, with a natural distaste for publicity.

When the court resumed after the postponement, Mrs. Potter's sad little corpse was sat upon by a dozen interested but busy people who, after all the available evidence had been placed before them, brought in a sane but not very satisfactory open verdict.

They found that the deceased had met her death by poisoning by nicotine, but that there was insufficient evidence to show if it were self-administered or no.

The testimony of the tremulous Miss Cunninghame concerning her friend's behavior on the last afternoon of her life did much to dispel the jury's doubt from the public mind at least, and, as there is hardly anything which the average man finds so dull and depressing as a tale of suicide, the whole business faded gently into obscurity.

The press, which has a gift amounting to second sight for detecting an unsatisfactory story when the first ripe buds are laid upon the editorial table, had relegated the yarn to the final news columns as soon as the customary outcry against police inefficiency had grown stale, and the authorities counted themselves blessed.

Campion and the inspector alone recognized the situation for what it was, and as the sensation died away and the atmosphere of Little Venice subsided once more into a false peace the younger man at any rate experienced the sensations of a maiden lady who sees the burglar's boots below the curtain as the last of the neighbours troop back to their homes after the false alarm.

He haunted the house for the next few weeks, drifting in on every conceivable excuse. Belle was always pleased to see him, while Donna Beatrice welcomed him with the thirsty affection of a performer for her audience. Mr. Potter remained in his room most of the time, a new uncouth creature with a secret life. Dr. Fettes shook his head over him.

The optimism of a healthy mind is indefatigable, however, and, as time went on, even Campion began to see the events here recorded from that detached distance so often miscalled true perspective.

The gentle procession of ordinary life swept them all along, and it began to seem as unlikely that violence would ever again assail Lafcadio's household as it had done on that Saturday evening when he and Belle had discussed the morrow's reception.

When the first trumpet of alarm came so crudely, therefore, it carried with it an element of shock.

Max put forward his ingenuous suggestion to the Lafcadio legatees with all the elaboration and hot air with which he usually invested business matters.

He phoned one morning, made an appointment for three o'clock, arrived at a quarter to four, and addressed the little gathering as if they had been a board meeting.

Donna Beatrice, Lisa, Belle, and the impatient Linda sat and listened to him in the drawing room. Mr. Potter, the only other member of the household, and D'Urfey, who was almost one, were excluded at Max's own suggestion.

The old room, with its comfortable decorations and faded curios, was very gracious and mellow in the afternoon sunlight streaming in from over the canal. Belle sat in her usual chair by the fire, Lisa at her side and Linda hunched up on the rug, while Donna Beatrice took the chaise-longue and prepared to enjoy herself.

Max took the floor, his small, graceful figure heightened by importance. His naturally picturesque appearance was considerably exaggerated by his latest sartorial fad, consisting somewhat astonishingly of a fully coloured Victorian fancy waistcoat. This gallant vestment was without question a thing of beauty. Its shades of mauve, old gold, and green were elegantly blended, and its workmanship lovely enough to account for its preservation, but on Max's attenuated form, beneath his flowing tie and in conjunction with his magnificently cut if somewhat loose new spring suit, it smacked altogether too much of affectation and the very peculiar, and even Belle, who took a childish pleasure in bright things, regarded its exuberance with doubt.

Linda, contemplating him sombrely from beneath her tawny brows, reflected that during the past month or so Max's conceit and overemphasis had become noticeably worse. Now and again there was a distinct touch of well-simulated foreign accent in his drawling utterances, and his swagger was becoming Irvingesque.

Looking at him posturing in the dusty sunlight, it occurred to her that it was really remarkable that he should not appear very ridiculous. She thought also that this was certainly not the case. Max Fustian's old strength, a passionate belief in his own magnificence and a force of personality which thrust this illusion upon all he met, had increased with the other eccentricities until the electric atmosphere which emanated from him was frankly disturbing. His opening remark was typical of this new super-affectation.

"My dear ladies," he said, regarding them as though they were at least partial strangers and not people he had known for twenty years, "we have something to face. John Lafcadio's great memory, which I myself have done so much to preserve, has been desecrated. It will take all my powers, all my skill, to put him back where he belongs. To do this I shall require your co-operation."

"Ah!" said Donna Beatrice with gratified idiocy.

Max shot a patronizing smile in her direction and continued in the same oratorical vein.

"Lafcadio was a great painter," he said. "Let us never forget that. A great painter. This calamity, this petty blot upon his household, this little smirch across his memory, must not be allowed to make any one of his admirers forget that. A great painter."

Lisa was listening, her quick dark eyes fixed upon his face in the fascinated stare of imperfect comprehension.

Linda, on the other hand, showed signs of restiveness and would have spoken had not Belle's plump hand upon her shoulder counselled her to be still.

Max continued, his head thrown back, the phrases falling lazily from his lips.

He had perched himself upon the arm of the great chair which Lafcadio had always pronounced, without any foundation at all, a part of the belongings of Voltaire. The faded crimson tapestry made a background for Max's eccentric figure and lent it some of its own gracious magnificence.

"Of course," he said easily, "you all realize that it will be impossible to continue the pretty Show Sunday conceit in future years. That amusing little idea has ended unfortunately. Lafcadio's beautiful work must never enter that tainted studio again. You will probably leave this house, Belle. The name must be preserved from notoriety. That is most important."

Belle sat upon her chair and regarded her visitor in mild astonishment. Waving her unuttered comment aside, Max went on with supreme confidence.

"I have given the matter quite a considerable amount of thought," he confessed, with a little condescending smile at the group on the rug. "As I am undoubtedly mainly responsible for bringing Lafcadio before the public, I naturally feel it my duty to do what I can to save the rest of his work from any contamination by this wretched little scandal."

"Quite," said Donna Beatrice faintly.

Max nodded briefly at that portion of the room in which she sat. He appeared to be enjoying himself.

As she sat looking at him, Belle's brown eyes seemed to grow larger and more dense in colour, but she made no sound, and only the gentle pressure of her hand on Linda's shoulder increased slightly.

"My plans are these," said Max briefly. "My name has been too long linked to John Lafcadio's for me to allow any private considerations to deter me from coming to his rescue at a time like this."

He had dropped the impossible artificiality of manner with which his opening remarks had been made, but a new matter-of-fact didacticism was if anything even more offensive. "At considerable personal inconvenience, therefore, I shall take the remaining four Lafcadio canvases to New York this autumn."

He made the announcement bluntly and continued without waiting to see if his audience agreed with him.

"Although times are bad, I think with my powers of salesmanship I can expect to sell one or perhaps even two canvases. The echoes of the distressing affairs in this house will have died down over there by that time, if they ever reach so far. After New York I shall take the remaining works to Yokohama, perhaps returning to Edinburgh with any that are left. I realize, of course, that I am taking a risk, but I am willing to do this as a last tribute to the man whose genius I have established."

He paused triumphantly with a wave of his long hands.

Belle remained perfectly silent, but Donna Beatrice leant forward, her thin face flushed, her necklace jangling.

"Dear Max," she said, her voice shaking with self-conscious sweetness, "keep his name green. Keep the Master's torch alight."

Max returned the pressure of her thin fingers and released them perfunctorily.

"The only reason I come to you at all," he remarked, slipping gracefully into the great chair, "is that written consent to break the terms of the present arrangement must be given by you, Belle, before I can take the canvases abroad. I have the documents with me. You sign them and I'll make all the necessary arrangements."

Donna Beatrice rose with a rustle and glided gracefully to the serpentine bureau in the corner.

"Sit here, Belle dear," she said. "*His* desk."

Mrs. Lafcadio did not seem to have heard her, and Max laughed softly and went over to her.

"Dear Belle!" he said. "Aren't you going to thank me? I wouldn't do so much for any other painter in the world."

When the habitually even-tempered suddenly fly into a passion, that explosion is apt to be more impressive than the outburst of the most violent amongst us.

Belle Lafcadio rose in the full dignity of her seventy years. Bright spots of colour burned in her crumpled cheeks.

"You preposterous little puppy," she said. "Sit down!"

The use of the old term of contempt was unexpectedly effective, and if Max did not obey her at least he slipped back involuntarily, his brows contracting.

"My dear lady—" he protested, but Belle was aroused, and Lisa and Donna Beatrice, who both remembered the last time Belle lost her temper some twenty years before, were silent.

"Listen to me, my boy," she said, and her voice was the vigorous, resonant thing it had been in her thirties. "Your conceit is turning your head. This is not a subject we talk about as a rule because politeness and kindness forbid it, but I see that the time has come for a little truth. You are in the position you occupy now because you have had the intelligence to cling to Johnnie's coat tails. I admire your intelligence in clinging, but don't forget the motive power is his, not yours. *You'll* do what you can to save his pictures! *You've* been mainly responsible for bringing his name before the public! Upon my soul, Max Fustian, you want your ears boxed.

"Johnnie left instructions about his pictures. For eight years I've obeyed those instructions, and for the remaining four I shall do the same, please God. If no one buys them, if no one comes to the parties, it doesn't matter. I know what Johnnie wanted, and I shall do it. Now go away, and don't let me see you for at least six weeks or I'll take the whole thing out of your hands. Be off with you."

She remained standing, breathing a little faster than usual and the colour still burning in her cheeks.

Max gaped at her. Her resistance was a thing he had obviously never considered. Gradually, however, his equanimity, returned.

"My dear Belle," he began stiffly, "I make every allowance for your age and the disturbing time through which you have passed, but—"

"Really!" said the old lady, her brown eyes positively flashing. "I never heard such monstrous impudence in all my life. Will you be quiet, sir! I have told you, no. The present arrangement holds. My husband's pictures remain in this country."

"Oh, Belle dear, is this wise? That angry red cloud in your aura! Max is so clever about business, don't you think—" Donna Beatrice's mild protest from the chaise-longue ceased abruptly as Belle glanced at her.

Mrs. Lafcadio smiled politely.

"Beatrice dear," she said, "I wonder if you'd mind going to another room for a moment. I see this is to be a business talk. Lisa, my child, you can go downstairs now. Bring tea, in fifteen minutes. Mr. Fustian will not be staying."

"Vivid crimson and indigo," muttered Donna Beatrice maddeningly. "So dangerous. So harmful to the Higher Consciousness!"

But she went all the same, rustling from the room like a startled bird. Lisa followed her, and as the door closed after them Belle glanced down at her granddaughter.

"I want to do what Johnnie told me to, Linda," she said. "You and I are the only people concerned. What do you think? If we lose a little money, does it matter?"

The girl smiled.

"They're your pictures, sweet," she said. "You do what you like. You know how I feel. Somehow I don't really care very much. If you don't want them to go away, that settles it as far as I'm concerned."

"Then not in my lifetime," said Belle. "While I live I shall do what we arranged all those years ago."

"Criminally absurd," Max declared. "Sheer stupidity. My dear Belle, even though you are Lafcadio's widow you mustn't presume on your position too much. Those pictures belong, not to you, but to the world. As Lafcadio's executor in Art I insist: they must be sold as soon as possible, and our only hope is in the other great capitals. Don't let obstinate sentimentality degrade the work of a man you obviously never appreciated."

His voice had risen, and in his anger his movements had lost their studied grace and become oddly childish.

Belle sat down in her chair. The old room which still breathed the presence of the turbulent Lafcadio seemed to range itself around her. She looked at the man coldly. Her anger had passed and taken with it all that radiating warmth and friendliness which made her what she was. In its place a new and unexpected Belle was revealed: a woman still strong enough to set her face implacably at anything of which she disapproved, still shrewd enough to see flattery for its tawdry self, and still sufficiently rich in friends to be able to choose.

"Max," she observed unexpectedly, "you must be over forty. I am over seventy. If we were both thirty years younger, as I feel we ought to be to make this disgraceful exhibition even faintly excusable, I should send for Lisa to put you in a cab and send you home. You mustn't come to people's houses and be rude. You make yourself ridiculous in the first place. Also they dislike it. You may go now. I want the remaining four cases which my husband left sent back here unopened within a week."

He stood looking at her.

"Are you really going to make that colossal blunder?"

Belle laughed. "Silly, pompous little man," she said. "Go away now and send the pictures back, and don't behave as if I were a Lyceum audience."

Max was angry now. His skin was very sallow, and the little muscle at the point of his jaw twitched ominously.

"I have to warn you, you are making a very serious mistake. To take the works out of our hands is a serious step."

"Bless the man!" said Belle in exasperation. "If Johnnie were here I don't like to think what would happen to you. I remember a man coming here once and behaving about as badly as you have done this afternoon, and Johnnie and McNeill Whistler threw him in the canal. If you don't go this instant I'll send for Rennie and have it done again."

Max retreated. He was livid, and his small eyes snapped dangerously. Halfway across the room he paused and looked back. "This is your last chance, Mrs. Lafcadio," he said. "Shall I take the pictures abroad?"

"No."

"Nothing will make any difference?"

"Only my death," said Belle Lafcadio. "When I'm dead you can all do what you like."

The words were spoken with peculiar spirit, and Mr. Campion, arriving on one of his many visits, heard them with all their significance as he came up the stairs.

He hurried forward to see who their recipient might be and was confronted by Max striding out of the doorway, his face contorted with uncontrollable rage.

19
The End of the Thread

"My dear, I must be getting old."

Belle patted her muslin headdress into position as she spoke. She was standing in front of the small oval mirror with its frame of white Dresden flowers which hung over the gilt console table between the two windows. She remained surveying herself, while the roar of Max's acceleration died away in the street below.

In actual fact she looked considerably younger than of late. The clash had brought out some of her old fire, and there was a trace of the "Belle Darling" of the Louvre in her quick smile as she turned to nod at Campion, who had just entered.

After the greeting she returned to the mirror.

"I like these bonnets," she remarked. "They make me look so clean, don't you think? Old women often look so mothy, put away for the summer without being brushed. That little whippersnapper, my dear! He talked to me as if I were a case of senile decay living on the parish."

Mr. Campion looked apprehensive.

"You behaved like a lady, no doubt?" he ventured.

"Not in the least," said Belle with satisfaction. "I washed my hands of him, absolutely, irrevocably. Johnnie and I never put up with people when we really disliked them, and I'm not going back on the habit of a lifetime. I have taken the rest of the Lafcadio business out of Master Fustian's hands. I've told him he takes those pictures abroad over my dead body."

"Oh, dear," said Mr. Campion.

Belle laughed, but Linda, who had not spoken since Max left, regarded the young man thoughtfully. The old lady reseated herself.

"Now I want a cup of tea," she said. "Touch the bell, Linda, child."

Five minutes later, as they sat round sipping out of the famous crackleware cups mentioned in so many books of reminiscence, the sensation of calamity which had returned to Mr. Campion as he came up the staircase burst into his fullest mind.

Max in the drawing room, Max at a reception, or in the gallery, might be a ridiculous, overexaggerated poseur; but there was another Max, a Max as yet unseen, but who, when reconstructed from the facts gathered about him, was certainly no person for a hot-headed old lady to offend.

Altogether it was not a very comfortable meal. Belle was stimulated and frankly pleased with herself. Linda remained unaccountably silent. Donna Beatrice sulked in her room, refusing to appear, and Lisa hovered round the tea tray, a gloomy, nerve-racked ghost.

Yet the presence of John Lafcadio was still apparent. If he had been forgotten in the storm which had burst over his house, as soon as it had subsided he had returned to his former importance.

For the first time in his life Mr. Campion was faintly irritated by that flamboyant, swashbuckling shade. Its presence conveyed an air of confidence and protection which was naturally not genuine. In spiritual dangers and mental pitfalls John Lafcadio's memory might be a tower of strength to his household, but in physical attack it was hardly so effective.

The appearance of Matt D'Urfey was a welcome diversion. He put his head round the door, a picture of mild reproach.

"I've been hiding in your studio," he said to Linda. "I didn't know you were all feeding. Is the conference over?"

"My dear," said Belle, fussing shamelessly, "come and sit down at once. Linda *dear*, you haven't looked after him."

Looking at the newcomer, Mr. Campion felt again a liking for this naïve, friendly spirit who regarded the world as an odd sort of party upon which he had dropped in by mistake.

He sat down by Linda and received the tea which Lisa handed him as his right, like a child or a puppy which has been overlooked and discovered just in time.

Even with his advent Linda did not become talkative. She sat looking into the fire, her elbow resting on her knee and her shabby painter's hand playing idly with her coarse, wild curls.

Suddenly she rose to her feet.

"When you've finished eating, Matt," she said, "come back to my studio. I want to talk to you."

She took a cigarette from the box on the table, lit it, and went off to her room with a nod and a smile at Belle.

D'Urfey stayed until he had finished his repast, neither hurrying nor being deliberately slow, but when he had finished he returned his cup and plate politely to Lisa, smiled engagingly at Mrs. Lafcadio, and rose to his feet.

"I've got to go and talk to Linda now," he said and went off.

Belle looked after him.

"Just like Will Fitzsimmons before he made his name," she said. "Success brought that man down to earth. He began thinking in terms of money and finally died of depression."

Campion grimaced. "What an outlook for D'Urfey!"

The old lady shook her head.

"I don't think so. Have you seen his work?"

"Does Linda like him?"

"Very much, I think." Belle seemed complacent about the suggestion. "They'd have a very happy, untidy sort of existence together, which is, after all, the main thing. She would have been miserable with poor Dacre. Love so seldom means happiness."

Mr. Campion was still reflecting upon this facet of the tragedy when Linda reappeared.

She looked a little more dishevelled than usual, and there was a note of underlying authority and purpose in her voice which Campion had not heard there before.

"Albert," she said, "I wonder if you'd mind coming upstairs for a moment."

"Anything wrong?"

"Good heavens, no. Why should there be? I only want to show you some drawings."

Her tone, although it was evidently intended to be so, was not particularly reassuring.

Belle nodded in response to Campion's unspoken question.

"Run along, my dear," she said. "I won't come with you. I've grown very tired of pictures. All painters' wives feel like that in the end."

Linda led Campion up to her little studio where he had found her on the day of the reception. It was in much the same state of chaos now, and as he came into the room the recollection of Mrs. Potter, briskly practical, came back vividly to his mind.

Matt D'Urfey was sitting on the window sill, his hands in his pockets, the expression in his china-blue eyes that of the intelligent but detached spectator.

Linda turned to him.

"I think I shall show him," she said.

"Very well," said D'Urfey.

"You think it's an idea, don't you?"

"Yes, I think so." In spite of his words, D'Urfey did not seem particularly convinced either way.

Campion's curiosity was whetted.

"What's up?" he enquired.

Linda went to her famous cupboard, which was believed in the family to contain somewhere in its depths everything which had ever been mislaid in the house, and produced a brown-paper parcel. She brought it to the table, swept aside a miscellaneous collection of paintbrushes, pots of paint, bottles of varnish, odd reels of cotton, and other débris, and proceeded to unpack it.

Campion looked over her shoulder.

What he saw was a careful pencil study of a woman's figure in a ragged blouse, a basket in her arms and a curious, half-horrified, half-eager expression on her face. Apart from the fact that the model had clearly been Mrs. Potter, he saw nothing unusual about it, except that the draughtsmanship was exceptionally fine.

He looked up to find Linda peering at him.

"Notice anything?" she enquired.

"No," said Mr. Campion. "Not particularly, I mean. What is it? A study for an oil?"

Linda sighed. "Wait a minute."

More rummaging in the cupboard produced an old number of *The Gallery*. She turned over the illustrated pages impatiently and finally pounced on the sheet she sought.

This was a full-page reproduction of an oil painting, showing the crowd round the Cross in modern dress. In the foreground was the completed figure from the sketch.

It did not take even Mr. Campion, who was an amateur in these matters, long to decide that.

Linda turned the magazine round so that he could read the descriptive paragraph upon the opposite page:

> "*We reproduce here the seventh of the Lafcadio pictures, unveiled in London in March last. This work, which is perhaps in some ways the most disappointing of the whole collection of posthumous pictures left by John Lafcadio, R.A., is nevertheless well up to the standard of that brilliant technician's later work. It has been purchased by the Warley Trust for the Easton Art Gallery and Museum.*"

"Now do you see what I mean?"

Mr. Campion picked up the study.

"Is this your grandfather's? I thought all his stuff was preserved somewhere."

"So it is," said Linda. "Sit down. When I was in Rome this time I came back through Paris. I told you I hadn't been very successful in finding any of Tommy's stuff. Someone had been round before me and cleared off everything. But when I was in Paris for a few days it occurred to me that he might have given a sketch or two to old D'Epernon, who keeps a filthy little café in Montparnasse. I looked him up. He lets lodgings as well, and Tommy used to take a room there whenever he came up from Rome."

Mr. Campion nodded to show that he was still attentive, and she hurried on.

"D'Epernon hadn't got a thing, but the wineshop people over the way were more helpful and finally fished this out. Apparently they had a daughter whom Tommy used to flirt with. He gave her this sketch as a parting present. I bought it and brought it home. Now do you see what I'm driving at?"

Mr. Campion had the uncomfortable sensation that he was being very stupid.

"How did Dacre get hold of it in the first place?" he demanded. "Did you give it to him?"

Linda picked up the magazine.

"You're not very intelligent," she said. "Look here. This picture, Grandfather's seventh posthumous exhibit, was solemnly unpacked at the Salmon Galleries just before Show Sunday last year. It wasn't supposed to have been touched or the original seals broken before that date. By that time Tommy had said good-bye to the wineshop girl for over six months and she herself was safely married and living in Aix with her husband, who's a baker or something. Her parents assured me that they'd had this sketch in the house for over eighteen months."

"Yes," said Mr. Campion, on whom the truth was slowly beginning to dawn. "Where is all this leading?"

"You'll see," said Linda grimly. "Look at the paper this sketch is drawn on." She held it up to the light. "See the watermark? That's Whatman Fashion Surface, slightly rough. That paper wasn't manufactured until about seven years ago. I remember it coming out when I was a student."

"Which would argue," put in D'Urfey from the window sill, "that Daddy Lafcadio didn't make the drawing."

Campion frowned. "You're sure Dacre couldn't have seen your grandfather's picture at some period before it was officially opened?"

"And copied it, you mean? I don't think so. The pictures were kept in the cellar at Salmon's. Max made quite a fetish of them. He'd hardly let a student see them, and no one else. Oh, Albert, don't you see what I'm driving at?"

Mr. Campion regarded her mildly through his enormous spectacles. "You're suggesting, I suppose," he said slowly, "that Dacre painted the picture?"

"I'm not suggesting," said Linda. "I'm telling you."

Mr. Campion rose slowly to his feet and stood looking out at the canal. His face was completely expressionless, and he appeared to be looking at something far away in the mist on the opposite bank.

"If this is true," he said at last, "it explains . . . well, quite a number of things."

Linda shot an appraising glance at him and was clearly about to speak, but a second thought occurred to her and she stood fingering the drawing meditatively.

Mr. Campion roused himself from his reverie.

"It's rather a dangerous yarn, isn't it?" he said with an attempt at his old levity. "I mean, I shouldn't go spreading it around. It might get you into a lot of trouble. There is probably some perfectly innocent explanation, anyway."

"I don't think so."

"But, my dear girl, how can you be sure?" Campion snapped the question intentionally. "I should keep very quiet about it if I were you."

The girl regarded him coolly, and he noticed, as one often notices irrelevant things in times of stress, that her eyes were quite green save for the little flecks of brown in them. She was really astoundingly like Lafcadio himself.

"I should keep quiet—I have, for two or three weeks— if I didn't think the time had come to talk. You see, Albert, I'm as sure as anybody can be sure that the seventh picture, which the Warley Trust bought last year, was painted by Tommy, and I'm open to bet that if there are any Lafcadios left in the Salmon cellars at least three of them were painted by Tommy, too."

"My dear girl, you mustn't make unfounded suggestions like this." Mr. Campion was shocked.

Matt D'Urfey, who had given up listening to the conversation and had been pottering with some drawings of Linda's in a corner, now returned to it to some purpose.

"Have you told him about Lisa?" he enquired.

Mr. Campion spun round.

"What are you two hiding?" he demanded. "Believe me, it's most dangerous at this stage."

Linda looked up at him.

"So you've guessed, too, have you?" she said. "I did, but not until this afternoon, and that's why I decided to talk to you. We don't want Max getting his teeth into Granny, do we?"

Her remark was so unexpected and echoed his own thoughts so completely that for a moment Mr. Campion was silenced. Finally he took the girl by the arm.

"What do you know about this business?" he said urgently. "What's this yarn about Lisa? That woman runs through this affair like a squib. You never know where she's going to explode next."

"Lisa's all right," said the girl carelessly. "She's very simple, though. People don't seem to realize that. She doesn't think like ordinary people. She's never had occasion to. She was a complete peasant when she came here. I don't suppose she knew more than a hundred words in any language. She doesn't mean to be secretive. She just doesn't know what's important and what isn't. When I came back from Paris I got her up here one night and made her remember quite a lot of things. She told me something which explains everything. You see, Grandfather didn't leave twelve pictures; he left eight. Lisa knows, because she helped him to seal them up."

Mr. Campion took off his spectacles and polished them. An enormous knot in the skein was unravelling before his eyes.

"It was very difficult to get it out of her," the girl went on. "It took endless questioning. But as far as I could gather, this is what happened: The year before Grandfather died— that is, in nineteen-eleven—Belle was very ill. She had rheumatic fever, and when she recovered she went down to stay at San Remo with the Gillimotts. He was a poet, and she painted. Funny, nervy people, I believe. Belle was down there for about six months, and it was during that period that Grandfather packed up the pictures and put the whole scheme in order. So Belle saw some of the pictures, and some she didn't. Mrs. Potter had seen them, because she was hovering about as usual. Old Potter was away somewhere, teaching, probably, in Scotland, and Lisa remained to look after the house. Grandfather was very secretive about the whole business. Everybody put that down to his age, whereas of course the old boy had a perfectly sound reason for keeping it all so dark."

She paused.

"There's one point you've got to understand," she said at last. "It may strike you as hard to credit, but it seems perfectly logical and natural—to me, at any rate. And it's this: The main reason why Grandfather did the thing at all was to get his own back on Charles Tanqueray. He really hated Tanqueray, and he left the pictures to discourage him. He wanted to leave a lot. He wanted to sound as if he were going to be in the limelight for a long time. He only had eight canvases he could spare, and so he labelled those '1924,' '1925,' and so on. But the last four parcels were fakes. Lisa says, as far as she remembered, one contained a kitchen tray, and one of the others a big cardboard sign advertising beer. Just anything, you see. The Victorians had that sort of humour, you know. It wasn't lunacy. He was that sort of old boy—a buffoon of a person.

"Lisa told me all this quite solemnly," she went on. "Apparently she promised him to keep quiet and helped him nail up the packing cases and couldn't understand what he was so amused about. She said he was in tremendously good humour when they'd finished and made her drink a whole bottle of Lafite with him."

"But the hoax was certain to be found out," said Campion.

"Of course it was," said Linda impatiently.

She seemed to share some of her grandfather's enthusiasm for the scheme.

"But that wasn't the point. Don't you see, Tanqueray was younger than Grandfather, and it had occurred to him that his hated sparring partner was only waiting for the Lafcadio demise to set up unpersecuted as the Grand Old Man of the art world. Grandfather gave him ten years to cool his heels, with the infuriating knowledge that at the end of that time Lafcadio was going to return with a spectacular stunt which would keep him in the public eye not for one year only but for another twelve. The fact that he had only eight canvases and hadn't the energy or the time to paint any more—he was portrait-painting right up to the time of his death, you know—made him slip in the faked packing cases for the last four years. I daresay he reckoned that eighteen years would about see the end of old Tanqueray. He overestimated it, poor darling. Tanqueray didn't live to see the first picture. Have you got that far?"

Mr. Campion signified that he had. The tangle was unravelling fast.

"Well, now," said Linda, "the rest is a sort of guess, I know, but it fits in perfectly. Some years ago someone at Salmon's—and I think it's pretty obvious who—had a peep into the packing cases and hit upon the obvious swindle. After all, as far as the authenticity of a picture is concerned, preconceived ideas are half the battle. If the fake's good enough you'd be surprised at the authorities who get taken in. Here was everything all ready. Everybody knew there were twelve Lafcadio pictures, everybody expected twelve Lafcadio pictures. Even if one of them was howlingly indifferent, why should anyone think that Lafcadio hadn't painted it? Whatever it was like, it was worth its price. Lafcadio's reputation was made. One dud, or even four, couldn't hurt it much."

"Quite," said Mr. Campion, who found these revelations very enlightening.

"Four years ago, before Tommy went to Rome, he took an extraordinary holiday. Matt'll tell you about it. He completely disappeared for about ten months. No one heard from him; no one saw him. At that time he was trying to be a portrait painter, very much in the Lafcadio manner. When he came back he gave up oils suddenly and went to Rome to study tempera."

"He got the Prix de Rome, didn't he?" said Campion.

"No. He didn't. That's the point. He got the other one, the Chesterfield Award, and Max was adjudicating that year."

Mr. Campion was silent for a moment, setting these facts in order in his mind.

"Where was Mrs. Potter when Dacre was on his mysterious holiday?" he enquired.

Linda nodded at him approvingly.

"You're shrewder than I thought," she said without discourtesy. "Quite remarkably, that period corresponds exactly with the time when Mrs. Potter had what was, as far as I can gather, the one stroke of luck in the whole of her life. She got a commission to go curio-hunting in middle Europe and was away for ten months. I never heard of anything she brought back. She was supposed to be moving around the whole time, and so no one wrote to her, nor did she reply. You know how casual people like us do that sort of thing. She did her curio-hunting for Max, of course. So you see she knew all about it, which probably accounts for . . . well, for everything."

"What about the last picture?" said Campion. "The Joan of Arc one."

"Oh, that's genuine. It was clever of Max, wasn't it, mixing the dud in with the others? There was a certain amount of criticism of last year's effort, and so this year out comes the genuine thing again."

"But look here," protested Campion, still bothered by the technicalities, "surely an expert could tell the difference? There's the paint, for one thing. And hang it all, the genius of the man. That couldn't be faked."

"You're talking like an amateur," said Linda. "Don't put too much faith in experts. They're only human. As for the rest, it was perfectly simple for Mrs. Potter to get hold of the Lafcadio paint. She was always begging little tubes of this and that from Rennie, anyway. The question of genius doesn't come into it. I've told you there was a certain amount of criticism of the seventh picture, but nobody thought of questioning its authenticity. It wasn't bad enough for that. As a matter of fact it was very good. Grandfather might easily have painted it. He didn't turn out a masterpiece every time.

"The question of technique is the most difficult of all. That had to be copied, of course. I think Tommy copied it deliberately. I think he was paid to. I've told you he used to imitate—or shall we say be influenced by?—Lafcadio, anyway. And he was particularly clever in oils. Really I don't see why he shouldn't have done it. In fact I'm perfectly certain he did do it."

"It would explain—" began Campion.

"It does explain," the girl corrected him. "One of the things it explains is why Tommy suddenly chucked up oils. It was part of the bargain, you see. If ever the question of authenticity arose in future years, one of the first questions everybody would ask would be who had painted the damn things. And if there was a competent painter very much in Max's pocket, who worked very like Lafcadio, the answer wouldn't be far to seek, would it? So Tommy had to give up oils. I'll never forgive Max for that."

"There are other things that'll take a bit of forgiving," pointed out Mr. Campion.

The girl flushed.

"I know," she said. "I haven't assimilated all that yet. The full explanation of the whole ghastly business only occurred to me when Max and Belle were having that row this afternoon. That was why I decided to tell you all this. I didn't realize you knew already. Something's got to be done before Max takes Belle at her word. He's got four pictures, remember; three duds and one good one. He knows his one real chance to dispose of them—and they're worth anything up to ten thousand pounds apiece—is to take them abroad and sell them before the hoo-ha dies down. It's a good selling tale, you know: 'to be disposed of quietly because of scandal.' 'All hush-hush, but the genuine thing, my dear boy.' "

Mr. Campion pulled himself together.

"You must keep quiet," he said. "That's the main thing. Let one breath of this get about and we may lose him, if nothing else happens."

"You can trust me," said Linda grimly.

"And D'Urfey?"

Linda regarded the affable, blue-clad figure with affection. "It wouldn't occur to him to talk," she said. "He's too lazy, for one thing."

"Not at all," said Mr. D'Urfey with dignity. "It's just not my affair, that's all."

"You'll do something, Albert?" Linda persisted. "You didn't see Max's face when he left Belle this afternoon. I did. He looked insane."

But Mr. Campion had seen and had formed his own opinion.

He went to see the inspector.

20
A Nice Little House

"Yes, well, there you are," said the inspector, kicking the fire, which in spite of its brightness did not take the chill out of his grim little office. "There's the whole story. We know nearly everything now. But what can we do?"

Mr. Campion looked as nearly excited as the inspector had ever seen him. He sat on the visitor's chair set out in the middle of the square of dingy carpet, his hat on the floor by his side and his hands folded across the knob of his stick.

"You can't leave it here, Stanislaus," he said earnestly. "The man's a menace, a sort of malignant germ which may produce an epidemic at any moment."

Oates rubbed his short moustache.

"My dear fellow, I don't want you to think I'm not interested," he said. "I am. We all are here. We've had conference after conference about this case. Your information completes a fascinating story. I can't promise to act upon it immediately because there's not a hap'orth of concrete evidence in the whole yarn. I needn't point that out to you; you know it as well as I do. You're not an amateur in the sense that you're a beginner. You must see the thing as we do here."

Mr. Campion was silent. In his heart he had known that some such answer must meet his demands, but he could not rid himself of the growing conviction that the matter was urgent.

"It would be most unfortunate for all concerned if a scandal about the Lafcadio paintings broke now," he said at last. "But if it meant that you could put that fellow under lock and key, then frankly I shouldn't hesitate."

"Good heavens!"—Oates was inclined to be querulous—"that was the first thing that came into my head, naturally. That's why I've been questioning you so carefully about this latest discovery. But as far as I can see, the only thing you have which looks faintly like proof is the figure study for the picture on recently made paper. What does that amount to in all conscience? Nothing at all. Fustian's only got to say that he gave the boy permission to see the pictures, confessing to a little irregularity, you see, and the mainstay of the whole case is swept away. It's not enough, Campion. There's no one more eager than myself to get an arrest. I'm badgered on all sides to make one. But one blunder now and we should lose him for ever. We've got to be canny. We've got to wait."

Mr. Campion rose to his feet and walked over to the window, where he stood looking down into the yard below.

"I feel it's urgent," he said obstinately.

"I agree." The inspector came and stood beside him. "Can't you persuade the old lady to go away somewhere or make her let the fellow have his own way? Meanwhile we've got our eye on him. Don't make any mistake about that. If he breaks the law in any way whatsoever—if it's only a motoring offense—we shall be down on him. And if he makes any serious attempt upon anyone, we're not unprepared this time and we shall get him."

He hesitated, his brow wrinkling.

"If Mrs. Lafcadio does succeed in getting those four cases from Fustian, I very much suspect that at least three of them will contain the original junk which the old man packed. But if by chance Fustian should be foolish enough to send the three fake pictures, and she can detect them—really detect them, I mean; not just personal-opinion stuff—she might possibly be able to hotch up some sort of case against him, though on what grounds I'm not quite sure. She'd have to go into that with a lawyer. However, in my opinion that'd be a dangerous proceeding in the present situation. As I think I've said before, when a man of that age suddenly takes to murder it means that there's a spanner in his mental machinery and God knows when he's going to stop. But then you know that, and that's probably why you came to me today."

"Yes," said Campion soberly. "That's why I came."

The inspector walked over to the desk, where he stood idly digging a pen into a piece of blotting paper before he spoke again.

"Thinking it over," he said, "I believe our only avenue of attack at the moment is through the pictures. There are one or two blanks we haven't filled in yet, you see. One is why Fustian should choose to kill Dacre when he did and not before the boy went to Rome at all . . . that looks like blackmail to me. And two, why was it, exactly, that Mrs. Potter came in for hers?"

"I don't think we shall ever know that," said Mr. Campion. "I don't think it matters. I think it's fairly obvious that she was with Dacre while he did the work for Max, serving as general factotum, model, and guardian, I should think. But whether he killed her because she guessed he had murdered Dacre or because she had threatened to give the game away about the pictures, I don't see that we can ever tell. Personally I incline to the former."

He looked at his friend helplessly.

"I'm at a dead end, Stanislaus," he said. "Man-hunting isn't my métier. It's a job for the police. I do see that you're hampered. If this fellow does it again, you'll get him. You've only got to watch him until he makes the attempt and fails or succeeds. I'm in a slightly different predicament. I want to stop him attempting."

"Then concentrate on the pictures," said Stanislaus

Oates. "Concentrate on Dacre. And that reminds me; I meant to mention it, but your story put it clean out of my mind. That Rosini girl, the little Italian he married: early on in this business I got the police of the Saffron Hill district to keep an eye on that bunch and let me know if anything unusual occurred. I had no special reason for this, you understand. It was just part of the ordinary routine. We like to keep an eye on anyone connected with a murder case, however remotely. I'd forgotten all about it, as a matter of fact, but this morning I had word that the erstwhile Mrs. Dacre, who seems to have an odd circle of friends, has been in the habit of going off for week-ends to the country with a whole crowd of them. It says on the report, 'Alleged destination some property left to Mrs. Dacre by her husband.'

"There is nothing remarkable about this, of course," he continued, "and so I didn't hear about it, but last week-end there appears to have been some sort of shindy, for the party returned to London in the small hours of Sunday morning looking as though it had taken part in a pitched battle. That's all the information we have at present. It may be nothing at all, of course, but it sounded odd, so I mentioned it. Did Dacre have any property?"

"None I ever heard of," said Campion.

He picked up his hat.

"I think I shall see Rosa-Rosa," he said. "You've no objection, I suppose, Stanislaus?"

"Oh, Lord, no. Be discreet, of course—but I needn't tell you that. And don't worry, my boy. That man's being watched at every step. I hope for everybody's sake that he doesn't make an attack on the old lady, but if he does we'll get him."

In the doorway Campion paused.

"Stanislaus," he said, "do you think that if you'd known as much as you know now you would have had a chance in ten thousand of saving Mrs. Potter?"

Inspector Oates was an honest man. He shrugged his shoulders.

"Perhaps not. But that was very ingenious," he said.

"Ingenuity seems to be a peculiarity of Mr. Max Fustian's," said Campion and went away uncomforted.

At six o'clock that evening he set out upon his search for Rosa-Rosa. For obvious reasons he did not want to visit her in her uncle's delicatessen store on Saffron Hill, but he had a very shrewd idea of where to look for her.

He started off down Charlotte Street with every hope of finding her at the Robespierre, and as soon as he turned into the side entrance of that most odd of all London pubs and pressed through the red-plush curtains which divided the outer bar from the holy of holies within he caught sight of her, seated on one of the shabby leather sofas in the corner by the fire.

The place was not crowded. Barely half a dozen men sat on the high stools round the bar, and the sketch-covered walls and coloured-paper-flecked ceiling were not yet obscured by a haze of tobacco smoke.

The largest party in the room was Rosa-Rosa's own. It consisted of four young men, among whom Campion recognized the sharp-featured Derek Fayre, the cartoonist, whose bitter, slightly obscene drawings appeared occasionally in the more highbrow weeklies. The others were unknown to him, although he was vaguely aware that he had seen the effeminate young man with the side whiskers on the stage at one of the Sunday shows.

The round man with the pointed beard and the real horn spectacles was a stranger, as was also the young Italian with the black eye who sat on Mrs. Dacre's left and held her hand.

Rosa-Rosa had not altered. Even the fact that her head was framed by an enlarged photograph of the 1920 Robespierre children's outing did not lessen the bizarre modernity of her extraordinary appearance.

She wore no hat, her strange immobile features were expressionless, and her yellow hair stuck out flat from the top of her head like the curls in conventional bas-relief.

Campion's immediate problem, which was one of introduction, was settled for him instantly.

As he stood hovering, glass in hand, the girl caught sight of him.

"Hello," she said. "I met you when my husband was murdered. Come and sit here." This greeting, which was uttered at the top of her harsh high-pitched voice, made a little stir in the room. The people round the bar paused to glance at her curiously, but the plump, capable woman who was serving did not bat an eyelid. Evidently the tragedy in Rosa-Rosa's home life was no news to her.

The plump young man made room for Campion at the table. Rosa-Rosa evidently regarded him as an old friend, and he settled down with his beer, the legs of his chair almost in the fireplace as he squeezed in on her right.

After her welcome, introductions seemed superfluous, and the conversation went on where it had left off.

"My uncle is taking me to his lawyer," said Rosa-Rosa, who appeared to be in the middle of a story. "When we go to the police court we shall raise hell. I will show that stinker!"

"What will you do, Rosa-Rosa?" said Fayre, smiling. There was something bantering in his tone, as if he were persuading her to perform.

"I will do this."

With one of her lightning changes into electric vivacity Rosa-Rosa did her trick, which consisted of a graphic and vulgar pantomimic display, rendered all the more vivid by the contrast with her natural immobility.

Mr. Campion was a little startled. It was evident that Rosa-Rosa's lack of English was no deterrent to her powers of expression.

"Dirty little beast!" said Fayre, laughing. "I'd like to see you do that all day."

"Get on with the story," commanded the young man with the beard with weary resignation. "I suppose we must hear it."

Rosa-Rosa stuck out a long thin tongue at him and beckoned to the barman.

When the question of further refreshment had been settled, the Italian boy cuffed her gently.

"It's your cottage, isn't it?" he prompted.

Rosa-Rosa choked into her glass.

"My husband who was murdered gave it to me," she declared as soon as she recovered. "Before we came from Italy he told me it was mine. 'We will live there and be happy,' he said."

"You loved your husband, didn't you?" said Fayre, still with the smile and as though he spoke to some clever animal.

Again Rosa-Rosa underwent one of her startling changes. She drooped, she crumpled, her body sagged, even her hair seemed to wilt. Her dejection was not so much exaggerated as epitomized.

She threw her arms out wide and remained very still, her chin resting on her breast.

"I loved him," she said.

It was an extraordinary exhibition; rather horrible, Mr. Campion thought.

Fayre glanced at him.

"Extraordinary, isn't it?" he said. "She does it every time. Carry on, Rosa-Rosa. Nothing's very clear in my mind except that your husband, whom you loved,"—he mimicked her grotesquely—"left you a cottage in his will. You went down once or twice and had a few disgusting parties. The second—or was it the third?—visit was interrupted very naturally by outraged neighbours, who were caretaking for the real landlord. Your uncle—disgraceful old basket—is getting in a shark lawyer, and when you get hold of the landlord, poor beggar, you're going to go like this—" He imitated her first gesture and rose to his feet. "I've got to go," he said. "I met my wife today and she said she might be coming home. If she's there when I get back I'll bring her along."

"Some hopes," said the man with the side whiskers as soon as the cartoonist was out of earshot. "Does he always talk like that to create an impression, or is it genuine?"

"Eve did marry him and did leave him," said the fat man with the beard languidly. "I don't feel his attitude towards it matters very much. Come, Rosa-Rosa, have you finished or is there more of this house-property idyll?"

Mrs. Dacre sat eyeing him sulkily. Then she smiled and began to swear appallingly in Saffron Hill English.

The fat man frowned with distaste.

"Horrible," he said. "Nasty, bad girl. Dirty. The management will throw you out on the street if you talk like that. Your difficulty seems very simple. Prove the will and claim your property."

"Fat beast!" said Rosa-Rosa venomously. She had noticed the cold eye of the lady behind the bar upon her, however, and lowered her voice.

"My husband made no will," she said. "He was murdered."

"Oh, God, how we know that!" said the actor, without bitterness. "Still, if he didn't make a will it's probably not your cottage. Why worry? Come and live in King's Cross. It's much more central and not nearly so insanitary."

Rosa-Rosa looked shocked. "When a husband dies,

everything that was his becomes the fortune of his wife," she said. "It is my cottage. My husband and I were going to live there, but he was murdered."

"That's nothing to be proud of," said the fat man.

"Huh?"

"I say it's not clever to be married to a man who was murdered," persisted the young man. "Unless you did it, of course. Did you do it, by the way?"

Rosa-Rosa gave her alibi, and this, too, Mr. Campion felt, was part of a performance which these feckless folk put her through whenever they saw her. His own curiosity about the cottage was thoroughly aroused, however, and he took a hand in the questioning.

"Where is this house?" he enquired.

"At 'Eronhoe. When I have seen my uncle's lawyer you shall come down to a party."

"Don't you go," said the slender young man from the stage. "It's miles away from anywhere, and the neighbours throw bricks at one. Look at that man's eye."

"Is it the Heronhoe in Sussex?" said Campion, making a guess.

The Italian boy answered him.

"No. It's in Essex. Near Halstead. I drove my cousin down there with some of our friends. We went several times. But on Saturday when we arrived the place was all shut up. People from the village were there. They wouldn't let us in."

"Very extraordinary," said Mr. Campion encouragingly.

"Most," said the boy, his solemn face with its one discoloured eye ridiculously solemn. "They said the owner was in London. We were cold, don't you know, and we'd got plenty to drink on board. We had a bit of a fight. Some of the boys got angry, the girls screamed, and the people came for us with sticks and dogs. We drove the car into 'em. Laid one bloke out. I don't think he was hurt. Anyway,"—he smiled engagingly—"we didn't wait to see. We came away. Perhaps they were right. Maybe it's not hers." He laughed at the prospect. "We tore the place up a bit," he said reminiscently. "They were good parties."

Rosa-Rosa had been listening to this recital, her head thrust forward between the two men and every line of her angular body expressing interest.

"It is my cottage," she said vehemently. "My husband gave me a little picture of the house when we were in Italy."

"A snapshot," explained the cousin. "It had the address on the back. That's how we found the place. It was furnished, but no one was there, so we broke in."

"A very stupid thing to do if you didn't know the place was yours," commented the bearded young man, who appeared to be bored to tears by the whole history.

Rosa-Rosa spat at him calmly.

"Stinkin' fat," she said pleasantly. "It is mine because my husband's things are there. All his drawings everywhere. My husband was a great painter. If he had not been murdered we should be very rich. On the day he died he told me so. We were to go down to the cottage and he was to paint four pictures like the others."

"What others?" enquired the man with the side whiskers.

Rosa-Rosa shrugged.

"I don't know. That's what he told me."

Mr. Campion took a deep breath.

"Are you sure they are your husband's drawings—the ones in the cottage?" he enquired.

"Oh, yes, they are my husband's. There are heaps—so high. Two big cupboards full."

"Heronhoe." Mr. Campion did not speak the word aloud, but it was printed indelibly upon his mind. "I wish you luck, Mrs. Dacre," he said. "You won't go down for some time, I suppose?"

"Not till she's seen the lawyer," put in the cousin.

His eyes had strayed to a red-headed girl seated at the side of the room, but he now tore his attention back to the topic which was evidently the principal subject of talk in the Rosini family.

"Afterwards we shall go back and see those country boys. Heh! It was a good fight. Bottles and everything. Not a flattie for miles. When we find out who the wet is who says he owns it there'll be a better fight still." Mr. Campion glanced through the shining window at the murky sky. He rose to his feet. Through the conflicting hopes and alarums in his mind the Italian's soft, thoughtful drawl reached him:

"It's a nice little house."

166

21
A Day in the Country

It was not so much the prospect of committing a burglary which disturbed Mr. Campion, as he steered his aged Bentley through the winding lanes of that part of Essex which is almost Suffolk, as the problem of the exact address where his project was to take place.

He had located Heronhoe on a survey map, but as he knew neither the name of the cottage nor its owner, its discovery promised a certain amount of difficulty.

It was for this reason that he had chosen to arrive in the daylight and had curbed his impulse to set off at once after hearing Rosa-Rosa's story.

He timed his departure from London at six o'clock the following morning, and it was nearly ten when he arrived at the village, having lost his way several times.

The tidy little main street, as compact and picturesque as the set for a musical comedy, lay fresh and bright in the spring sunlight. The air was chilly but sparkling. There was a crisp, invigorating wind. The fat, bursting buds on the chestnuts were wet and cold and radiant. It was altogether as fine a day for a felony as Mr. Campion had ever known.

He pulled up at the White Lion, a big, straggling hostelry which took up more than its fair share of the southern side of the street, and succeeded in persuading the landlord to admit him at least to the Commercial Room.

Wm. Pudney, according to the minute board over the doorway, was permitted by a gracious government to dispense wines, spirits, and tobacco, and, by immemorial custom, food, to all who should pass, but at ten o'clock in the morning he seemed disinclined to do any of these things for the pale young man with the rakish motorcar.

Mr. Campion was not drawn to Mr. Pudney. He was a spare, pink, youngish man with a masterpiece of an accent which betrayed at once both his ambitions in this direction and his complete lack of the ear by which to attain them.

"Me mother," said Mr. Pudney at last, "will find you somethin' to eat in the pentry. You may sit in the Commercial Lounge."

He led the way to a chamber of horrors on the right of the bar. This room smelt faintly of beer and strongly of oilcloth. The decorative scheme was, properly enough, in keeping with the atmosphere and achieved its devastating effect by lace curtains and vast enlarged photographs of past phases of the Pudney ménage, helped out here and there with cheap mahogany and coloured-glass ornaments.

Mr. Campion felt that the White Lion, commercialism, and Mr. Pudney were not good mixers. He attacked the problem on hand, therefore, without loss of time.

"Many visitors this way?" he enquired artlessly, attacking the limp bacon and anemic egg which Mr. Pudney's mother had found in the pantry.

"Not motorists," said the landlord with disdain. "We're not very keen on motorists litterin' up our beautiful countryside. Trippers lower any place."

In self-defense Mr. Campion ventured the information that he was going to Ipswich to see his father.

"He's in the Church," he added as a grace note to the fable.

"Reely?" Mr. Pudney showed surprising respect. "I thought you was a commercial. You'll pardon me, sir, but we get so many persons round here takin' orders for this and that and demoralizing the cottage people."

Mr. Campion graciously accepted the apology, and Mr. Pudney became chatty.

"We have the cycle club 'ere in the summer," he said modestly. "Me mother does quite a lot of caterin' then. Toppin' chaps they are; nothin' tripperish about them. Very tidy fellows. Never leave so much as a bottle about."

"Good," said Mr. Campion absently.

"We had a party of hikers once," continued Mr. Pudney. "Very intellectual persons, all of them—and there's the hunt, of course, in winter. That's very nice, but we don't tolerate common trippers from London. The village boys set the dogs on them."

It was borne in on Mr. Campion that Heronhoe was eminently unsuitable as a site for a week-end cottage for Rosa-Rosa.

"Really? Have they ever actually set the dogs on anyone?" he enquired.

Mr. Pudney eyed him sharply.

"There was very unregular behaviour at Spendpenny last Saturday night, I 'ear," he said at last. "Quite a fracas."

"Oh? Is Spendpenny a house?"

"Oh, dear me, no." Mr. Pudney's contempt was magnificent. "It's a dirty little old place, a labourer's dwelling. Some people came down and behaved shockin'ly—very common persons. The caretakers in the next cottage couldn't do anything with them, so they got some villagers down there on Saturday and when the persons came there was quite a fight."

"Where is this dreadful place?" enquired Mr. Campion with ghoulish interest.

"Down Pope's Lane. That little path on the left just through the village. It's never had a nice name. An artist had it once."

Campion raised his eyebrows.

"Very lowerin' to the locality," said Mr. Pudney, adding darkly, "artists mean models."

"Quite," said Mr. Campion sagely, and paying his exorbitant bill he went away in his car to turn down Pope's Lane.

The cottage Spendpenny, named after some improvident past owner, lay a good half mile down a steep lane whose banks were heightened by great walls of elder and ash. It was a postcard cottage with a roof like the back of a camel, and boarded walls which had once been tarred but were now mellowed by thirty years' weather to the comfortable greenness of the country verger's frock coat.

As far as Mr. Campion could see, as he drew up in the lane, there were no other houses round about. Spendpenny lay under a fold in a green meadow. The wild patch of garden before the door was still brown with the dead spears of last year's weeds, but the perennial polyanthi and an occasional tulip showed among the ruin.

He had no doubt that this was the cottage he sought.

The small wooden gate to the lane was smashed, the newly splintered wood showing yellow against the grey-green of its surface. Moreover, the place itself had an air of desertion, while there were yet ragged curtains at the small square windows, and the grass-grown path was tramped flat.

The loneliness of the countryside descended upon him as he stepped over the ruin of the gate, for like many travellers used to much wilder country he could recognize the peculiar emptiness of the green meadows and the tiny hidden lanes; an emptiness different from the cold freshness of virgin soil, since it is the emptiness of desertion, of the unfurnished room or the forsaken camp.

He stood for a moment looking at the cottage and then stepped forward, his lank figure casting a very small shadow in the bright cold sunlight.

When he was halfway down the path he stopped abruptly. The cottage door had opened with a clatter. For an instant the figure within was indistinct in the shadow. Then it moved out onto the cobbled step.

"My dear fellow," said Max Fustian, "but how delightful!"

The immediate thought which came into Mr. Campion's mind was typical of him. It occurred to him that the emotion of pure surprise was rare, and that when it did come it cleared the consciousness of everything else. But this was obviously no time for introspection. Max was coming to meet him.

Max in tweeds, with his hands dirty and shreds of cobweb in his hair, was in many ways a more fantastic figure than Max in his black hat and fancy waistcoat. The crofters' cottages produce many opulent, not to say exotic, weaves, and Max in heather pink and green plus-fours looked as though he were in fancy dress.

"How nice of you to drop in," he said. "Come inside. The house is obscenely dirty, and I'm afraid there's nothing to drink, but at least there's a chair."

It occurred to Mr. Campion that he ought to say something.

"Are you the landlord?" he enquired, somewhat baldly, since they were the first words he had spoken.

"Of such as it is, yes," said Max lightly as he led the way into the main room of the dwelling, a low, brick-floored apartment sparsely furnished and incredibly dusty. Much of the furniture was broken, and there were quantities of beer bottles about.

"I'm looking for a cottage," said Campion, without hope or even particular intention of sounding convincing. "They told me in the village that this was empty, so I came along."

"Naturally," said Max happily. "Do sit down."

He was evidently tremendously pleased with himself, and his visitor had the impression that his own unexpected arrival was not of the least consequence to him. Campion experienced a sense of futility. He looked at the man and wondered what on earth he could possibly be thinking.

Anyone less like the popular conception of the murderer some weeks after the crime, it was difficult to imagine, yet he experienced the uncomfortable conviction that if he should suddenly say: "Look here, Fustian, you killed Dacre and Mrs. Potter, didn't you?" Max would smile and reply airily: "Yes, I know I did. My dear fellow, what can you do about it? Think about something else."

It was an impossible situation.

Max had produced a case of yellow Cyprian cigarettes, and when Campion begged leave to stick to Virginian he shrugged his regret and lit one himself.

"I don't know if this place would suit you, my dear boy," he said. "It's very remote and quite devastatingly insanitary. But come and look over it. Look in every hole and cranny."

Campion raised his eyes without turning his head, and for a dizzy moment he thought Max had given himself away, but the bickering smile had vanished from the wide mouth and Max was his elated self again.

"I keep this place to lend to artists," he said. "It's so fantastically lonely the beggars simply have to work. There's a wash house out at the back that I converted into a studio. Come along. There's just this one room down here and a scullery. What a hovel, Campion, what a hovel!"

He led the way to a cupboard staircase and clambered up the awkward way to the two small rooms above, Campion following.

Here the disorder was incredible, and Max shuddered. "I've had uninvited visitors," he explained. "I lent this place to Dacre years ago, and that monstrous little slut of his, Rosa-Rosa Rosini, seemed to imagine it belonged to him. Anyway, I heard from the Ravens, the good peasants

171

who keep an eye on the house for me, that someone had been here, and I came down to find out that 'Mrs. Dacre had come to take possession.' She seems to have brought half the rabble of Clerkenwell with her. However, you can see the rooms."

He turned, and they went down again. Crossing through the minute scullery, they went out into the weed-grown yard and entered the studio.

The fine old wash house had been very simply converted. The warm rose brick floor, coppers, and big open fireplace had been left, and the big north light let into the tiles and a wooden platform at one end of the place were the only alterations as far as Campion could see.

There were two great presses, part of Victorian giant wardrobes, on either side of the fireplace, and the doors of these hung open, revealing them to be empty.

"Charming, isn't it?"

The elaborate drawl at his side drew Campion's attention from the tragic cupboards.

"Very nice," agreed Campion.

"Not cold," said Max unexpectedly. "Not a bit cold. Look at the fireplace."

Mr. Campion's eyes followed the sweep of the graceful hand and rested upon the ruin of his hopes.

The immense fireplace was of the early cavern variety, consisting of a square hole cut at the base of the chimney and furnished with a huge iron basket for the fire itself.

The whole square was a mass of fluttering grey and black paper ashes, still warm it would seem from the faint heat exuded by the chimney.

"Destroying something?" enquired Campion.

Max met his eyes. He was frankly happy.

"Everything," he said. And then, dropping his voice so that he spoke in a stage whisper, half serious, half bantering, "All my sins, my friend. All my sins.

"When would you like to take possession of the place?" he went on more normally. "Five shillings a week. You pay the Ravens. You can't grumble at that, my dear boy. If you take up painting I'll lend it to you. Come along and give me a lift to the Ravens' cottage down the lane. I left my car there and came over by the fields."

Mr. Campion went meekly.

On the London Road Max's new sports car shot away

from the old Bentley at something over eighty, for Mr. Campion drove soberly, almost cautiously. As he sat he thought.

The last straw of evidence which might possibly have led to Fustian's arrest had been destroyed, possibly less than an hour before he himself had arrived. Moreover, he had undertaken to rent a white elephant. The honours of the day lay with Max.

That evening, however, he received a note from Fustian making what seemed to Campion an astoundingly naïve suggestion. He said he had been thinking it would be nice if they should drink a cocktail together some time.

22
Invitation

"I've told Belle, Mr. Campion, I've told Belle over and over again that she must compose her Higher Consciousness, bring herself in tune with the Cosmic Universe, and then her aura will return to its natural blue and rose and everything will be quite all right."

Donna Beatrice delivered herself of this somewhat remarkable confession of imbecility and sat back in the high brocade chair before Belle's bedroom window and smiled up into the strong sunlight as if she placed herself on an equal footing with it as a human comforter.

Belle sat up in her small Dutch bed, a shawl round her shoulders and a crisp muslin bonnet on her head. The coverlet was strewn with letters.

Campion, who sat in the doctor's chair, shook his head at her flaming cheeks and overbright eyes.

"You get some sleep," he said. "Clear the room of all visitors and refuse to see anyone. Wash your hands of the whole business. Forget it."

Belle glowered at him like a fat, rebellious baby.

"Not you, too, Albert!" she said. "I did think I'd get a little intelligence from you. Old Dr. Pye has been here talking like that—silly prim little man! We always call him Mince

Pye, and I nearly told him so this morning, only I thought he probably wouldn't have enough French to see the joke, even if his humour rose to the occasion. I don't want to stay in bed. What's a temperature? We never bothered about them when I was a girl. I want to go down to that gallery and fetch those pictures. I won't be treated like a doddering, drooling old half-wit by a posturing little ninny who ought to be spanked."

"I can't stay in the room with such an aura," said Donna Beatrice faintly. "It stifles me."

She made a dignified exit, sighing heavily just before she closed the door behind her.

"Thank God for that!" said Mrs. Lafcadio truculently. "The woman's a fool."

"Why don't you get rid of her?" enquired Campion not unreasonably.

"For good?"

"Yes. Send her right away. It must be very trying to live with a lady of—er—her convictions."

"Oh, no, I couldn't do that." For a moment it was the old Belle who peered out from beneath the organdie. "She's old, poor darling. This is her life. Johnnie gave her a false conception of herself, and she's been living up to it rather misguidedly ever since. When he died he said, 'Belle, darling, look after that damn fool Beatrice for me. She was so lovely once.' No, I mustn't send her away, but I'm glad she's gone out of the room. Now, Albert, you tell them that I'm quite all right and bring your car and we'll go down to Bond Street and take those canvases away. Johnnie wouldn't have hesitated."

"No, Belle, you can't do that." Mr. Campion was embarrassed. "Look here, you leave it to the lawyers and meanwhile get some sleep. If not, you know, you'll die."

"Rubbish," said Mrs. Lafcadio. "If Johnnie were here we'd get the pictures, sell them for what we could, and go away to Capri until the money was spent. I should lie in the sun and listen to him telling the story and improving it."

She was silent for a moment or two, and then she laughed.

"Second childhood, my dear. I *do* know how different it is now I'm old, but I forget when I get cross. Now, Albert, advise me. What shall I do?"

She leant back among the pillows, and the colour gradually faded from her cheeks, leaving her pale and exhausted.

"I can't leave everything to the lawyers," she said plaintively, "because they say leave it alone. You see, the whole thing is in such a muddle. Johnnie thought I should be dealing with old Salmon, who was a pet, so he didn't bother much about the legal aspect of the business, and now they've come to examine it they find that Max and I are both responsible for the things. He can't do anything without me, and I can't do anything without him. It's all so annoying."

"You're still very angry with Max?"

Mrs. Lafcadio was silent for a moment while her lips moved ruminatively and her eyes grew dark again.

"Yes, I am," she said. "Yes, definitely. Very, very cross."

"What are you thinking of doing?"

"Well, I don't know. I don't know at all. If he takes the pictures out of the country I shall have to proceed against him, I suppose, and that's such a lengthy business and such a nuisance."

"You just want things to go on as they are, then?" said Campion. "I mean, you're really only anxious that the pictures should stay in England and be shown every year as Lafcadio wished?"

"Yes." She nodded emphatically. "Albert, my dear, you see to it. You speak to Max. You make him do what I want. I never want to see the man's hideous little face again, but I give you full powers to act for me. You see to it. Linda is worse than useless. She advises me to let him have his own way."

In view of everything, this was a somewhat awkward mission, and Mr. Campion could hardly fail to recognize it.

There is an optimistic belief widespread among the generous-hearted that the average human being has only to become sufficiently acquainted with another's trouble or danger to transfer it to his own shoulders not merely unhesitatingly but gladly. The fact remains, of course, that the people who say to themselves, "There is real danger here, and I think it had better confront me rather than this helpless soul before me" are roughly divided into three groups.

There are the relatives, and it is extraordinary how the

oft-derided blood tie decides the issue, who, moved by that cross between affection and duty, perform incredible feats of self-sacrifice.

Then there are those misguided folk, half hero, half busybody, who leap into danger as if it were the elixir of life.

And finally there is a small group of mortals who are moved partly by pity and partly by a passionate horror of seeing tragedy slowly unfolded before their eyes, and who act principally through a desire to bring things to a head and get the play over, at whatever cost.

Mr. Campion belonged to the last category.

"All right," he said slowly. "All right, I'll see to everything."

"Oh, my dear! Thank you so much. I can just go to sleep then and know that everything will be all right and the pictures will stay here in England?"

He nodded. Having reached a decision, he felt much easier in his mind about the whole business. He rose.

"You go to sleep now and I'll see to things. It may take a day or two, so don't worry."

"Of course I won't."

Belle was very weary, but there was still a gleam of amusement in her eyes.

"He is an odious little beast, isn't he, though?" she said coaxingly.

"I think you underestimate him, at that."

"Do you? Oh, I'm so glad. I didn't like to feel I'd made a fuss about nothing, especially after so much dreadful trouble in the house."

As he reached the door she called after him:

"Did you read his evidence in the Stoddart case yesterday? He was an expert witness for the defense, you know."

He had read the case—everyone in London seemed to have done so—but he let her repeat the story.

"The prosecution said: 'Mr. Fustian, you were called in, I understand, by the defendant to give, as it were, a counsel's opinion,'" came the faint voice from the pillows. "And the little mannikin smiled and said: 'I'm afraid you underrate me, Sir James. I was called in as a judge.' I think he's mad, don't you?"

"Very likely," said Campion absently. "Very likely. Goodbye, Belle. Sleep well."

Mr. Campion sat before the telephone in his own room in Bottle Street for some time, considering, before he drew the instrument towards him and called Max Fustian.

It was now a full week since he had visited Spendpenny, and he had not yet replied to the note he had received on reaching home after that excursion.

As he had hoped, Max was in the Gallery, and, after giving his name to a minion and waiting for some considerable time, he heard the famous voice, rendered, it would seem, even more soft and liquid by the phone.

"My dear Campion, how nice to hear from you! What can I do?"

Campion gave Belle's message simply and without excuse.

There was silence from the other end of the wire until he had finished. Then a soft, affected laugh reached him.

"My dear fellow," said Max Fustian, "must you mix yourself up in that musty business? It's really a matter for experts, don't you think?"

"I don't know that I have any opinion," said Campion cautiously. "I only know that I have been commissioned by Mrs. Lafcadio to prevent the pictures leaving the country."

"Such a charming, stupid woman," sighed the voice over the wire. "I suppose that in your new capacity you take up the same uncompromising attitude that she affects?"

"Yes," said Campion, adding with unnecessary deliberation, "over my dead body."

"I beg your pardon?"

"I say you take them out of England over my dead body."

There was in infinitesimal pause. Then the gentle laugh reached him again.

"How conscientious, Campion! We must meet."

"I should like it."

"Of course. Well, we shall see each other at the Cellini Society's party tomorrow. We can fix something then."

"The Cellini Society?" enquired Campion.

"But of course—the cocktail party to celebrate the new life by Lady du Vallon. Urquhart has done the illustrations, and the White Hart Press have turned out an exquisite book. Haven't you had your card? I'll send you one at once. I shall get there about six-thirty."

"Fine," said Campion, and added with intentional deliberation, "By the way, Fustian, you needn't trouble about the Dacre drawing. The 'Head of a Boy,' you know. I have one."

"Really?" The voice was plainly cautious now, and Campion persisted:

"Yes. A most interesting little thing. A study for a big oil. There's a sketch of the whole picture in the corner—a crowd round the Cross. I recognized it at once."

"I should like to see it."

"You shall," promised Campion airily. "You shall. See you tomorrow."

23
Night Out

Campion left the inspector and went down to Brook Street for the cocktail party.

It had been in full swing for some time when he arrived, and it was a weary servant who led him up the marble stairs with the wrought-iron balustrade, and jettisoned him into the green-panelled double drawing room with the exquisite ceiling and the Georgian sconces.

The noise was terrific.

The theory that the art of conversation has died out in modern times is either a gross misrepresentation of the facts or an Olympian criticism of quality alone. Three-quarters of the gathering seemed to be talking loudly, not so much with the strain of one trying to capture an audience, but with the superb flow of the man who knows all creation is trying to hear him.

Lady du Vallon, a crisp little woman with sharp eyes and red elf-locks, rustled across in her burnt-sienna tea gown to shake hands perfunctorily and pass him on with a murmur which might have been his name or a good-natured "Look after this" to a lonely-looking man who happened to be standing near.

This individual did not speak at all, but contented himself by looking gratified and leading the way through the gesticulating throng to the cocktail bar.

Mr. Campion accepted a dry Martini from a scowling barman and looked about for Max. His guide, having accomplished his duty, had disappeared, and the next time Campion saw him he was at the entrance again, and it occurred to him that he was probably his host.

Fustian did not seem to have arrived, and he was looking about for a convenient corner in which to stand, for the eddying mass about him was a trifle tempestuous for a lone rock, when he saw Sir Gervaise Pelley, the Cellini authority, standing a few feet away behind a bank of famous stage folk.

The great man looked a little pensive, but his eye flickered as he sighted his acquaintance, and they waded towards each other.

"In an awful hole," he muttered as he came up. "Look."

He half opened his hand, held surreptitiously low at his side, and Campion caught sight of a handkerchief loosely enwrapping a mass of sticky broken glass.

"Ice cream plate," he muttered. "Don't know what to do with it."

"Put it in someone's pocket," Campion suggested helpfully.

Sir Gervaise looked round gloomily.

"There seem to be only women near enough," he said.

In the end it was Campion who took the handkerchief and handed it to the barman in exchange for a couple of cocktails.

Disembarrassed, Sir Gervaise became his old truculent self again.

"Don't know who everybody is," he said, staring with unconscious offense at the nearest celebrity. "This isn't much like the usual Cellini Society show. Very different. I want to see a copy of the book, by the way, and I hear there are some very fine exhibits downstairs. Shall we go along?"

Campion excused himself on the plea that he was waiting for Fustian, and the announcement seemed to dismiss for ever any claims he might have had to Sir Gervaise's interest.

Once more he was left alone. He observed several acquaintances in the crowd but did not go out of his way to speak to them, since he was concentrating on the interview ahead.

The talk continued at fever pitch all round him. Old Brigadier General Fyvie was bellowing his latest *mot*, which seemed to be something about a daring escape from the British Legion; and a little rhyme, "God in His loving arms enfold us—Contrary to the belief of the Huxleys, Julian and Aldous," was going the rounds.

No one seemed to be mentioning the book, and he never discovered its title, but he saw at least two famous publishers and one rather sad-looking critic.

Unexpectedly, he came upon Rosa-Rosa clinging to the arm of a very famous painter whose tongue was quite as much paragraphed as his brush. He was exhibiting the girl as though she were an unusual type of pet and obtaining the same sort of notice for her. She did not see Campion, but swept on, large-eyed and strange-looking in her bright clothes.

The amount of energy, vivacity, and sheer personal force discharged in a single room impressed Campion again, as it always did at these functions, and he wondered idly how long the walls and ceiling and battered carpets would tingle after everyone had gone.

He found himself waiting for Max in very much the same mood as one waits for a train to an unknown destination: with doubts and impatience. There was too much gin in the cocktails, he decided, and reflected that the fault was a common one among unprofessional mixers, the outcome, no doubt, of a horror of appearing economical.

It was very late, and although one or two people seemed to be leaving they did not keep pace with the late arrivals, and the crowd was growing thicker than ever.

Max came at last, pausing to speak to the servant in the passage so that he should make his entrance alone and not in the midstream of a file of guests.

He stood for a moment framed by the great doorway with its beautiful moulding and sculptured cornice.

A number of people turned to look at him, and for an instant something like a hush swept that portion of the room. If it was not quite the silence of delighted or respectful recognition, at least it showed a momentary interest and curiosity, for he was a picturesque figure.

Campion, who had taken up a position by the far window where he could command the door, had a clear view of him.

He was wearing a grey lounge suit, rather light for the season, and a new and dazzling waistcoat. The MacDonald tartan in silk, a little faded, mercifully, but still brave and gay enough in all conscience, was fastened across Mr. Fustian's slender middle with onyx buttons. His dark face, long hair, and mercurial bearing saved him, perhaps, from looking an ordinary bounder, but they increased his oddity considerably.

His hostess 'recognized him and fluttered over, and Max, enjoying his little sensation, made the most of it.

Their conversation seemed to be common property, and Campion listened, as did most other people within earshot.

Lady du Vallon had not struck him as being a fool when he first saw her, and now, as she went up to Max, hand outstretched, he had no reason to change his opinion. Only the informed seemed to take Max seriously.

"How very very nice of you to come!" she said, allowing him to kiss her hand without embarrassment.

"Absurd, my dear Erica." Max waved away her gratitude self-consciously and added, with the air of one announcing a delightful surprise: "I've read the book!"

The lady's expression was suitably humble and shyly glad.

"Really? Oh, Mr. Fustian, that's too nice of you. I really didn't expect that. I do hope you weren't too disappointed."

"Not at all." The Fustian drawl had reached the point of becoming indistinct. "I found it quite adequate. Even more—dignified. I congratulate you. You have only to work to be a second Vasari. I think I may say that."

"Vasari? The historian? Er—do you think so?"

For a moment something approaching polite bewilderment flickered in Lady du Vallon's bright grey eyes.

"I've said so," said Max grandly.

The conceit of the man was never more apparent, and someone who felt it must be intentionally exaggerated laughed audibly, only to look uncomfortable when no one else smiled.

Lady du Vallon, who knew that she had only written a monograph on the goldsmith to knit some fifty or sixty woodcuts into a book, clearly felt a little at sea, but she was a woman of courage.

"I always saw you in that rôle, Mr. Fustian," she said, taking the bull by the horns. "As Vasari, you know."

"I? Oh, no, dear lady. Not Vasari." Max smiled.

In his tartan waistcoat the man looked like a barrel-organ monkey, Campion reflected.

"I see myself more as a patron of the arts—a Medici, shall we say. Lorenzo de' Medici."

He laughed, and his embarrassed audience were glad to join in with him and turn back to their own more human and more interesting conversations.

"And yet the damn feller gets away with it!" muttered old Fyvie to Campion as he passed. "Can't understand it. Something fishy somewhere."

Max was still chattering to his hostess with a wealth of gesture but in a lower tone and not so publicly as before, while a thin, shy young man had joined the group. This was Urquhart, the cutter of the woods, and Max was evidently much employed.

As Campion waited he watched the exotic little figure and considered him.

He was puny, ridiculously dressed, insufferably or laughably conceited according to one's temper, and yet there was hardly a soul in the crowded room who would willingly offend him. Moreover, he had murdered two human beings in the past three months; one impulsively in an insane fit of hatred, and one in cold blood after considerable preparation. Also he had got clean away with both crimes. Looking at him now, it seemed quite impossible.

Mr. Campion considered murder.

The chief deterrent to private killing, he reflected, was probably the ingrained superstitious fear of the responsibility of ending a human life, but in a man of Max's inordinate conceit this objection could no doubt be swept away by being decided a necessity.

Then, nearly if not quite as strong a deterrent was the fear of apprehension, but here again sufficient conceit and belief in one's powers might easily make one insensible to this second terror also.

The third difficulty, of course, was the practical side of the business.

Concerning the murder of Dacre, Mr. Campion was inclined to think that the astonishing luck attending that affair was one of those tragic chances whose results are even more far-reaching than might be at first supposed. If ever a beginner received encouragement, he thought grimly, Max had certainly not lacked it. The impulsive stab in the dark had come off with fantastic ease, and in the consequent enquiries not even suspicion had ever really touched the killer.

Fustian's second essay, on the other hand, the murder of Mrs. Potter, had been ingeniously carried through, ruthlessly and without a slip, but, Campion realized suddenly, the actual details had been no more neat and ingenious than those of a hundred delicate business intrigues which Max must have carried out in his time.

In fact, once the two main objections to murder had been overcome the rest required merely that subtlety and lightness of touch of which Max was admittedly a master.

Campion frowned. As a possible third victim he found the subject extraordinarily interesting.

It was at this moment that he noticed that Max had left his hostess. He went over to join him.

Fustian greeted him effusively.

"My dear fellow!" he murmured. "My dear fellow, what an impossible crush! No room to breathe or move or talk. Why do we come to these herdings of the little brains!"

He spoke affably and loud enough to be heard by all his more immediate neighbours, who shot him resentful or contemptuous glances according to their humour.

At the same time he was forging through the throng. Mr. Campion partook of another cocktail while Max demanded sherry and, after some little delay and trouble all round, obtained it.

He was in excellent spirits, chatting and nodding graciously to everybody whether he knew them or not. Mr. Campion got the impression that he must be almost universally disliked. His affectations seemed to have broadened to the point of farce, and there were people about who laughed at him openly.

He was standing, glass in hand, his head thrown back, surveying the throng and commenting on it as though he were watching it through a microscope, when Bee Birch, the militant painter of athletes, came up with fire in her eye and a magazine in her hand.

She was a picturesque figure herself in her puce stuff dress and outrageous sailor hat lying flat on her soft grey hair. The tales of her battles were many, and her habit of never leaving a thought unsaid was the terror of her hostesses.

She descended upon Max like a very nice war horse and thrust the open magazine at him.

"Fustian, did you write this disgusting piece of effete snobbery?" she demanded.

Campion, who was wedged in by the bar and Max himself, saw that the magazine was the current issue of *Life and Letters*, and the article was headed "The Coarse in Paint, by Max Fustian." Moreover, there was a photograph of him, very dark and dramatic.

It seemed as if a certain amount of unpleasantness must ensue, but Max was unruffled.

"Dear Miss Birch," he murmured. "Of course I shall be delighted."

And then, before anyone realized quite what he was about, he had set down his glass and taken an enormous gold pencil from the pocket of his dreadful waistcoat, signed the photograph with a flourish, and handed the paper back to her with the hint of a bow.

Rendered completely speechless with indignation, Miss Birch stood silent, and seizing Campion's arm, Max made an unhurried but purposeful getaway.

"We must discuss our business over dinner. I insist," he said as they came down the stairs together. "One can't talk in a bear garden like that. I can't drink a sherry these days without getting a crowd around me."

Campion glanced at him sharply, but he was apparently perfectly serious.

"We must drop in at my flat first," he went on. "Between ourselves, I want to change my waistcoat. Then we'll go on to Savarini's. I have a table there."

Mr. Campion did not demur. He wondered how Max was thinking of killing him. Savarini's sounded safe enough.

The flat in Baker Street proved to be one of those luxury apartments on the top floor of a giant block.

The room into which Max conducted him, with a murmured apology for his absent man and a languid comment on the servant problem generally, had much of the ascetic elegance of the Bond Street gallery: that is to say, it only just escaped being definitely bare. Its lovely stripped-pine walls were decorated by a single Matisse over the fireplace, and the plain pale green carpet was reflected more etherreally still in the slightly domed ceiling.

Campion seated himself in one of the two chairs as big as Austin Sevens on either side of the hearth, while his host slid back a part of the panelling to reveal a small bottle cupboard.

"If you don't mind, my dear fellow, I'll stick to sherry," he said, his fingers moving deftly among the paraphernalia of refreshment. "But I have an excellent cocktail here, my own invention. You must try it."

Mr. Campion felt a fool.

"I don't think I will, if you don't mind," he said. "I've been drinking all the afternoon."

"Really? Oh, but I know you'll change your mind. You needn't be afraid. I know what these home-made concoctions are so often like, but I assure you I'm an expert. I shan't give you the recipe. I guard that most—most jealously."

On the last word he shook a few drops of poisonouslooking green stuff from a bitters bottle into a minute shaker and fastened it up.

"There," he said a moment or so later as he filled a glass and poured out a sherry for himself.

Campion, leaning back in the Gargantuan chair, wondered at himself and his host. The chances of a man poisoning one in his own flat were remote, of course, but in so serious an issue the most unlikely eventualities were worth considering.

Max was still talking. His drawl was less noticeable, his guest thought, and his languor had given place to vivacity.

"Now the cherry," he said. "This is the one cocktail in the world in which the cherry is an integral part."

"I don't like cherries," said Campion feebly.

"You'll adore this one. This cherry," said Max firmly and with an inflection which gave his guest an uncomfortable sensation, "is like no other you have ever tasted—or ever will."

He took a stick with a red blob on the end of it from

some recess in the cupboard and dropped it gently into the glass.

"There, my friend," he said, placing the potion in Campion's hand. "If you'll excuse me I'll leave you to enjoy it while I change my waistcoat for something a little less festive."

Campion sat looking at the glass, conviction of the complete unreality of the whole scene creeping over him.

He reproached himself for undue jumpiness, for seeing innuendoes in innocent remarks. Nevertheless, he did not drink from the glass in his hand but, removing the cherry stick with its burden still attached, sniffed the contents cautiously.

It seemed perfectly normal; a little odd in colour, perhaps, but otherwise very much the ordinary flavoured gin which he had been drinking all the evening.

He was about to replace the cherry when a fleck of white upon it caught his attention. He set the glass down and examined the fruit.

Its secret became obvious almost at once. The hole where the stone had been was now filled with a greyish white paste which certainly did not look wholesome.

Campion stared at it, and his emotion was at least half disappointment. The whole ridiculous business was so unbelievably crude. Was this the man who had engineered the death of Mrs. Potter? It seemed hardly credible.

He wondered what exactly the stuff was and what symptoms his host might expect him to show when he returned.

He emptied the contents of the glass in the back of the fire and watched it blaze. Most of it was spirit, anyway, he reflected. The cherry he placed carefully in an old envelope from his pocket and stowed it in his wallet.

Max could hardly be hoping for him to die in the flat, he decided, however much his methods might have deteriorated.

He was still contemplating the amazingly puerile attack when it occurred to him that more than likely Max had no conception of the completeness of his own discovery. He must know now that the authenticity of the later Lafcadios was under suspicion, but he probably had no idea that his part in the deaths in the household had been traced.

In this case was the present attempt so childish after

all? Campion shuddered to think of the concoctions he had thoughtlessly swallowed down in the houses of acquaintances.

The subtlety might come later—in the disposal of the body, no doubt. Or perhaps it was one of those slow-working things; a culture, even, although that would be difficult for anyone but a doctor to obtain. It would be interesting to see what Max intended to do next.

Max intended to go to Savarini's, that latest love of the moneyed intelligentsia. That was evident as soon as he returned.

He had changed not only his waistcoat, but his whole suit for a set of darker garments, and seemed very happy.

"Did you like it?" he enquired, picking up the glass. "Not very much, perhaps?" he added, as his guest hesitated. "You don't like bitters? I do myself. They seem to give to a drink what minor disappointment gives to life, just that touch of the unsatisfactory which makes it worth one's going on. It's nearly half past eight. I must apologize. You must be positively starving."

Savarini's was crowded, as usual, and at the little tables, under the famous ceiling painted by Du Parc, sat many who had been at the cocktail party. Campion recognized at least a dozen people, including young Farquharson, the shipping heir, dining with a party. He looked hard at his friend and harder at his friend's friend, and raised his eyebrows questioningly. There was a lot of the snob about young Farquharson.

Max himself had something of a royal entry. Preceded by Joseph, the pontifical head waiter with the sabre cut, he strutted among the crowded tables, nodding at every face turned towards him.

Evidently it was to be a special occasion. The table in the alcove of the farthest window was reserved for them, and as they settled down on the upholstered bench they had a complete view of the whole restaurant. Joseph himself superintended their meal, which appeared to have been ordered beforehand. Mr. Campion decided that perhaps after all he was not expected to die at the dinner.

Max was speaking in his new role of the perfect host.

"I took the precaution of leaving the food to our good maître, my dear Campion. We're to taste the Cantonetti tonight, and to appreciate it one must eat the right things with it. This is to be a gourmet's meal, a fitting prelude to the discussion of the Lafcadios."

Campion expressed his willingness to enjoy whatever Joseph should set before them and enquired about the Cantonetti. The name was vaguely familiar to him, but he could not place it.

"The Cantonetti?" Max appeared suitably shocked. "My dear Campion, the greatest gastronomic discovery of the age. The one wine our generation has given to the civilized world. Of course in Rumania, the place of its birth, it has been known for generations, but the disastrous effect of old-fashioned transport ruined it completely. The coming of the aëroplane has altered all that."

He beckoned Joseph, who, Campion was grieved to see, was positively hovering.

"Has the Cantonetti arrived?"

"Quite safely, Mr. Fustian, by Monsieur Savarini's private plane."

"And it has been kept at sixty-five?"

"Sixty-five degrees exactly, Mr. Fustian."

Max nodded his gracious approval. "Bring it," he said. "We'll have it with the omelette."

Joseph sped away like one of his own service boys, and Mr. Campion tried to remember. Among the odd information in the back of his mind there was the word "Cantonetti." It was a red wine, he fancied, and the particular possession of a great family, and there was something odd about it, some anecdote, something mildly funny. He gave it up. Whatever it was it had escaped him entirely.

The dinner arrived, and Mr. Campion privately decided that the cherry in his pocket contained some poison with a delayed action; a botulistic culture, no doubt, or one of the fungus poisons. There were mushrooms in the omelette, which strengthened this idea.

Yes, of course, that was it; one of the fungus poisons. How extremely ingenious, and particularly unpleasant. Also, incidentally, how very hard on poor old Savarini.

He eyed Max thoughtfully as a waiter slid the delectable gold-and-black mass onto his plate.

"You like crêpes, I hope?" enquired his host with something that was surely more than ordinary interest.

Campion decided to play.

"Very much indeed," he said, and Max seemed pleased.

The omelette was just in situ, as it were, when a small procession walked up the room to their table.

Joseph came first, dignified and intent, his eye glassy and his bearing superb. Behind him, and in a pathetic imitation, strode a small boy bearing a tray on which stood two beautiful glasses. They were fully ten inches high and lily-shaped, with long, slender pedestals and curved lips.

Finally came the Savarini wine waiter, a solemn portly soul, carrying a broad flat basket lined with vine leaves. In the basket reposed the bottle.

Mr. Campion, the most modest of men, was slightly embarrassed by this homage so publicly paid to his stomach.

Joseph made the uncorking an occasion.

The bottle was frankly enormous, and with its dusty sides swatched in a napkin the size of a cot sheet it was probably sufficiently ostentatious even for Max.

"You are prepared for it, Mr. Fustian?" the head waiter murmured, smiling, as he poured a little of the thick crimson stuff into the host's glass and filled his guest's to the lily's brim.

"We've been in training all day," said Max happily. "Haven't we, Campion?"

If four or five cocktails constituted a training for anything, Mr. Campion supposed he had.

He nodded, and Max raised his now full glass.

"Your health, my dear Campion," he said.

The young man smiled. The toast might have been more appropriate, he thought.

They breathed, savoured, and drank, Joseph still standing before them to give the moment its due solemnity.

The wine was remarkable. Campion found himself astonished. So much preparation he had feared could only herald a minor disappointment, but this vintage seemed not only to excuse but even to merit any amount of palaver.

It was heavier than the wines of Bordeaux; deeper in colour and more soft, but without the weight of a Burgundy, and although completely different from either was yet without eccentricity to alarm the palate.

Mr. Campion, who knew the strong vintages of Spain and the odd wines of the East, found himself unable to think of anything with which to compare it. It was really a discovery, and he gave Max due credit.

"Amazing, isn't it?" His host leant back, a gleam of pure

189

pleasure in his little dark eyes. "The secret is to drink it. Don't sip it like Tokay, but drink it like the divine draught it is."

It seemed such excellent advice that Mr. Campion took it, reflecting that the fungus poisoning could hardly be expected to take effect for another two or three hours at least.

The Cantonetti was admirably foiled by the tournedos and afterward by a curious savoury mess of sweetbreads and chicken liver, and it was not until the end of the third glass when Joseph was superintending the presentation of the flat oat biscuits and the little round red cheese of the Danubian plain that Campion noticed anything odd about himself.

His first indication that he was not perfectly normal was the fact that when Max mentioned Lafcadio for a moment he had the greatest difficulty in remembering who that eminent painter might be.

He pulled himself together. The Cantonetti was evidently much more potent than its sisters of France. He felt irritated with himself and glanced at Max, who had drunk considerably more of the stuff. Mr. Fustian was obviously perfectly sober and was surveying the world with the gracious tolerance of one who has dined wisely quite as much as well.

Mr. Campion jibbed at a word and fluffed it badly, and alarm seized that part of his brain which is the last to succumb to alcohol or anesthetic.

He wondered wildly if he had been drugged in the restaurant, but one glance at Joseph reassured him. That monument of dignity would never connive at anything which might harm the prestige of the beloved business in which he was reputed to have a considerable share.

Besides, he decided furiously, he was not drugged: he was drunk, and moreover he was rapidly becoming more and more deeply sunk into that unenviable state.

Cantonetti. He stared at the bottle. Something about Cantonetti was coming back to him. Now it was gone again. Something—something mildly funny. He knocked over his empty lily goblet and laughed to see the little splinters of fine glass sticking in the cheese.

He pointed out the joke to Max, who laughed, too, tolerantly and with graceful good humour.

And then suddenly Campion was ashamed of himself and angry that he had broken the glass, and he put his napkin over the cheese and tried to change the subject and talk about pictures. Only he couldn't think of the names of any artists except a man with an unpronounceable name of whom Max had never heard.

He ate a wheat biscuit, and for an instant his mind cleared. He remembered everything, the cocktail, the cherry in his pocket, and the whole ghastly business. He glanced sharply at Max and saw that he was looking at him narrowly.

He felt suddenly cold. It had dawned on him at last. The second degree of subtlety again. The old trick which had Fustian's characteristic all along. He had meant his ridiculous poisoned cherry to be discovered; he had laid particular stress on it and had gone out of the room so that it would be discovered, and his victim, poor beast, put off the scent of the real attack.

The real attack lay somewhere in the Cantonetti. Campion wished he could remember. The whole of the main restaurant had become indistinct. He was aware of vast planes of misty, chattering ghosts to whom, he supposed fatuously, he was as invisible as they to him.

Max he knew. Max was just beside him. There was something that Max was going to do that he did not like. He could not remember what it was. It was something that he must stop him from doing. It was all very sad and difficult. He ate another biscuit.

Out of the gaily-coloured fog which seemed to have enveloped the table he caught a glimpse of Joseph's face. He felt like laughing at it because it had no body and because it looked so worried. It was saying something to Max to which Campion would have liked to listen but found it difficult because the waiter was speaking indistinctly. He caught one or two phrases.

"He did not take you seriously, Mr. Fustian—the strongest head cannot stand it if . . ."

Max was saying something now. He seemed to be apologizing.

"Of course I had no idea—he gave me his word . . ."

Once again Mr. Campion became himself, but only for a moment, for the absorbent powers of one small biscuit are not great.

Although his vision was still impaired, the scattered phrases he had heard made sense and awakened his memory.

The Cantonetti.

Old Randall talking about the Cantonetti—most marvellous stuff in the world if you haven't had any spirit within twenty-four hours. If you've had any, though, or especially if you've had any gin—then, oh, my hat!

Campion broke into a sweat. The world was beginning to fade again.

"If you've had any gin—"

Was the mixture a poison? Hardly. Savarini's would hardly risk it.

Confound this idiotic tendency to laugh unreasonably. No—that was it—Randall had said it made one tight but not ordinarily tight. Mr. Campion fancied he had said "gloriously tight," or was it "fantastically tight"? Well, he was fantastically tight now, and Max was going to do something to him. What was it? Oh, what was it? Max was going to— Good God, Max was going to kill him!

He stared at Max now, Max grotesque and misshapen with a yellow haze round him. He looked so ridiculous like that that Mr. Campion could not think of anything else. He laughed uproariously.

Max echoed him, and so did the people behind the curtain of coloured lights. Everybody laughed like anything. It was all very jolly.

Campion flew out of the restaurant, a most exhilarating experience. His feet did not touch the ground, but he hit the top of a chair once with his knee and knocked it over. No one minded. Everyone was so happy, nearly as happy as himself. They were all giggling except Joseph. Joseph's face was gloomy and shocked, and very humorous floating about without its body.

Max was there close beside him, but not flying. Max was walking rather fast, bobbing up and down and knocking into one, but he was happy, too, and did not care.

Only once Campion remembered what it was that Max was going to do, and that was when in the foyer he suddenly saw young Farquharson's face not a foot from his own. The startled expression on the familiar face sobered him, and he clutched at the man's arm as though it were the proverbial straw, and which of course it very well might have been.

"I'm—I'm in danger," he said seriously, and Farquharson's face split into a smile.

"I know you are, old boy," he said. "In danger of falling down if you don't look out."

Then Max was there again, silly Max in his comic clothes. Mr. Campion roared with laughter at him and flew on.

Outside it was lovely.

The wet streets shone as the lamps raced by. All connections with the sordid trappings of earth deserted Mr. Campion. He was a disembodied spirit, and Max was his mortal guide.

Of course there were amusing incidents. There was the time when Max lurched against him and he fell over on a street refuge, and a policeman helped to pick him up and told him to be careful. And there was the man at the embassy who told him he wouldn't like it inside because everyone would be in evening dress and laughed when he offered to take off his waistcoat.

There was the excruciatingly humourous moment when his aunt's butler in Grosvenor Square did not recognize him at first and rushed away and shut the door when he did.

By and by the glory diminished. Campion realized he was walking, and not walking too well, either. Then he noticed his hands were filthy from the refuge incident and he had lost his gloves.

He became increasingly aware of Max about this time. Max was hurrying, he fancied. He was not talking so much, either. Mr. Campion began to distrust Max. At the back of his mind there was something that warned him not to like Max. Something most unpleasant about the fellow; he couldn't remember at all what it was.

They were in a darker part of town now. There were not nearly so many lovely dancing lights. It was familiar, though. Very familiar.

Max spoke.

"Now we must go see that girl in Watford," he said clearly.

"No," said Mr. Campion definitely.

"In Bushey, then."

"In Bushey, but not Watford," agreed Mr. Campion indistinctly and for some reason which he could not bother about. "How will you get to Bushey? You don't know, do you?"

Max's voice was different, more compelling. It seemed

to Mr. Campion that it was hardly a voice at all but rather the promptings of his own mind.

"No," he said foolishly. "No, I *don't* know." The remark seemed at the moment to sum up a great tragedy.

"Ask," said the voice again. "Ask at the club."

This wonderful suggestion seemed to solve all Mr. Campion's troubles. Then, marvel of marvels, there was the club right in front of him.

He staggered to the steps and had great difficulty in climbing up them. Max was no longer with him. But the idea was still fixed in his mind: how to get to Bushey? How the hell to get to Bushey?

He put it to old Chatters, sitting in his box, his newspaper on his knee.

But Chatters was stupid and seemed to want him to go away, although he did not say so. Puffins was a rotten club, he decided. A rotten, stuffy club.

He went out again and fell down the steps, and Chatters came and helped him up, but the fool was not clear about the way to Bushey but wanted to call a taxi and send him home.

There were no taxis, though, and Mr. Campion got away from him and wandered down the road into the dark, and then Max was there again.

Mr. Campion did not like him, and said so, and Max suddenly seemed very anxious to hurry. He gave him a drink from his brandy flask, which was kind and generous of him and showed Mr. Campion that he was at heart a decent fellow.

In the hurry Mr. Campion had to think about walking, which had become increasingly difficult because the pavements now gave beneath his feet as if they were mounted on swaying piles.

They came back to the lights, which did not please him so much now, since their motion was giddy rather than the delirious speeding onward which they had affected before. Also, there were more people about. The theatre crowds filled the streets uncomfortably, and they and the unsteady pavements made progress unpleasant.

Suddenly he was aware of a familiar smell. It was the hot used air belching out of a tube station. The vast bright mouth seemed to suck the crowd down and himself and Max along with it.

In the doorway of the lift some inner sense warned him of impending danger, and he stood still, swaying unhappily, but the crowd thrust him on and supported him with its vast sides throughout the descent, which was like the descent into hell.

Afterwards, too, it swept him along giddily down the steep path to the iron trellis which parted wide open before its stream like the gates of a surrendering city.

Max was on his left, holding his arm, and a vast man in a tweed cap fought his way on the other side.

The crowd was so great that they missed the first train, which thundered out of the tunnel. In fact, Max dragging on his arm prevented Mr. Campion from attempting to catch it, and they, with all those in their immediate vicinity, moved forward to the edge of the platform to wait for the next.

Meanwhile, another lift load of homing playgoers had been jettisoned onto the narrow way behind them, and the centre of the long platform was a solid mass of straining people.

In front of the exits, at intervals where the doors of the trains were estimated to pause, were short iron railings made for such occasions, little barriers to prevent outgoing passengers from being forced back into the train by the sheer weight of the incoming mass, but Campion and his guide avoided this protection and stood midway between two barriers on the very edge of the granite. Before them yawned the track with the raised live rail in the centre and the curving poster-covered wall beyond.

Campion was giddy. The world reeled and swayed like a plane in bumpy air. His intense physical discomfort was intensified by the heat and the breathing, rustling crowd like some great weary animal behind him.

Yet his wretchedness was not all of the body. His subconscious mind was struggling to tell him something, to warn him of something. It made him feel futile and afraid.

Max nudged him.

"Look at that poster. Can you see it?"

He raised his heavy eyes from the track at his feet and stared in front of him.

An insurance firm had commissioned an artist to draw a series of rounded doorways, one inside the other, stretching, it seemed, to infinity. An inscription, *The Arches of the*

Years, sprawled across the design, but even the lettering had been drawn to heighten the illusion. The first *T* was at least a couple of feet high, and the last *s* only just readable. The curve of the wall increased the oddly inviting effect, and unconsciously the drunken man swayed towards it.

"Can you count the arches?" Max whispered and slipped behind him, the better to indicate what he meant by pointing over his shoulder.

Campion had to move forward a little to make room for him, and Max's place was instantly filled by another traveller forced from behind. He seemed to move instinctively, since he did not take his eyes from the evening paper he held.

Count the arches. Count the arches. Count the arches. Mr. Campion tried.

One, two, three, and three more, and three more and four, and— One and two more and three and six . . . twelve, thirteen, fourteen— One again, one and two—

He stretched out his hand to help him to count. From the distance came the roar of the train.

One and two and five more and . . . One—

People farther down the platform were looking at him, some laughing, some nervous.

One arch, again, and two . . . he must get closer.

The train was screaming now; nearer and nearer and nearer.

One and two and three more . . . He was almost amongst them now—

Campion saw the train, saw the great eye in the cab, saw the whole fiendish business, the devilry of the second degree of subtlety; saw the faces in the witness box, Farquharson, the policeman, the butler, old Chatters. *"He was certainly drunk." "He fell down." "He was not himself." "He was trying to get to Bushey."*

He staggered back and met resistance; more than resistance—force.

The man was pushing him. He was falling. Someone screamed . . .

A great weight struck him in the stomach and jerked him up. It was the arm of the man with the newspaper. The train passed him like a monster and screamed and stood still. There was commotion behind him. Max. Max and a screaming crowd. Max in the arms of the man with the cloth cap.

In all his mental vicissitudes Mr. Campion had never remembered the subject of his morning's chat with the inspector—the plain-clothesmen who had been following him patiently ever since he had left Scotland Yard.

24
In the Morning

"Almond paste," said Inspector Oates. "That's what it is, almond paste. What a clever, clever devil!"

He was standing by the desk in the sitting room at Bottle Street, prodding a sticky cherry with a nail file.

It was past two in the afternoon of the following day, and he had already spent half an hour in the flat.

Mr. Campion was himself again in all but one particular: his naturally affable temper had undergone a complete change, and it was a bitterly angry man who confronted his friend.

"Now you know everything," he said shortly. "I've told you my story, and you have your men's reports, I suppose."

A faint smile passed over the inspector's face.

"I have," he said. "One day you shall see them, but not now. You wouldn't appreciate them. In honest P. C. English the history of your night out makes good reading, especially the beginning. There's quite a lot you seem to have missed yourself. You were tight."

"Tight!" said Mr. Campion with disgust.

The inspector did not smile.

"If ever you get nearer to Death than you were last night you'll be able to steal his scythe," he said seriously. "Harris says the train brushed his sleeve when he caught you, and the resistance from behind was extraordinary. For a moment, he says, he thought he must go over with you. That chap Fustian—"

He shook his head as words failed him.

"He beat me," said Mr. Campion briefly. "Beat me with all the cards in my hand. I was taken in by that fake poisoning, taken in by the old second-degree-of-subtlety trick. It didn't dawn on me until I was too hopelessly tight to do anything except make a fool of myself."

"Beat you?" enquired the inspector. "You're alive, aren't you? Harris and Richards were there, weren't they, even if you had forgotten them? You were dragged out from under a train, and Fustian is under arrest. What more do you want?"

"Under arrest, is he?" Mr. Campion brightened. "What charge?"

"Attempted murder. That's enough to go on with."

Campion sat down.

"I'm still a little vague," he said apologetically. "But frankly, on the face of the evidence, I don't see how you dared do that. As far as I can see, the case must resolve into my word against his. The fact that I had a couple of plain-clothesmen trailing me shows that I had the idea in my head all day. It seems to me that his solicitor could make out a very good case against me for attempting to frame him. He's beaten us again, Stanislaus. Don't you see it?"

"Well, he's been charged," said Oates obstinately. "He came up before Mr. Masters this morning, and now he's detained. I want you to come down and see him."

"But damn it, man,"—Mr. Campion was still irritable—"unless you tell the whole story, which is impossible, there won't be any earthly reason apparent to explain why I had the idea he was out after my blood. As for witnesses of the actual pushing we all know the value of police evidence in a question of that sort, and as for independent testimony I should think practically everyone on that platform was shoving the man in front of him."

The inspector did not comment on this disquieting argument.

He put the remains of the cherry back into its envelope and pocketed it.

"I may as well have this analyzed," he remarked. "But I think there's no doubt about its being non-poisonous, if not particularly wholesome. Are you coming down to see him? We've got him at the Yard at the moment."

"The Yard? Whatever for?"

"After coming up this morning he wanted to make a statement, and what with one thing and another it seemed the best place to take him."

The inspector seemed to be intentionally uncommunicative.

"A statement! Good heavens, has he made a statement?" Campion was becoming bewildered. "What sort of a statement?"

"A long one."

"Look here, Stanislaus, are you telling me that he's confessed?"

"Not exactly. At least, I don't know."

Mr. Campion's ill temper increased.

"What's the matter with you this morning?" he demanded. "You're as secretive as a green detective on his first case."

Oates remained affable.

"It's afternoon now," he observed. "Come along down and see Fustian."

Campion rang for his hat and gloves.

"I don't want to see him," he said. "It may be childish, but I feel so vicious that I doubt if I shall be able to keep my hands off him."

"We'll risk that," said the inspector. "Come along."

They went out, and ten minutes later, in a long, concrete-lined corridor lined with many small and heavy doors, they passed a little, hurrying man with a hooked nose and gold pince-nez. He looked both pale and startled, and, shooting a glance at Campion, would have passed by with his policeman guide had not Oates stopped him.

He was J. K. Pendle, the solicitor. Campion recognized him and felt resigned. Max had a legal loophole, and it looked as though he had already found it.

"All right, Mr. Pendle." Oates was finishing a murmured conversation. "In my office upstairs in ten minutes."

He returned to Campion. Just before they reached a door near the end of the row, before which a large, helmetless police constable sat on a ridiculously inadequate chair, two men, conversing animatedly but in low tones, came out. Campion thought he recognized one of them, but the name escaped him.

Oates had a few minutes' chat with the newcomers, and as Campion drew away he heard his own name and the phrase "responsible for bringing the charge."

"I see." The man whose name and calling he had forgotten looked after him with the same half-curious, half-secretive expression which had characterized Mr. Pendle's glance. Then he lowered his voice and went on talking earnestly to the inspector.

"All right, sir." Oates spoke clearly. "I shan't be a moment. In ten minutes, then, in my office. Mr. Pendle is already there."

Mr. Campion turned to the inspector as he came up.

"Do you know, Stanislaus, I don't think I'll see him after all," he said. "I still feel unreasonable. What good can it do, anyway?"

The inspector did not seem to hear.

He signalled to the constable, who had risen at their approach, and the door was unfastened.

Mr. Campion was still angry. The emotion of personal hatred, which is after all practically unknown among sophisticated folk, had descended upon him, making him ashamed. Slowly he went in to his enemy.

Max was the first thing he saw, the first and the only thing. Campion was naturally observant, and training had intensified this attribute so that whole scenes were wont to photograph themselves on his mind in minute detail, but on this occasion he saw but one thing only, one thing lifted out of its surroundings.

He never knew what the room was like. The heavily barred window, the two men in white coats sitting silent in the shadows, the protected light were all lost upon him. He did not see them.

From the floor all that remained of Max Fustian smiled slyly at him with drooling lips.

Mr. Campion stood very still. His anger dropped from him. In its place came the strange horror which is purely instinctive, a primitive terror of that which is not a right thing.

The creature spoke, soft, slurred, meaningless sounds delivered with awful, secret confiding.

The inspector took Campion's arm and led him into the passage again.

"Sorry to spring it on you," he said apologetically. "He's worse than he was when I left. They found him when they took him some food to the cells this morning. He was truculent last night, so they left him there to cool his heels. He was only taken before the magistrate because they thought he was foxing. He wasn't quite like he is now, of course, but pretty bad. He says he's Lorenzo de' Medici. Says he's known it for some time."

Mr. Campion did not speak.

"They're like that, you know," the inspector went on slowly. "As long as all goes smoothly they get away with it, but as soon as they come up against something they can't sweep aside, a police-station cell for instance, they go over the edge and—there you are."

Mr. Campion wiped his face. He had remembered now who the man in the passage was.

"What will happen?" he asked unsteadily.

"Infirmary—Pentonville—remanded until fit to plead. Waiting for the ambulance now," said Oates briefly. "There's his statement, you see. Five thousand words of it. It took them all the morning to get it down. He confesses to everything: your murder, too, incidentally, and also instigating the assassination of Girolamo Riario, a prince of Romagna—but that was in the fifteenth century."

"When he recovers," said Mr. Campion, "will you press the charge?"

Oates shook his head.

"He won't recover. Did you see old Braybridge just now? He's been in to see him. He was very guarded, of course—all these specialists are—but he said 'undoubtedly genuine mania,' and I saw his face. Fustian will get worse and worse and finally curl up and die. I've seen scores of 'em."

"But it's so quick," Campion muttered. "Yesterday—"

"Yesterday he was a genius," put in the inspector, "and today he's a lunatic. Well, there's not all that amount of difference, is there? Besides, it's not so sudden as you seem to think. I've had his partner, Isidore Levy, down here this morning. Poor little chap, he was worried out of his life. He told us Fustian had been growing more and more peculiar for some time. Apparently he used to drop his affectations in private, but lately he kept them up always.

There have been other things, too. Only yesterday he went to a party in a scarlet tartan waistcoat. What could be madder than that?"

Campion glanced over his shoulder at the closed door, and there was something very honest in the expression in his eyes.

"He was my dearest enemy," he said gravely, "but I wouldn't have wished that for him."

The inspector smiled.

"No, old boy," he said affectionately. "No, I didn't believe you would."

25
Good-bye, Belle

Some days after Max Fustian died in a prison infirmary, and the Crescent was dusty and littered with autumn leaves, Mr. Campion went to visit Mrs. Lafcadio.

They stood in the great studio and looked at the picture which had been returned from Salmon's and hoisted into position over the fireplace.

It was a cool, dark interior, the figures subdued and the lighting superb.

Belle nodded at it, her white bonnet reflecting the light from the gallery windows.

"Such a nice picture!" she said. "He meant it to be the last to be shown. I remember him painting it quite well, in Spain. I always liked it."

"What will you do with it?" said Campion. "Keep it?"

"I think so." The old lady spoke gently. "There's been such a lot of trouble through this Show Sunday idea of Johnnie's. Poor Johnnie! His ideas always brought trouble. Next year he and I must have our party alone with Lisa and poor Beatrice."

Mr. Campion hesitated. He was on delicate ground.

"Did you see the—the other three?" he enquired at last.

"No," said Belle. "Mr. Levy and Mr. Pendle and Inspector Oates told me about them, and I quite understood. They're still at Salmon's, I suppose."

She paused, her faded brown eyes troubled and her wrinkled lips pursed up.

"I heard he was dead," she said suddenly.

Campion realized that she was deliberately avoiding Max's name and did not mention it himself.

"Yes," he said. "A bad business, Belle. I'm sorry you had to know about it."

She did not seem to hear him, but went on talking in the same quiet voice:

"The inspector hinted that Tommy Dacre was trying to blackmail him, and he lost his temper, saw his chance, and killed the poor boy. I didn't think Tommy would have blackmailed anyone, did you? He was so nice as a child."

Campion shrugged his shoulders.

"I don't suppose he looked upon it as blackmail," he said cautiously. "As far as we can find out from Rosa-Rosa and—and the confession, Dacre had been paid for the four pictures he had done and had finished his scholarship. He needed money and simply announced that he was going to paint another four pictures at the same price and in the same cottage. That's how it happened. If—if his murderer hadn't had an opportunity to hand at that moment, it would never have occurred."

"And Claire?" said Belle, her lips working. "Poor, clever Claire, how did she offend?"

Campion frowned.

"Ah, she was a more serious menace to him," he said. "She knew everything, you see. She had been a confidante in the picture-faking and had taken care of Dacre in the cottage. She guessed and let the man see she guessed, probably on that day he came to see you and told us about the Van Pipjer. Her nerve seems to have gone to pieces, so when she got a telephone message from him telling her that the police were making dangerous enquiries she did exactly what he hoped she would do, and so she died."

Belle folded her hands over the little cretonne workbag she carried, and for a moment she did not speak.

"Her poor man!" she said at last. "Poor Claire's poor man! He's just beginning to take a little interest in his work again. It's actually a little better, I think; just a little, so that's something for him. But oh, Albert, the wickedness—the dreadful wickedness and the waste!"

She turned away from the picture, but, before they went out, paused before another. The portrait of Lafcadio smiled down at them. "The Laughing Cavalier's Big Brother": again Campion was struck by the resemblance.

There was the same bravura, the same conscious magnificence, the same happy self-confidence.

A thought occurred to him, and he glanced down at Belle, to find her looking up at him.

"I know what you're thinking," she observed.

"No," he said. "I mean, I'm sure you don't."

"I do." Belle was laughing. "You're thinking of the seventh picture, the one the Easton Museum bought, aren't you? None of the facts have been published, and you're wondering what I'm going to do."

The young man looked startled. The thought had been in his mind.

Mrs. Lafcadio opened her cretonne bag.

"This is a secret," she said and handed him a slip of paper. Campion glanced at it curiously.

It was a receipt for four thousand, two hundred pounds, seventeen shillings and ninepence from a very famous artists' charity. The date particularly interested him.

"This is nearly two years old," he said wonderingly. "Oh, Belle, you knew!"

Mrs. Lafcadio hesitated.

"I knew Johnnie hadn't painted the crowd round the Cross," she said. "I didn't see the picture until the party, as it happened, because I was in bed until the very morning, and then I was too busy to look at it closely. When I did see it properly, it had already been sold and everyone was chattering and praising it. I didn't realize what had happened. It never occurred to me to doubt the Gallery."

Mr. Campion was still puzzled.

"Whom did you doubt, then?" he said, not unreasonably.

Mrs. Lafcadio glanced up at the Sargent.

"Johnnie," she said. "My bad old Johnnie. I thought it was a pupil's effort. Johnnie would have laughed so—hoaxing them all like that—all the clever, pompous people."

"So you said nothing?"

"No. I thought perhaps I wouldn't. So I sent every

penny I received to a charity, and I made a rule that in future I was to see the pictures before anyone else. Of course the one this year was genuine, so I thought the last was one of Johnnie's naughtinesses and I tried to forget it."

"How did you tell?" enquired Campion curiously.

"That the seventh picture was not genuine?" Mrs. Lafcadio's brown eyes were bright like a bird's.

"Because of the child on the shoulder of the figure in the foreground. I never understood the technique of painting. I'm no expert. But Johnnie never painted a child on a grownup's shoulder in his life. It was one of his private fetishes. He didn't care even to see it. There's a mention of it in one of his letters to Tanqueray, that dreadful book which everyone said was in such bad taste. He says somewhere: *Your disgusting habit of painting sentimental, elderly yokels supporting their bulbous and probably insanitary offspring on their shoulders repels me. Whenever I see a bloated child carried thus, its head exalted above its father's, I want to tear it down and dust that portion if its anatomy which is always so adequately but unbeautifully covered in your pictures with the sole of my boot.*"

"I see," said Mr. Campion. It seemed the only comment in the face of such irrefutable proof.

"He wasn't altogether a kindly person," Belle remarked.

"Who? Tanqueray?"

"No—noisy old Lafcadio," said the painter's wife. "But he loved my little John. Poor little John."

Campion had never heard her mention Linda's father before, and now she did not dwell upon the subject.

"Never tell about the seventh picture, will you?" she said. "After all, what does it matter? Oh, dear life, what do all these pictures really matter?"

Mr. Campion promised on his oath.

As they walked up the covered way to the house, he looked down at her.

"Well, is everything all right now?" he asked.

She nodded and sighed.

"Yes, my dear," she said. "Yes. And thank you. Come and see me sometimes. I shall be lonely without Linda."

"Linda?"

"She and Matt were married at Southampton on Monday. I had a card yesterday," said Mrs. Lafcadio placidly. "They found that separate cabins on the boat to Majorca would cost so much more than a special license, and they're set on painting down there, so they married. It seems very sensible."

Mr. Campion took his leave. Belle came to the door with him and stood on the steps, plump and smiling, her crisp bonnet flickering in the breeze.

When he turned at the corner to look back, she was still standing there, and she waved a little pocket handkerchief to him.

When he was out of sight she came in and closed the door.

She pulled the mat straight with the heel of her buckled shoe and trotted down the hall. At the kitchen door she paused and looked in.

"Beatrice and Mr. Potter are out tonight, so you and I will have something easy, Lisa," she said.

"Sí, sí," said the old woman, without looking round from the stove. "Sí, sí."

Belle closed the door softly and went up to the drawing room. The yellow evening sun was streaming in, mellowing the faded Persian rugs and caressing the upholstery of the Voltaire chair.

The old lady went over to the bureau and, taking a small key from a chain round her neck, unlocked a narrow drawer under the writing flap.

It slid open easily, and from its green-lined depths she lifted out a small unframed canvas.

She seated herself and propped the little picture up on the desk.

It was a self-portrait of John Lafcadio, painted in the impressionist technique only appreciated in a much later day. It showed the same face which smiled so proudly from Sargent, but there was a great difference.

John Lafcadio's famous beard was here only suggested, and the line of his chin, a little receding, was viciously drawn in. The lips were smiling, their sensuous fullness overemphasized. The flowing locks were shown a little thin and the high cheekbones caricatured.

The eyes were laughing, or at least one of them laughed. The other was completely hidden in a grotesque wink.

It was cruel and revealing, the face of a man who was, if half genius, also half buffoon.

Belle turned it over. Written across the back in the painter's enormous hand was a single phrase:

Your secret, Belle darling.

The old lady returned to the portrait. She touched her lips with her forefinger and pressed it on the painted mouth.

"Oh, Johnnie," she said sadly. "Such a lot of trouble, my dear. Such a lot of trouble."

ABOUT THE AUTHOR

MARGERY ALLINGHAM, who was born in London in 1904, came from a long line of writers. "I was brought up from babyhood in an atmosphere of ink and paper," she claimed. One ancestor wrote early nineteenth century melodramas, another wrote popular boys' school stories, and her grandfather was the proprietor of a religious newspaper. But it was her father, the author of serials for the popular weeklies, who gave her her earliest training as a writer. She began studying the craft at the age of seven and had published her first novel by the age of sixteen while still at boarding school. In 1927 she married Philip Youngman Carter, and the following year she produced the first of her Albert Campion detective stories, *The Crime at Black Dudley*. She and her husband lived a life "typical of the English countryside" she reported, with "horses, dogs, our garden and village activities" taking up leisure time. One wonders how much leisure time Margery Allingham, the author of more than thirty-three mystery novels in addition to short stories, serials, and book reviews, managed to have.

Kinsey Millhone is...

"The best new private eye." —*The Detroit News*

"A tough-cookie with a soft center." —*Newsweek*

"A stand-out specimen of the new female operatives."
—*Philadelphia Inquirer*

Sue Grafton is...

The Shamus and Anthony Award winning creator of
Kinsey Millhone and quite simply one of the hottest
new mystery writers around.

Bantam is...

The proud publisher of Sue Grafton's Kinsey Millhone
mysteries:

☐	27991	"A" IS FOR ALIBI	$3.95
☐	28034	"B" IS FOR BURGLAR	$3.95
☐	28036	"C" IS FOR CORPSE	$3.95
☐	27163	"D" IS FOR DEADBEAT	$3.95
☐	27955	"E" IS FOR EVIDENCE	$3.95

Special Offer
Buy a Bantam Book
for only 50¢.

Now you can have Bantam's catalog filled with hundreds of titles plus take advantage of our unique and exciting bonus book offer. A special offer which gives you the opportunity to purchase a Bantam book for only 50¢. Here's how!

By ordering any five books at the regular price per order, you can also choose any other single book listed (up to a $5.95 value) for just 50¢. Some restrictions do apply, but for further details why not send for Bantam's catalog of titles today!

Just send us your name and address and we will send you a catalog!